Kel!

"You're not one bit sorry you insulted me, are you?"

Rita started to touch her temple, but froze the instant her fingers hit her beauty pageant crown, still knotted up in her hair. What made her put that darn thing on, anyway?

He continued. "You've got nothing to feel sorry about. Your pals there cooked up my coming by today without telling you what they had in mind, didn't they?"

"I had no part in asking you here."

"I get that. You didn't ask for my help at all." And he knew she sure needed his help, but she wouldn't ask. Not Rita. "Do you know what I have to say about that?"

"Why should I care what you have to say about anything, Mr.—"

"I say you've just sealed a deal to get your Pig Rib Pigsty a bargain-rate makeover."

"You don't have to . . ."

"But I *do* have to, Rita." He reached up and freed the crown from her hair. "I do . . ."

LUANNE JONES

the DIXIE Belle's Guide to LOVE

AVON BOOKS
An Imprint of HarperCollinsPublishers

AVON BOOKS
An Imprint of HarperCollins*Publishers*
10 East 53rd Street
New York, New York 10022-5299

For Bob,
my sweetie, best friend,
and a man who understands that sometimes
a girl has to be the B-word—a real Belle!

Acknowledgments

A multitude of thanks go out to the good folks who helped me with everything from achieving authenticity to not giving up on me throughout the process of putting this book together.

To my cohorts on the Southern Porch, thank you for helping me get the details right. Thanks to my princess pals—Lynn Bulock, Sharon Gillenwater, and Diane Noble—for their encouragement, laughter, and listening. Thanks to Bill for his input on Memphis-style ribs and to Denise Camp for all the little tidbits of local color she came up with whenever I hit a snag. Also to the friends and family members who shared recipes: Nancy Henneke, Patje Lentz, Janella Price, Jody Henneke, Maxine Shorter (my mama, who was able to share by way of notes in the cookbook—the one with the cover almost burned off!—she passed on to me before she died).

Pernel Stark Offers a Prologue
(of sorts)

Ask anyone in Hellon, Tennessee, about Rita Butcher Stark and they will tell you first about the tornado. They'll tell you the other things, of course, like how she and that Stark boy—*nobody* calls me *that Stark boy* anymore, thank you very much—had to get married when they were seventeen. It never was much of a marriage, and no one was one bit surprised it didn't last, but it did produce one mighty fine daughter. Our girl graduated a full year ahead of her high-school class and not without fanfare, I might add. Not to mention how her beauty and poise won her the coveted Miss Strawberry Belle crown.

Every girl—and just maybe a boy or two—in Hellon yearns to be Miss Strawberry Belle. Rita herself held the title when she was barely sixteen. A year later she took the Tristate Teen Dixie Belle

Duchess pageant by storm and won with ease.

Her talent nailed it for her. Rita sings like an earthbound angel mourning for heaven, a hell-hot temptress longing for love, and, bless her heart, Tennessee's own Patsy Cline all rolled into one.

She could have gone a long way in the pageant circuit, a smart, pretty girl like Rita. She could have used the scholarships to fulfill her dreams of going off to college and taking on the world. But life (and our raging teenage hormones) gave her an unexpected spin. The next year she took on the title she has worked the hardest at, which suits her like a gold-and-crystal tiara complements big hair and high heels, and which she cherishes above the rest—Mom.

Mention Rita today and fellow Hellonites (Hellonese?) will use phrases like "salt of the earth," "downright dependable," "steadfast and loyal." To the point of being almost immovable, I'd add. That woman's goal in life seems to be nothing loftier than finding perspective and keeping her wheels between the ditches.

People around here would agree with me on *that* much, at least, and tell you so. But not a word of it will come your way until they lay the proper groundwork by telling you about that tornado.

That's how it is if you live in a town with one zip code, a handful of places where you can eat *and* get gas (or so say their roadside signs), and just seventy miles of highway between you and the promised land of Memphis.

Somebody knows one or two good stories on

everybody who ever lived, loved, lied, lusted, or just laid over for more than twenty-four hours in this smudge on the back road. And everybody, even those just passing through, has heard about "The Tornado."

It was her mama and daddy's story, by all rights. Rita and I had already married and had the baby the year three separate funnels bore down on Hellon in the space of less than an hour.

The air was so charged up it prickled on the skin. The sky had gone dark as midnight in the middle of the afternoon. The funnels appeared, seemingly out of nowhere, and hung low above the horizon. Two together fast and furious, then, just when you thought it was over, the last and most horrible cut loose on the town.

The next day, the phrase "They roared through like a freight train out of hell," got repeated more times than a man could count. People who probably never heard the terms outside of professional wrestling on TV spoke of "mass mayhem" and "pandemonium." Church was full to the rafters that next Sunday with grateful souls. No one was killed, and there was only superficial damage, except for Rita's mama and daddy's house.

For years after that awful day you could come across a bent piece of silverware or a perfectly preserved knickknack in the oddest places, forks of trees, the window ledge outside the bank building, in the middle of a farmer's field. If you did, that object more than likely came from Tammy and Rydel Butcher's home. Or the pile of rubble that was left after the third and final tornado had done its worst.

Of course that's just the lead-in to the good part, the part where everyone moves in a little closer, holds eye contact a little longer, and lowers their voices, like they're letting you in on prime gossip. Because it isn't the tornado that makes this story worth the retelling sixteen years later, it's what happened next.

The story goes then that Tammy Alice Butcher took a long, thoughtful look at the wreckage that had been her home. Then she looked at the man who had been her husband for more than half her life. Then she looked at the debris again. Then at the man who had made a shambles of their wedding vows time and time again over the years.

Finally, she looked—one could only guess at this bit, but you can't leave it out cause it makes the story—finally, she looked long and hard at what her life had been there in that two-bedroom ranch with that two-timing man. And damned if she didn't up and walk away from it all.

Used her part of the insurance money to get a divorce and buy an RV. She took off to find herself and must still be looking to this very day, because she never has come back to Hellon. Rydel married the only one of his hootchie galfriends who'd have him and moved off to Birmingham. He died a few years later.

With them gone, the story just naturally got glommed onto Rita. It's the first thing folks tell you about her, even if you only asked for directions to Pernel's Pig Rib Palace, the barbecue joint I ran for years before up and leaving it to her so I could pursue . . . other interests.

That tornado is why, they will tell you, she has let that place sit all spring and not done a thing about fixing it up or converting it to the kind of restaurant she is so capable of running.

It's why they say she mopes around the apartment over the Palace, reading and singing into that portable karaoke machine of hers, speculation goes. That and cook up a storm—always adding "but it's not like she needs the calories." Yes, folks around Hellon use that tornado story to rationalize everything about Rita from her failure to find wedded bliss to her weight.

Pleasingly plump is the way I look at her. Big and beautiful are the words her friend, Cozette Harvey, would proclaim. Cozette is on the big-boned side herself and prone to the dramatic.

"Cute as a ladybug's ear but built with a Volkswagen Bug's rear," is what her other closest gal pal, Jillie West, has been known to say—and right to Rita's face, no less. Though you can't go by Jillie, as she's the original stick-figure girl. She thinks a healthy woman's body with shape and curves and jiggle rates the triple "S"—shame, starvation, and Spandex undergarments. Having experienced all three, I wouldn't recommend a one of them.

Rita's unlikely relationships get attributed to the whole tornado aftermath, too. Why else could anyone as good and decent as Rita stay hooked up to an earth-mother type who don't know the summer of love is over and a self-absorbed wild child from a family who takes excess to an extreme, even for moneyed Southern folks?

Knowing all that, you can understand, of course, why the real trouble began when Cozette and Jillie decided that what Rita needed to stir her out of her recent bout of complacency was her very own, heart-pumping, knees-a-knocking, life-as-she-knew-it-was-uh-oh-over . . . tornado!

You see, her mother's lifestyle might have been turned upside down by that awful ill wind, but it was Rita's life that has been defined by it. Seems all Rita's choices stem directly from that moment when her mama up and left.

Those choices have kept her rooted and rigid. But take it from me, there's a turbulence just under the surface of Rita Butcher Stark. Others see it, too, and we are watching her and waiting. Waiting for that day when she finally steps out of the shelter she's made of her life and soars.

Chapter 1

EVERY DIXIE BELLE KNOWS:
When loved ones overstep bounds or your ego needs a little oomph nothing flat out puts the frosting on the cake and says you mean business like a four-inch-high glittering headpiece of gold and rhinestone.

"No, no, no, no, *no*." Rita pushed past Jillie. They were standing in the kitchenette—kitchen-*not* was more like it—but it was all the cramped apartment over Pernel's Pig Rib Palace had to offer.

"What are you trying to tell us, sugar?" Cozette's words dripped like honey from her smiling lips, but her eyes shimmered with tart mischief.

Rita went on tiptoe to reach to the back corner of her top cupboard and hauled out a big red-and-white mixing bowl. She clunked it down on the table. "I'm saying no. No, no, and no." Cozette and Jillie exchanged disbelieving glances.

Rita huffed and reached inside the bowl to fish out the dazzling object she kept hidden there. Gently, she placed it on her head. Then she grabbed up her best wooden spoon and pointed it directly at Cozie, who had sprawled her long body over the sagging green couch in the other half of the room. "And in case you think that's the least bit ambiguous, let me say it again. No!"

"You know when she says it like that?" Jillie leaned back against the baby blue fridge, ruffling the clippings and photos of Rita's daughter covering the door. "You can almost believe she means what she's saying."

"It's that . . . that . . . thing on her head," Cozie said.

Rita touched the Dixie Belle Duchess crown she had just perched precariously over what she felt sure was an adorably messy topknot. She'd seen a lot of years and a lot of pounds since it was first placed on her head. She didn't put the thing on every day—not *every* day. But it still held magic for her. Wearing it, even as a gesture of pure smart-assness for her friends, never failed to remind her that she still had dreams and life still held possibilities.

Besides in times like these, when loved ones overstepped their bounds nothing flat-out puts the frosting on the cake and said she meant business like this four-inch-high glittering headpiece of gold and rhinestones.

"That crown and the way she waves that spoon around." Cozie twirled her hand in the air. "Gives her the illusion of authority."

"It gives her the illusion of insanity."

"That's no illusion." Rita tugged at the strings of the old hospital gown she wore as a lightweight robe. "My so-called friends have driven me stark raving mad."

"Then our work is done." Cozie rolled her eyes.

"Oh, no." Jillie wagged a manicured finger. "Our work here has not even *begun*."

"Heaven help me!" Rita hiked her sagging pajama pants up by the broken elastic waistband. "How could I be this big a peanut brain? Stupid, stupid!"

"Don't talk like that, Rita!" Cozette sat bolt upright, her long black braid flipping down to rest on the soft slope of her breast. "The things you repeat to yourself silently and outwardly to the world become your reality. If you want to change your reality, you have to change the way you speak to and about yourself."

"That *is* my reality." Rita shook her head.

"Stop it," Cozie demanded.

"Rita, really . . ."

"Well, I must be thicker than molasses in January, right?" She wiped the mixing bowl out with a soft cotton hand towel. "Here I am, a grown woman who doesn't know whom to trust and believe in anymore."

Even Cozie didn't dare deny that one.

"Who, according to you two, cannot figure out how to get her life back on its safe, reasonable track without your intervention."

Jillie had the good form to look sheepish.

"And most importantly someone who, despite

far too many intrusions by well-intentioned friends, has still not learned to keep the door leading from the restaurant to my apartment locked if I want to be left alone."

"Being left alone is the worst thing that could happen to you, Rita." Jillie spoke with a conviction that told more of her own fears than of her concern for her friend.

"Well, I don't know about the *worst*." Cozie's warm maternal expression changed as she looked from Jillie to Rita and narrowed her eyes. "But it certainly is the least likely."

Rita thought of throwing a house shoe at her, but the way this day had begun she'd probably hit her friend smack in the head. Then Rita would feel sorry and need to fix things, to put any bad feelings right before they threw the friendship off-balance. Then Cozette would start with the touchy-feely stuff about only having the power to forgive yourself and the need to embrace life where you are at while you can.

And then Rita would have to kill her.

Rita clucked her tongue.

"How a fiftysomething woman who only wears scratchy, voluminous, hand-loomed clothes and has not shaved her legs or armpits for twenty years could pull off an attitude worthy of one of Miss Peggy West's country-club cronies, I cannot understand."

"You don't *shave*?" Jillie paled.

"We're not talking about me, here, we're talking about Rita." Cozie shifted her weight and visibly sank a little lower into the sad old sofa.

"Sorry, were we talking about me?" Rita pointed the spoon at her chest. "I thought we were talking about you two and your harebrained idea to barge into my life and run roughshod over my careful, considered plans."

Rita grabbed the handle of the refrigerator door.

"What plans?" Jillie stepped out of Rita's way. "You don't have any plans."

Rita took out a carton of eggs and set them on the table by the large mixing bowl, humming nothing in particular.

"If you had any plans at all, Cozette and I never would have been driven to such . . ." Jillie attempted to push the refrigerator door shut with her entirely-inadequate-for-the-job backside. "Stop that humming and what do you think you're doing?"

"Cooking breakfast." Rita came to the rescue and sent the fridge door swinging shut with one well-aimed hip. "Cooking is my therapy. It's my calm in the storm, my eye in the middle of the hurricane."

"You don't have time for that now. Tell her, Cozette."

"We don't have time for breakfast or hurricanes, Rita."

"Don't you tell me what I have time for. That's not your place." The shell made a delicate crackle as Rita tapped it to the rim of the gleaming white bowl. "Not in my kitchen."

The yolk plopped into the bowl with a soft splat.

"Not in my restaurant."

The egg white drizzled down slowly, without a noise.

"And certainly not in my life!" Rita tossed the empty shell over her shoulder without looking. The rustle of the brown bag lining her garbage can told her she'd made the shot. "Is that clear?"

Both Jillie and Cozette started to protest at the same time, but Rita did not give them the chance.

"If and when I choose to remodel the Palace is not for you two to say." Rita winced as her tiara snagged deeper into her hair. She went on talking like nothing was wrong as she worked with the headpiece, pulling one way, then the next, only managing to wind more and more wayward strands around the rhinestones. "I will decide when it will be remodeled and who will do the job. Understand?"

"Fine. Then decide." Jillie fluttered the pages of the two-year-old calendar on the wall. People all over Memphis kiss butt, connive, and expend outrages amounts of cash to say my brother is their contractor. He is the best in his field and willing to work for you. "If you don't want him to take this project on, knowing full well he'll do the best job possible with a guarantee not to go over your—and I say this with all due respect and empathy to your situation, sugar—pissant little joke of a budget, then that's okay by me. Cozie?"

She sat on the couch with her hands clasped between her knees. "Fine by me as well."

"Good." Rita gave up on getting the crown off without a mirror and maybe a pair of scissors to help, and sighed. She folded herself safely into the comfy old hospital gown.

Jillie's heels clicked for a couple steps before she stepped from the linoleum to the well-worn beige carpet.

"Thank heavens that's settled. Now, who wants waffles?"

Cozie studied the tip of her braid like she could read the future in its ends. "It's not quite settled, Rita."

Rita held a second egg over the bowl, her hand frozen in mid-crack. "Why not?"

"My brother is downstairs."

"Your . . . ? Oh." Gently, with the expertise of one of western Tennessee's finest cooks, Rita dropped the egg, shell and all, into the mixing bowl.

Jillie's brother was waiting downstairs? If only she had memorized some of the swear words scrawled on the bathroom walls down there. Maybe then she would have a full enough vocabulary to voice her honest opinion of that situation.

"He's here to help you, Rita. If you don't want that help, you at least owe it to him to tell him no thank you to his face."

"Why should I have to tell . . ." *Wild Billy.* She couldn't even say his name. "What could I possibly have to say to a man who is . . ."

Arrogance on wheels. Fast wheels, the faster the better. He roared through Hellon whenever it suited him, but he never stayed long enough to make a difference. When he tore out of town, he left the people who cared about him behind in his dust without a backward glance. That's how Rita saw him, how she pretty much had always seen him. She saw it in the way he practically ignored his mother and sister to his reluctance to take responsibility for his choices. She'd told him as much once, not that he'd heard her. Or, if he had heard her, he had not stuck around long enough to acknowledge it.

Afterward, just thinking about her audacity in taking him to task made her feel . . . all the things she hated to feel. Even now just standing here her face grew hot and she had to battle back the emotions the memory, the very man, called up in her. *Stupid, stupid, dumb, and unworthy. Not good enough—never nearly good enough.*

All those things she worked so hard to keep at bay in order to retain whatever quiet dignity she could manage in her train wreck of a life washed over her again. Just thinking about him churned her doubts and fears and regrets so close to the surface she didn't dare even look her best friends straight in the face as they talked about him.

Now those friends were suggesting she march down into Pernel's Pig Rib Purgatory and throw

Wild Billy out on his—oh, merciful heavens, it was probably still one of the top ten finest creations since the beginning of time—ass! "No."

"No?" Cozie stole a sidelong glance at Jillie perched on the arm of the couch. "No what?"

"I can't go down there."

Jillie folded her arms. "Not looking like this you can't, but . . ."

"Not at all! I can't . . . I can't face him *at all.* Don't you understand, there's something about him that just . . ." *Sets my teeth on edge. Makes me want to slap his careless-with-everything-precious-in-life cocky grin into next Tuesday.* Rita rejected the troublesome truth of things and settled on a more diplomatic, nonverbal explanation. She shuddered.

"I told you this was going to work!" Jillie clapped her hands together.

"What are you talking about?" Rita clutched the gold band tangled in her hair.

"After all these years, my big dope of a brother still makes her . . ." She sat on the arm of the sofa by Cozie, shut her eyes, sucked her breath in between her teeth, and gave a shimmy.

"No, no, not . . ." Rita did a passing imitation of Jillie's rapture.

"Liar. This is Wild Billy West we're talking about here, girl." Cozette gave her own nature-girl-gone-downright-feral quiver. "That man puts the beef in beefcake. And coming from a lifelong vegetarian, that's saying something!"

"No! *No beefcake!* Look at me!" Rita extended

her arms. Her hospital gown gapped open over her knee-length sleep T and her pants drooped low enough that the hem almost covered her fuzzy pink slippers. She shook her head. The tiara pitched forward, and her hair fell into her eyes. "Is there *anything* about me that screams 'bring this woman beefcake'?"

"There's something about every woman that screams for beefcake, honey." Cozie laughed.

"If it makes you feel any better, Billy . . ." Jillie held up her hand. "Uh, he goes by Will now. Apparently that's some kind of issue with him, but don't worry about it. Anyway, Billy isn't built like a quarterback anymore himself."

"More like a lineman," Cozie said like she, who hated all forms of competitive sports, had an inkling what she was talking about. "Little more to get your hands on, but he still has the best backfield in the county, if you ask me."

"I did *not* ask you! I did not ask for any of this." This was not happening. This could not be happening.

Jillie shook back her perfect hair and smoothed her hand along her silk lapel.

Cozie picked a cocklebur off her sandal strap.

"I can't believe this! Up until now you two have gotten along about as well as two cats in a bag."

"What can we say? I was visiting Jillie's mama the other day, and we crossed paths and got to talking about you."

"And found out we didn't dislike each other nearly as much as we thought we would."

"We both care so much about you, Rita. We figured somewhere that meant we had some common ground, and we decided to try to find it."

"And sticking your grubby fingers in the big pie of my life is what you came up with?"

"Hard to believe, isn't it?" Cozie threw one hand up.

"I know. Our first attempt and we got it abso-freaking-lutely perfect." Jillie slapped a high five on Cozette's much larger palm like they'd played on the same team all their lives.

"Perfect? A perfect disaster!" Rita grabbed up the mixing bowl and hugged it to her chest. "I do not want to be set up with your brother, Jillie."

"It's not a setup," Jillie protested.

"It's not like we expect you two to actually . . ." Cozie waggled her eyebrows and lowered her voice. ". . . *date*."

"Oh, that makes it so much better. You're not setting up your brother, you're pimping him."

Jillie crossed her legs and arms tighter than chains on a miser's money box. "Oh, hell, Rita, not *everything* is about sex!"

"Yeah, but the really good stuff is." Cozie put her chin in her hand and sighed.

If looks could kill, Jillie and Rita would be arguing over where to hide the corpse of the only woman in the room with a bona fide love life.

"Besides, don't kid yourself, ladies, this *is*

about sex." Standing up, Cozette dominated the room.

Jillie leaned in.

Rita swallowed, hard. She held her breath and waited.

"This is about *passion*. It's about tension and longing and looking for something more." Cozie spread her arms out.

"Yes," Jillie whispered.

The older woman drew her fingers into fists and shut her eyes, smiling. "It's about tearing everything down that doesn't work any longer, about getting tired and sweaty and when it's done, about producing something worthwhile."

Rita had to admit it sounded promising whether they were talking fornication or construction.

"This is about rebirth and bursting through to the next level."

"Bursting?" The only bursting Rita understood was bursting her bubble, and she didn't need that. "Look, ladies, I don't want . . ."

Cozie raised her hands like an artist describing a mystic vision. "It's about a six-foot-one shot of testosterone poured into a pair of butt-grabbing jeans."

Okay, maybe she'd let her friend finish that thought.

"About having a tightly muscled but loosely moraled man, capable of building you a house or rocking your world, standing by to inspire you while you do the work of putting your life back together."

"You almost had me up until my world rocked." Rita sighed. "That and putting my life back together . . . no."

"Ah, Rita, you're as stubborn as Billy himself, and that is *not* a compliment." Jillie jiggled her foot.

"Rita, it's time." Cozie reached out. "I know how much it smarts that Pernel swapped your home and security for a few low-cut sequined gowns, a second-rate Dolly Parton wig, and way too much flashy makeup, but you have got to move on now."

Rita planted her feet firmly.

"C'mon, Rita." Cozette snapped her fingers like a pinched-cheeked schoolmarm. "Don't you see how a summer in the presence of a certain wild man could refurbish the Palace *and* mend your battered ego?"

"Why do you always have to be the one helping people, Rita? Why can't you just let someone else do the helping for a change?" Jillie stood up to steal a glance at the stairway door. "If it matters, this will be good for Billy, too. Did you ever think of that?"

"Yeah, sure. Like he needs yet another woman lusting after him."

"Oh, please!" She rolled her eyes and fluffed her red curls. "If this had just been about lust, I'd have gone and hired a rippled twentysomething blond Adonis with sawdust for brains. Then I could have ogled him right alongside you all summer long."

"This isn't about you getting laid, Rita. It's about you laying down your defenses and feeling alive again." Cozie motioned toward the door.

Still clutching her mixing bowl, Rita lifted her face heavenward. "Why me, Lord?"

"Because we care about you, Rita. And we believe that somewhere in that woman who has become so careful that she has practically ceased to exist, somewhere under the heartache and the disappointment and the longing to inch her way along the edges of life, is your mother's daughter."

"Oh, no. No-ooo," Rita groaned, her eyes closed. "I am not my mother. I have worked all my life to not *be* like my mother. Why does everybody keep insisting that somewhere, someway, somehow, someday I am suddenly going find my inner Tammy and transform everything in my life?"

"Because we know you can," Cozie said softly.

"Damn it, y'all," Rita murmured. Suddenly the mixing bowl felt like it carried the weight of her lifelong frustration in it. Sighing, she plunked it down—right on top of the carton of eggs.

"Go get your brother." Cozie snapped her fingers, and Jillie headed off down the stairway. "I'll try to get Rita into some outfit that looks a little less like she got it from the escaped-lunatic collection."

First one and then a second broken egg oozed from the carton under the bowl, then began the slow, inevitable slide toward the short-legged side of the table. Sunny yellow goo dripped onto Rita's fuzzy pink house shoe while she fixed her eyes on her remaining friend. "I am so glad you two have worked out your differences enough to talk this over."

"Why is that, hon?"

"Because I'm no longer speaking to *either* of you."

"Good." Cozie folded her arms, tipped her head until her silver-laced black bangs swept to one side, and grinned. "Because if we can get you to shut up long enough, it will be much easier to pull this whole thing off."

"Okay, you've had time to look around the place." Jillie breezed in from the kitchen, not looking one bit guilty over abandoning him in this deserted diner for the last fifteen minutes. "Be honest. Got any ideas about brightening up the place?"

"Yeah."

"Really?"

"A gallon of gas and a lighted match."

"Oh, come on. It's not all *that* bad." Jillie threw open the curtains on the front window. A piece of the fabric tore loose in her hand.

Will tried to take in all of the old barbecue restaurant with one broad, unrelenting look. Instead, he found himself squinting, trying not to look too closely at the splotches on the yellow-papered walls. He really didn't want to know if they were cheap beer and barbecue or bug guts and bloodstains.

"Okay, it's bad. But *you* can fix it, can't you, Billy?"

"Will." He slipped his dark glasses back on. A callus on his thumb snagged on the lapel of his black jacket as he dipped two fingers into his breast pocket. He tugged free one of his business cards and flicked it at his baby sister.

She let it fall to the floor. The gray paper blended with the pocked linoleum, making the embossed message stand out all the more: WILLIAM WEST, CUSTOM CARPENTER.

She wrinkled her nose. "Maybe I'll use the name most of Hellon knows you by . . ."

"Don't. I mean it."

"Wild Billy." She narrowed her eyes at him like a cat perched just out of reach while licking the last bit of stolen cream off her paws.

He swore but kept his jaw tight enough to deprive her of the satisfaction of hearing just how foul a word she'd provoked from him. *Wild Billy West*. The name dredged up more bad feelings in him than this place had greasy spoons. "You wanted my opinion of this place, and I gave it. Torch the sucker."

Jillie stepped between him and the front door. "Don't be so mean about this . . ." Her lips went thin ". . . Will."

Then she did one of those damn prissy woman things, flipping back her gaudy red curls like a princess who'd just ordered some poor jerk's head—or worse—cut off.

"How'd you get your hair that color?" He tugged on a strand just like they were nine and five years old again. "I recall you being born with a head full of coal black hair, just like everyone on Mama's side of the family."

"So I was born with Mama's family coloring and the West family nose." She touched her made-to-order features and gave him a going-over that she clearly thought as scathing.

Will adjusted his sunglasses. He turned his head, knowing it put both his nose—which by West family standards was unimpressive—and the waves of black, shaggy hair in unashamed profile.

Jillie folded her arms. "I was also born naked and shoeless but I certainly didn't see any reason to stay that way either, not when God created so many avenues to correct it."

"Yeah, Fifth Avenue, Park Avenue. Aren't you so proud to have *something* to show for tearing through your trust fund?"

"There's plenty left." She gave that same back-handed wave their mother gave when she wanted them to leave her alone.

"What are you doing with your life, girl? Don't you have any goals, ambitions, a desire to make something more of yourself?" He would not at-test to it in court, but he thought he saw her lower lip tremble.

Then she jerked her shoulders up straight and went full-blown bored-with-the-likes-of-you debutante on him. "I *do* things with my life. I sup-port my charities. I travel. Just this spring I took a college extension course. One night a week over in the church basement."

"It boggles the mind. A course in what?"

"Art appreciation."

"Ah, yes. Now it makes sense. Something practical you can apply in your day-to-day life here in Hellon." He looked out the door, not seeing anything in particular. "Where you have the chance to appreciate such fine works of art as the advertising mural on the Feed and Seed Store or the concrete slab where the cannon used to stand in front of the VFW. Let me see, what else could you appreciate around here?"

"Paul says . . ."

"Paul?"

"My . . ." Her hesitation said more than any words ever could. "Professor."

"I see. So it was Paul appreciation got you into that church basement."

"He's a married man, and I don't have to tell you another thing. I brought you here to discuss you, not me."

"Looking around here I'd say you've done your job. I'm about as disgusted as I can get this early in the morning."

"Would you for one minute stop being such a *Billygoat* and shut up and listen to me?"

"Why should I listen to you, Jillie? What could you possibly have learned in that class, or in your travels? What could you have bought in some overpriced store or learned by living far too long in our mother's house that applies to *me*?"

"I'm not here to tell you a damn thing, you big jerk. I'm here to ask you for a big favor."

"Then you've wasted your breath." The greasy floor eased the way for him to turn on his heel without so much as ruffling his hair or his jacket. "Nobody *asks* me for anything, baby sister."

"Will, you don't . . ."

"I do not let myself be held hostage to owing favors or put myself in a situation where I have to produce what is asked of me in order to win anyone's approval or satisfy someone else's idea of what I should be, do, say, or give."

"Don't you do that in your work all the time?"

"My work is precise. There are standards. There is an objective result. Things can be measured, and if they are not up to snuff, there is a clear, understandable reason why. Favors, little sister, are never like that. Favors always come with some deeper expectation than most people are able to meet."

"Honestly, Will. You are making a bigger deal of this than needs be. If you would just let me explain what I want from you and why I'm asking *now* . . ."

"I know why you're asking *now*." He touched his dark glasses and looked out at the road. "You saw the opportunity to use my annual guilt trip to Hellon to twist me around your finger until you got your way. Mama would be so proud."

"Billy!" She wedged her bony shoulder against the door opening.

"Step aside, Jillie. Clearly you've called the wrong man for the job."

"That's not true." She stood up straight, not a

trace of deception or pride in her eyes. "I called *you*. I called the only person I know who could come into this town and get done what needs doing without anyone throwing up roadblocks or making trouble. Wild Billy, you are the *only* man for the job."

"The only man for the job?" She made him sound like freaking Superman. Worse yet, she reminded him that he was and would always be Wild Billy West, with all the unashamed intrusions into his life, the damnable obligations, and the unrealistic expectations that went with the title of small-town hero. He wondered if his little sister knew how much he hated that feeling—or how powerless he felt to walk away from it?

Jillie's brow wrinkled enough to undo a month's worth of creams and treatments.

He stepped back from the door, but just one step.

"Billy . . . *Will* . . . please." She looked back over her shoulder. "You came this far. I didn't really think you'd come, but you did, and I . . ."

He followed her line of vision. Across the narrow road the morning sun glinted off the cars coming and going from the gas station. A faded metal sign pointing directions to a bank that went belly-up twenty years ago still swung from a post by the road.

Above the treetops he could make out the steeple of the Second Street Baptist Church. Time and the realities of a dwindling population had caused the two Baptist churches in town to merge a few years back. The racially divided congregations had voiced reservations about that solution, but somehow, in time, they made it work. Now they even had a sign out front in Spanish to welcome the migrants and new immigrants.

Some things did change here, Will conceded, but so many things never would. He would always be Wild Billy here. Football legend and only son of the town's most respected family. A handful, but basically a good kid, they would always say of him. Always forgiven by the town, his family, and even the local law for things other boys caught hell for.

He sighed. "I've come this far and what, Jillie?"

"And I just wanted to thank you."

"So help me, Jillie, if this is some big show to butter me up to get your way . . ." He had no threat to finish that sentence.

"It means more than I can tell you that you're here, Will." He could only nod to acknowledge her words.

"Because the person we're doing this for means more to me than I can ever say."

"Pernel Stark?" He couldn't even muster a believable laugh at that.

"No, Rita."

Rita. Just her name made his chest seize up and his breathing grow shallow. Rita Butcher Stark, Lord have mercy. "I thought this place belonged to . . ."

Jillie shook her head. "The house was in Pernel's name—he inherited it from his mama, you know, and she never did like Rita. But they always had joint ownership of this place, though Rita never set foot in it if she didn't have to."

"A woman of uncommonly wise judgment."

"Attested to by her choice in friends, no doubt." Jillie smiled. "Long story short, Pernel wanted money. He sold the house out from under Rita and gave her his share of . . . *this*."

Will would have cursed, but he couldn't think of any word hard enough to convey his thoughts about Pernel at that moment.

"See, I'm not asking anything for myself, Will. I'm asking for Rita."

He shut his eyes.

"Rita is my friend, and there is no reason for her to be. She never lets me skate by on my family name or money or looks because she sees something more in me. And that gives me a kind of hope I can be more. Do you . . . do you have any idea how dear that makes her to me?"

He knew. Damn it, he knew better than anyone alive how precious that kind of friend would be. Not the first time today, it felt like he had a fist stuck high in his throat.

"Please, Will. Do it? Help fix up this place . . . for Rita?"

He scratched the back of his neck. "I'm guessing she doesn't have a lot of money to spend."

"She has a little nest egg, but it's hardly the kind that came out of the golden goose."

"She'll need what's called sweat equity, too. She does have friends she can rely on to help?"

His sister's face went absolutely ashen. "With money or sweat?"

"Either. Both."

Her cheeks pinked up again, and she nodded. "She has friends."

"I'd waive my fees, of course. Maybe call on a few business associates who owe me favors." Everyone everywhere owed Will a favor. In his drive never to be asked to do for others, he made a practice of finding every opportunity to give to others freely. To be the first to volunteer, the hardest worker, and the man everyone trusted to have the deepest pockets when he learned of a need. "I could get her the work and materials at cost."

"Does this mean you're going to take the job?"

"It's not the best use of my time and talent."

She laughed and clapped her hands, claiming a triumph he had not actually granted her. "Don't underestimate yourself. This project is exactly how you should be using your time and talent."

He inched his sunglasses down on his nose and shook his head.

"You won't regret a minute of this."

"I never committed to sinking as long as a minute into this dive and its renovation."

"Don't think of it as renovation, brother, think of it as . . . ." She raised her open palms in the beam of sunlight streaming in the front window and laughed before concluding, ". . . redemption."

"Redemption? Mine or Rita's?"

"Does it matter?"

Redemption. Him? He ran his hand along the

lunch counter then rubbed the gritty dust between his thumb and fingers. Naw. Renovation, nothing more. But still . . .

His gaze strayed to the front window. Even with the torn curtain hanging down over one corner it gave him a wide-open view of the intersection half a block away. Winter Road cut a lopsided semicircle around the edges of Hellon. From this intersection a right turn sent you toward the highway and on to Memphis. A smart man would be on that route right now. Will's gaze, however, fixed on the other direction. The way he had just come.

He tugged at his jacket collar. He wiped the dirt of the place off his hands and onto his faded jeans. His heart ached.

"Damn it." He had thought after all this time he would have made peace with his life and his choices, but it had not come.

He'd all but given up on finding his way back. Then Jillie talked of redemption and gave him a way to help Rita find the same, if she needed it. And it did seem clear that she needed help.

Some tiny spark of longing for that very thing still burned deep, deep inside of him. He did not know whether to curse or thank his sister for wrenching that up after all these years.

Six years. In the small, silent cemetery a few miles down Winter, he had buried the baby boy who bore his name six years ago today. That was a long time to wait to feel whole again.

Charging blindly on with life had not done it.

Hard work had not done it. Recommitting himself to the things he hoped to be true and right had not done it. Seeing his child's mother make a new life and find happiness with another man had not eased his guilt or diminished his pain. Why on earth did Jillie think remodeling this dump would make one bit of difference for him or for Rita?

"Pig Rib Palace." The name caught in his throat like the low growl of a fight-scarred dog. He looked around. The place reeked of age and artery-plugging food. It had probably waited as long as he had—longer maybe—for its redemption.

And Rita. If she needed his help, how could he refuse? He owed her more than anyone—perhaps even Rita herself—could comprehend. "Tell Rita I'll do it."

"Tell her yourself." She motioned for him to follow her through the kitchen, pausing at a half-open door to say, "I think she's had enough time to get used to the idea by now."

Chapter 2

"I hate the smell of raw eggs." Cozie picked up the soaked and battered egg carton by one corner and pitched it into the trash.

"It's not the eggs that stink around here." Rita wiped a sponge through some shell-speckled gunk. What didn't smear seeped off the edge of the table and splattered on her shoe. "It's the advice."

"Who are you to judge advice? It's not like you ever take any." She took Rita's sponge and tossed it in the sink. "Go fix yourself up a little. You may be able to take on the world in a pair of comfy house shoes but you cannot think straight if your hair's a mess. Go on, do as I say."

"I never take advice, but go on and do as you say?"

"What?" She shrugged, and the layers of her

outfit shrugged with her. "I'm a mom. I'm allowed to say stuff like that."

"Don't give me that. Your kids have been out of the house for years now."

"Doesn't matter. You never lose the ability to apply mom-logic to any situation because once you're a mama, the job never ends."

"I know. I know. I'm that way with Lacey Marie. Rinse off that bowl for me will you, sugar?"

"Does it take a long time for the water to get hot?" Cozie turned taps on the chipped enamel sink.

"No, but it does take a couple minutes to let the rust wash out of the pipes." Realizing she had just left an opening for her friend to tell her again why she needed to renovate this dump, she scrubbed at the table with her egg-slimed paper towel—and changed the subject. "Sometimes I think of my little girl off at that big old college and . . ."

"And you get so jealous you could pop."

"No!"

"Admit it." Cozie swished water over the bowl and took a few swipes at its underside with the sponge.

"I *miss* my child!"

"Of course you do. One thing has nothing to do with the other. You love her and miss her, but that doesn't mean you don't harbor some secret longing to be *like* her, out having new experiences." She leaned back against the counter, tipped her head toward the stairway door, then, seemingly satisfied no one was coming up yet, grinned slowly. "You could be having new experiences, of course, like for instance with Jillie's brother."

"If Lacey Marie is having the kind of new experiences that you expect me to have with Jillie's brother, jealousy would not be my first reaction."

"Why are you fighting this so? Nobody is forcing you to do anything? Just to consider working with the man and getting a fresh start."

"I'm afraid it's too late for Billy West and me to have a fresh start."

"You two have history?"

"In the sense that history is just riddled with unresolved conflict, then yes, we have history."

"Oh?"

"It's nothing! It's . . ." *Stupid.* She sighed. "It goes back to when he came back to Memphis seven or eight years ago and moved in with—oh, you know, that woman who tried to be a country singer for a while."

"Norrie Walker."

Rita remembered but nodded like she'd just heard it after years of never thinking of it.

"Honey, you should hear Miss Peggy go on about that girl. Apparently one of the reasons Norrie never became Mrs. West was that she had a rather relaxed approach to fidelity."

"Really?" All the gossip that went around this town and Rita had missed that one. Rita looked at the table, now dull with dried egg and then at her sticky hands, then at her awful mess of a house shoe. The crown tangled in her hair had started to make her head ache, and adding that poignant little tidbit of fact about Wild Billy to the mix did not help things one bit.

"So, what went on between you and Jillie's brother?"

"It goes back to the time when Norrie was pregnant. The last time Billy spent more time in Hellon than at home in Memphis, drinking with his old buddies, living off past glories that weren't really all that glorious if you ask me."

"I'm not one to be judgmental." Cozie shook her head. "But he acted a first-class asshole back then."

Rita had to laugh at her friend's *nonjudgmental* assessment.

"Everybody said so. Nobody to his face."

Rita shut her eyes. "Almost nobody."

"What did you do?"

She wet her lips and wriggled her foot out of her soggy shoe. "I told him his place was with Norrie. That he was thirty-two, a grown man with responsibilities, *and* I told him what I thought of his behavior."

"That doesn't sound too bad."

"Well, I didn't give him the sweetened condensed version, nor did I wait until he was alone."

"Rita! I'm shocked at you."

No more shocked than Rita had been. But something about that man brought out the fire in her. "And you wonder why I resist my mother's impulsive streak?"

"It couldn't have been *that* bad, honey."

"I tried to tell myself I did him a favor because then when his baby was born so early and the poor thing only lived a few weeks, well, he *was* there for Norrie and the child."

"So some good did come of it."

"I had hoped that was the case, but after I tore into him, that's when he stopped coming to town at all. When does he come here, now? Three or four times a year? And then he doesn't stay long enough to play any kind of role in his family."

"What?" Cozie pulled Rita into a sidelong hug, laughing. "You think he stays out of Hellon 'cause he's scared of you?"

"I think he stays out of Hellon because he's all the things I accused him of being that night. *I'm* no more significant to the likes of him than—" She bent down and took up her yoke-matted slipper. "Than a discarded eggshell."

"You're creating your own reality again, Rita. You should speak your wants, not your fears."

"Fine. I want waffles."

Cozie stepped away, listening again at the doorway. "Rita . . ."

"I want another carton of eggs." Rita lifted her chin and held out her hands. "I'm speaking them into reality even as we stand here."

"Go change. I can hear them coming right now."

"Where are my eggs, Cozie?" She tipped her head up. The crown slid back. Quietly she beseeched the heavens, her slimy house shoe held aloft, "Eggs. Where are my eggs?"

"Where is your mind? I can hear them on the steps. Any second now Wild Billy West will be . . ."

"Wild Billy West can kiss my red-hot . . ."

"Yes?" The man braced his arm against the doorframe and put one boot over the threshold. And yet he seemed to fill up the whole room and suck most of the air out of Rita's lungs.

"Waffle iron," she whimpered. *Stupid, stupid, stupid.* All he had to do was show up and that became her self-fulfilling prophecy. But she'd be damned if she'd let *him* know it.

"Hello again, Rita. Hope I haven't caught you at a . . ." He took the long route to give her the once-over head to toe—or should she say tiara to toe?

Even from behind the cool dark shades, she felt the heat of his gaze.

Finally, he smiled, dipped his head just enough to peer over the top of his glasses and nail her with a smirk. ". . . bad time."

She tossed her house shoe to the floor and squared her shoulders. He could look askance at her, but she would not let him look down on her. "Not at all, Mr. West."

"Good to hear it." He stepped forward, hand outstretched.

She never let her smile waver as she fit her hand in his and pressed a glob of gooey egg yoke into his warm, callused palm.

"Oops, I forgot! Had a little accident with a raw egg a minute ago." With a gleam in her eyes and her dimples flashing, Rita cranked that killer smile of hers up a notch.

She might as well have handed him his ego in that handshake. No one else in Hellon would dare do such a thing. Damn, but Will admired this woman.

She withdrew her hand and cleaned it off on what looked like an old hospital gown that she had thrown on over her nightclothes. "I am *so* sorry about that."

"No, you're not." He didn't remove his sunglasses or even so much as glance at the mess covering his palm. He simply took the gown's hem from Rita's grasp.

She let out a little gasp that left her full lips pursed.

He edged in close to her and wiped his hand on the soft fabric.

She didn't pull away.

"You're not one bit sorry. Are you?"

"Well, I . . ." Her gaze dipped to his hands on her clothing. She started to touch her temple but froze the instant her fingers hit a crown knotted up in her hair.

He kept on cleaning his hands and tried not to decide if he was alarmed or impressed with the sight of so much sparkle this early in the morning.

"You're not sorry." No woman wearing a damn pageant tiara in her kitchen would feel the least bit of regret over an action like that. "You've got nothing to feel sorry about. Your little playmates there cooked up my coming by today without telling you what they had in mind, didn't they?"

"I had no part in asking you here."

"I understand that. You didn't ask for my help at all." She damn sure needed his help, but she didn't ask. She wouldn't. Not Rita. He dropped the hem of her gown. "Do you know what I have to say about that?"

"Why should I care what you have to say about anything, Mr. . . ."

"I say you've just sealed a deal to get your Pig Rib Pigsty a bargain-rate makeover."

"Wh-what?"

He had a vague awareness of some feminine squeals and laugher in the background, but his focus remained with Rita. "I'm not a man to weigh every pro and con before making up my mind. I decide what I want to do, and I do it. I want to help you fix up your place, Rita."

She blinked and somehow her big brown eyes grew bigger, deeper, more compelling. "If you said that to impress me, you've wasted your breath."

"I know."

"You . . . you *know*?"

"I know you're not impressed with me."

"I didn't exactly say . . ."

"You've gone out of your way more than once to make sure I know it." He held his open hand up. He tried not to grin at her, but he couldn't hold it back.

She pressed her lips together and looked away.

"That's the reason I can't say no to this project. I wanted to say no, believe me. I tried to say no." He reached toward her.

She flinched.

He raised his hands to show his innocent intentions.

Her face clouded but she didn't stop him.

Reaching behind her head, he began to unwind Rita's hair slowly, meticulously from the gold and rhinestones. "For anyone else I would say no."

She shifted to keep some space between their bodies. "You don't have to—"

"But I *do* have to, Rita." He freed the crown. For a minute, he turned it this way and that, studying how it glittered in the light of the cramped kitchen's window.

"My Dixie Belle Duchess crown. I only put it on my head because . . ." She took it from him and shot Jillie and Cozette a scathing glare.

"I think I understand." He didn't. Not really. But then, he didn't really give a damn about the crown or why she had it on. "So, when can we talk about my suggestions for redoing the restaurant?"

"When pigs fly."

"I . . . I beg your pardon?"

She set the crown on the table and cocked her head. Her rat's nest of a hairdo fell forward. Then, seemingly oblivious of the fact that she looked like a walking laundry pile, she gave him a look so sweet he wouldn't need sugar in his tea for a month. "Not that I don't appreciate the offer. I mean a man of your repute and your obvious"— she cleared her throat— "talent, willing to fritter away a few hours—"

"Days. In fact, it will probably take a few days

just to come up with the rough ideas for what needs doing."

"... of your precious time on a person like me—"

"You mean a person I respect and want to help?"

"... and place like mine, well, I should certainly feel grateful, right?"

"I don't know about grateful, Rita. I feel like mostly we make our own way in this life. If we see an opportunity to make that way better, we should grab it."

"So, you think I'd be foolish not to grab this opportunity?"

"Actually, I was thinking about me."

Her deep brown eyes opened wide. "You think I should grab *you*?"

Jillie and Cozette hooted like frat boys at a kegger.

Rita shot them a look that neither shut them up nor left any question that they would pay later for their part in this. Her newly cooled gaze targeted him again. "Maybe this would work better if you simply explained your thinking, Mr. West."

"What's to explain, Rita?" He used her given name to try to shame her into dropping the mister business. "I was thinking of myself."

"Yourself?"

"Some people believe I am always thinking of myself. You know like the self-involved bastard I can be."

She had the decency to wince at that, but just fleetingly.

"That is what you called me that day you told me off, right? A self-involved bastard?"

She folded her arms. "An immature, irresponsible, self-loving donkey-headed bastard."

He nodded. "How kind of you to have remembered."

"No bother."

"So, didn't it ever occur to you that an 'immature' and so on bastard would not be so quick to give his time away if he didn't think he'd get something out of it?"

"I see."

"I don't think you do."

"Oh?" Her lips remained rounded after the whispered syllable faded away.

"No." He adjusted his sunglasses at the temple. "This is something I just have to do, Rita."

"Remodeling *my* place is just something *you* have to do?"

"Yes."

"*Have* to do?" Her voice came out soft as a shared confidence. "The only thing you have to do, Wild Billy—"

"Will."

"Is get the hell out of my apartment."

He glanced behind him, then leaned just one shoulder against the fridge, careful not to bother the photos and school papers stuck on it. "But you invited me so cordially to stay for breakfast."

"Now, I'm inviting you, cordially, to eat dirt and die."

"Eat *dirt* and die?" He stroked his chin like he

had to contemplate her G-rated version. "Now see, you didn't tell me Jillie would be cooking."

Cozette's squawk of a laugh again reminded him that they were not alone.

"Very funny," Jillie muttered from her seat on the couch across the room.

"Yes, you are a very funny man." Rita turned away from him and in a single step stood facing the sink. "Why don't you take your act on the road?"

The less she wanted him around, the less likely she became to ask him now—or ever—for help, the more determined he became to change her mind. "Why don't I stay here and help you get the meal on the table?"

"Why don't you"—she turned in time to press the bowl she'd taken from the counter right into his midsection—"bite me?"

"Maybe I will." He set the bowl aside, then leaned in close so that no one but Rita could hear him whisper, "After breakfast."

Miracle of miracles, he'd left her without a single smart-ass comeback. If she were any other women, he would have taken advantage of that one instant of vulnerability to kiss her senseless.

She stepped away and put her back to her friends. "I won't abide your pity, Will."

"My pity?" She had his respect. His gratitude. His sudden, astounding desire to take her in his arms and kiss her until neither of them could stand. But pity? He lowered his head and his voice to further exclude the others. "You haven't got it."

"I'm not ready," she whispered.

He brushed his thumb along the neckline of the hospital gown. "Then get ready."

"I don't mean my clothes. I am not ready inside of me. I have to give this some thought."

"What's to think about? You want to renovate the restaurant, don't you?"

"I have to. It's all I have after Pernel's latest escapade. I can't keep on paying Lacey Marie's tuition if I don't have income. I can't sell the business in the shape it's in now."

"You want to sell the Palace?"

"I don't know what I want. I do know that I have to get the Palace up and running and turning a profit again before I can even consider what to do next."

"You don't have a lot of money to spare."

"I have my share of our savings and money from the sale of the house. I think I could get a business loan if I wanted to sink myself in debt up to my earlobes for this place."

"Or you can accept my help for nothing. I can find friends in the business to give you a discount so deep you'll hear an echo when you open the bill."

"Either way, I'll be beholden to someone, won't I?"

"The devil you know or the devil you don't know."

She narrowed her eyes at him. "Which are you?"

He laughed. "Of all the people in this mudhole

town, you are one of the very few I can say does know me, Rita."

"Me?" She put her hand just below her throat.

"You saw right through me from the git-go."

"Well, maybe not from the git-go." The corners of her lips lifted, just slightly.

He had no idea such a subtle gesture could wrap itself around a man's heart with the warmth of a long-overdue welcome home. He smiled back at her. "At least you know what you're getting when you deal with me."

"I can't just throw caution to the wind and let myself get swept up in this." She reached past him and touched a photo on the fridge.

He craned his neck to check out the picture of Rita standing next to a lovely young girl wearing a Hellon High maroon cap and gown. Her daughter, he decided. He thought of the child in the graveyard he'd come to remember today and the familiar hurt flooded his chest again.

"I am not sure of what I want to do, yet." She ran her fingertip over the young girl's cheek.

"That's too bad because I need a decision today." He knew he had to push her for her own good—and for his.

She looked from the photo to his face. She pressed her lips tightly shut and started to shake her head.

At last after all this time standing in her home, he slowly slid his sunglasses off, trusting that she would understand and accept what she saw in his eyes. "Tell me what you want to do, Rita."

Her hand went to her mouth. She blinked. She looked down, then met his gaze again. "Nothing really seems about what I want anymore. It's come down to a case of ready or not I have to do something, hasn't it?"

He supposed he nodded, though he was so lost in her eyes he couldn't have sworn he'd done that.

"I *have* to do this. *We* have to do it, don't we?"

"Do what?" His voice hardly made a sound. Clearing his throat, he went on. "Breakfast or letting me come in for a few days as a consultant on the renovation?"

"Both, I guess."

"Can I get a rain check on that breakfast?"

"Um, yes, I . . . uh, I don't see why not."

"I'm in kind of a rush to get back to Memphis." Across the room Jillie stood up. He sucked in a quick breath and slid his glasses back on. "Well, not so much of a rush as I don't really want to hang around, not today."

She nodded.

"But let me clear my schedule and I'll be back in a few days and we'll get down to it. Deal?" He held his hand out to her.

She stared at it for only a moment before she raised her gaze to his face and surrendered the most sincere but skeptical smile he'd ever seen. "Deal."

Chapter 3

EVERY DIXIE BELLE AGREES:
*When a Southern woman tells you she is not going to tell
you what to do that is precisely what she has in mind.*

"The key word I want you to keep in mind is simplicity." Rita stood in the center of the Palace's serving floor. She'd had roughly forty-eight hours to adjust to the fact that Wild Billy would be in her life—or at least in her place of business—to help her sort things out.

She'd spent two days since she'd agreed to his help steeling herself to tell him *thanks but no thanks*. But as soon as he showed up to begin work, those words failed her. "I want this handled with a minimum of fuss and bother."

"The floor has to be ripped up." Will paced off a few steps, his head bent. "No getting around that."

"Nothing complicated."

"The place needs light, too. Maybe a second picture window in that wall left of the door."

"Only the very essential improvements, nothing drastic. A couple coats of paint here, a half dozen new fixtures there."

"One well-placed sledgehammer."

"Sledgehammer?"

He pantomimed breaking through the front wall.

She could not help but notice the play of his muscles, the ease with which he moved his body.

He spread his arms to gauge the size of the could-be window.

Rita fought off a sigh of pure satisfaction at the sight of him practicing his craft.

He scratched under his chin, then ran his thumb over his lower lip, his gaze trained on the wall in front of him.

How comfortable he appeared with himself and his work. Strong. That described him. And capable, she decided without needing proof of it. But not rigid or overbearing. The man looked . . .

He stood on the bench of one of the booths and spread both his hands over the rough, red bricks.

He looked . . . like a grown-up! A big, sexy—without even being aware of his sexiness—all-American male.

"I think somebody took a sledgehammer to my head." She pressed her cool fingertips to her temples but kept her veiled watch on the man making plans for her livelihood.

Folks around town often said Will belonged in the movies. If Rita were to cast Billy West in a role, it would be as the darkly sexy outcast who lived by his own set of rules and no visible sense of honor.

She eyed the man who filled the empty room with just his presence and felt the knots in her stomach. Obviously he had some sense of honor, or he wouldn't be here. Will wasn't some central casting version of a rebel bad boy anymore. He was something far more dangerous. He was a real, flesh-and-blood, doing-the-right-thing-for-God-only-knew-what-reason, fully grown adult man. The way they are supposed to be, not like a cutout from a magazine or a dreamed-up character, but a real man.

Thinking that way about him only intimidated her even more. From her father's immaturity to Pernel's eccentricities, life had not prepared her to handle a real man—well, not to *handle* him, but to—

"That's it, baby." Will interrupted her thoughts. He stepped away from the booth and aimed another imagined swing at the dingy brick wall. "It'd be over before you knew what hit it."

Rita liked the way his black hair curled against his tanned neck in stark contrast to his soft white shirt. He no longer had the long, lean lines of a young athlete, but that only heightened his appeal to her. If, she quickly corrected herself, a man like that could ever even remotely appeal to a smart, principled, down-to-earth woman like her.

"We can do this, Rita." He faced her. "I know we can do it."

"You think?" The driest whisper she'd ever heard came from her lips.

"I know we can, if you want to pursue it."

"Pursue . . . it?"

". . . *don't kid yourself, ladies, this is about sex. It's about passion and tension and longing for something more. It's about tearing everything down that doesn't work any longer, about getting tired and sweaty and when it's done about producing something worthwhile. It's about rebirth and bursting through to the next level.*" Cozette's words came back to haunt her.

"Yeah, pursue it, follow through, go after it. What do you say?"

"Let's do it!" She said it, all right. But danged if she had planned to say it, at least not with that much energy. "But let's not get too carried away. Can't we take it nice and easy? Do a few things and see how that goes then decide if it needs more work after that?"

"We'll have to yank those out." Will scratched something down on his already crowded legal pad, then pointed his pencil at the row of shabby booths in the back. "Yank 'em out and have ourselves a great big ole Tennessee bonfire."

"Baby steps, that's what's in order here." She pinched her thumb and finger together, but he did not even look her way.

"And while we're at it let's toss this lunch counter onto the flames as well." He slammed his palm onto the worn surface.

Their half-empty glasses of iced tea shuddered at the impact.

He took a drink from his, then clunked it back down as he swept his gaze over the room. The air around them practically shimmered with his enthusiasm. "I bet I can come up with a working list of recommendations by nightfall. Tomorrow we can go over specifics and talk budget, and then I can get moving."

"Don't feel you need to hurry on my account."

If he picked up on her sarcasm, it didn't show as he settled down on a vinyl-covered stool at the counter. He fanned the pages of his notes a few times, his shoulders hunched forward and his back to her. "No need to drag my part in all this out. At this rate I can be back in Memphis in time for a late dinner at the Rendezvous."

"Good. Hate for something as trivial as my uprooting and reordering my entire life to put a cramp in your plans for the weekend."

He spun halfway around to look her way. "What?"

"Nothing."

"Yeah, I thought it was nothing." He grinned, more with his eyes than with his lips.

He had heard her. He just wanted the satisfaction of making her say something so ungrateful and rude to his smarmy, smug, drop-her-dead-where-she-stood handsome face.

"I think you actually like it when I say something meant to put you in your place, Mr. West."

"Call me Will." He took another slug of tea, which was mostly sugary dregs and melting ice. He cracked one of the round pieces of ice in his mouth and gave her a wink like they'd shared some naughty secret. "*Especially* when you're saying something intended to put me in my place."

What a truly twisted individual. Unless, of course, that was his way of showing her he knew the truth about himself. Could Wild Billy, at one time every inch the self-loving donkey-headed bastard she'd pegged him for, have changed?

"Anyway, you'll probably be glad for me to get gone from here quick as I can, right?"

She shrugged, sort of. More like lifted her shoulders slightly and tipped her head and hummed a nonanswer answer.

"I know I'll be glad to hit the road that much sooner."

"Why?" She did not ask as a way of accusation. Though some part of her wanted to do just that—come right out and accuse the man of providing his family the emotional stability of a dust devil. "Why are you always so het-up to get out of Hellon?"

"Because it's Hellon."

"It's also where your only family lives. Your mother isn't getting any younger, you know."

"As long as the grandest beauty salons and finest plastic surgeons in the region remain open for business, she ain't getting any *older* either."

"And what about Jillie?"

"She actually prefers to go up north for her beauty treatments."

Glib. She should have known that's how a man this shallow and self-involved would respond. He hadn't changed. But he was right about one thing, she'd definitely be glad to get shed of him as quick as possible. "Never mind. Sorry I even brought it up."

"Jillie is an adult, Rita. I don't see how my hanging around Hellon until I'm stifled within an inch of my life with phony hero worship is going to have any effect on her."

"Maybe if you showed her there was something genuinely heroic to look for in others, to strive for in herself. Maybe if you were more of a presence in her life, you'd counteract some of the other . . . influences."

He laughed, but not brightly. "In other words, Mother."

"Miss Peggy isn't a bad sort, really, she's just . . ."

He held up his hand to stop her. "I don't need another lecture from you on my responsibilities to my loved ones, thank you."

"Your family is a mess. You know that much, don't you?"

He rubbed his hand over the back of his neck.

"You know a lot of your mother's stirring up trouble all the time stems from pure loneliness."

He conceded as much with a nod so curt it hardly qualified as a head movement.

"And did you know that Jillie has decided that since there are no good men left on the face of the earth, she'd rather take up with outright rotten ones? Just to save herself a lot of heartache?"

He clucked his tongue. "That's her choice."

"Well, it's a bad one." She didn't have to tell him that, did she? Surely he had enough moral grounding to know this was a bad, bad thing and enough concern for his sister to want to know the truth. "She's dating a married man. Did you know that?"

"Paul?" His features clouded.

"You *do* know?"

"I teased her about him but, no, I never thought she'd . . ." He rubbed the spot between his eyebrows with one crooked knuckle. "Damn it, Rita. What is wrong with her?"

For an instant she actually felt bad for unloading the specifics on him.

But he shook it off before she could so much as backpedal an inch. He let his shoulders drop and scored his thumbnail over the gouged lunch counter's surface. "You're her friend, why don't you talk to her?"

"You think for one minute I've stayed silent on the subject?"

He laughed.

"But it all boils down to the fact that a friend is not family. She needs her family. She needs *you* to talk to her."

"I wouldn't know what to say. I'm not exactly . . ." He let the thought trail off.

"And you think *I'm* a prime example?" She leaned one elbow on the lunch counter. "You think I'm the person to stand up and lecture anyone on how many good men are out there looking for decent women to become their lovers and lifelong helpmates?"

His expression gentled. "I see your point."

She straightened her back. "Don't take that as a slap at Pernel, now."

"No, I wouldn't."

"That's about me and my faults."

"I know that's how you see it. You take on the blame and worry for far too much of your loved one's problems."

"And you won't take any of either." The man brought out the fire in her, for sure. Fire and foolhardiness. Still, once she'd blurted her true opinion out she couldn't take it back, so she rushed on. "You accept none of the blame. None of the worry."

"Why should I?" He rubbed the heel of his hand down his jeans, his gaze distant. "In the end what Jillie does is her call, too. Not much I can do about it."

"Should that stop you from trying? If my family was in the kind of disarray yours is in, and I could do anything, *anything* to help them, nothing short of an act of God could keep me from it." Now it had gone personal. She blinked and cursed the tears welling in her eyes. "Of course, I wouldn't presume to tell you what to do—"

"Uh-oh." He laughed.

"What?"

"When a Southern woman tells you she is not going to tell you what to do that is precisely what she has in mind. Stridently, ardently, no holds barred, she's going to tell you *just* what she thinks, what you should do and probably offer to kick your butt into gear to get it done, as well."

"Maybe we should stick to talking about the Palace renovations."

"Good idea."

"Like I said, I want to keep things uncomplicated."

"If that's really what you want—gut the place and walk away. Can't get much simpler than that."

"That's your ultimate solution, isn't it?" She wasn't just talking about the Palace. "Trash it all. Move on. Don't look back. Leave trying to make things better to somebody else."

"That's all I committed to do here, Rita. Consult on the remodel and put you in touch with the professionals who can do it."

How could she argue with that? She looked around her. He made it sound so easy when to her it was the most difficult task she'd ever faced—getting herself on the right track for the rest of her life.

"You want this?" Will had snatched the last chicken leg off the platter she had brought down for their lunch and held it up.

"No." She folded her arms not caring that it made the bib of her baggy overalls gap down to show her cleavage in her scooped-neck T-shirt. "As a matter of fact I don't want any of this. If you recall this was all your sister's doing. Hers, Cozie's, and yours. Not mine."

"Uh-huh." He made no pretense of looking away from her breasts. He didn't even have the decency to act the teeniest bit contrite at wangling her into accepting his assistance. "What about the chicken?"

"What about it?"

"Best damn fried chicken I ever had. Best meal I've had since I don't know when. Mind if I polish it off?"

"No." Good gravy, how could you stay mad at a man who liked your cooking that much?

"Guess if you can't make a pig of yourself at a place with a princess of pork as its symbol, where can you do it?" His fork scraped the plate as he got up every last bit of potato salad for one man-sized bite.

Rita sighed and plunked down on the stool next to his. "I do like to see a man who enjoys eating."

"Way you cook, darling, it'd be a sin not to enjoy it."

"Still, seems like nobody enjoys eating anymore, they've gotten so all-fired worried about fat and cholesterol and carbohydrates."

"I could stand to think about those things myself." He hooked one thumb under the waistband of his jeans but kept a firm grip of the chicken leg in his other hand.

"You?" She snorted. She set out to laugh deep and sexy in the back of her throat but snorted instead. Still, she tossed her hair back the way she had intended to if she'd actually pulled off the husky flirtation. "What would you worry about? You're fine just as you are."

He leaned on the counter with both elbows, his gaze fixed on her. "Not like I was when I played football for the Hellon Hurricanes."

"Why would you want to be like that? So you're a little thicker in the middle, a little broader in the chest." She held her hands apart.

"Those aren't the only places I've grown since adolescence." With one leg braced straight and the other on the footrail of the lunch counter, he gave the sense of someone relaxed yet ready to manage anything thrown at him. "If you're measuring."

He spoke of personal growth, personality, depth of character, of course. Still she found herself struggling against the powerful urge to glance at his jeans.

He put the chicken leg down and began lazily to lick his fingertips. "But then not many of us look the way we did at seventeen."

She tucked her hair behind her ear. She wondered if she suddenly sucked her tummy, would he catch her at it and tease her? Instead of risking it, she went on. "You were a scrawny, snot-nosed kid then. Who wants that? Now you're a man, a real man with a real man's needs and appetites."

"True enough, Rita." His dark eyes glittered,

and his smile—if you could call that slow, smirky tilt of his lips an authentic smile—never faltered. "True enough."

She felt a perfect fool. All her blustering the past few days, all the speeches she had made to herself about how she would stay in control and not let him rattle her, and she had not lasted through their first lunch before blurting out something dumb. "All right, you win. Clean your plate. Take your notes. We'll go over them tomorrow, then you can be on your way."

"With the satisfaction of having done my good deed for the decade and not having had to spend more than a single night in Hellon." He said it in an undertone, like a commentator filling in what Rita had kindly left unspoken.

"I didn't say—"

"But that's what you thought, and we both know it. Despite my efforts on your behalf, Rita, you don't really think any more highly of me than you did six years ago when you told me off."

"Eat the last biscuit, too. No sense in its going to waste."

He took the biscuit in one hand and turned it over once, then again. "You're the one who insisted you wanted things uncomplicated. Well, this is about as simple as it gets. I make my recommendations and a list of people who will give you a break on costs. If you choose to follow through, you follow through. If you don't . . ."

You're a damned fool. It always came down to that with her and Wild Billy, didn't it? He was cool and sexually smoldering. He said and did all the right things. She was cautious and a little too lumpy to have inspired lust even in her own husband.

"If I don't follow through on your suggestions, you'll never know the difference." She smiled at him. "So why make an issue of it now? Do what you came to do, then tomorrow we will go over your ideas, I'll thank you as sincerely as I can, we'll shake hands, and say—"

"I hope you're happy!" The front door banged open and Jillie stood in the threshold, her hands on her hips. "Because now the shit has really hit the fan!"

Chapter 4

EVERY DIXIE BELLE HAS HEARD:
Only an untrained hound sinks his teeth in a decoy. The harder you try to fool people into thinking you're on the high road, the more down and dirty the gossip is going to get.

"First rule of life in a small town." Jillie pointed her finger at his face and walked into the Palace, a diva taking center stage. "When you are up to something you don't want absolutely everybody to know about, you should never, never, *never* park your car in a place where just anyone can come along and clap their eyes on it."

"I'd have thought you of all people would know that." Rita went up on tiptoe to peer out the front window, then lowered her lashes to nail him with a glance over her shoulder.

Will wasn't looking at her eyes or her shoulders. "I've never been one to hide my light under a bushel. I thought the two of *you* would know that."

Jillie snorted.

Rita didn't say a word, though her lips parted

in a way Will found absolutely riveting. Or was it tempting? His gaze wandered downward over her body again.

A sudden flush spread over her cheeks. She sucked in her lower lip.

Tempting. Definitely tempting.

She turned away, glanced behind her, then took a step to place a chair between them, hiding her lower body from his eyes.

Will frowned at the predictable reaction. He wanted to tell her to knock it off. He wanted to challenge her the way she had challenged him in the past. He wanted to rant at her for buying into the belief that if a woman's body didn't fit into that ever-narrowing mold, that she should feel ashamed of it.

Rita didn't fit any mold, and that made her all the more remarkable. She was round and ripe and . . . full. That's what he wished he could make her see. Her breasts were full, her hips, too, but more to the point her heart and mind were full and rich with the things that really mattered in life. If he could convince her of that, he'd have given her a gift greater than any business expertise he had to offer.

"Listen, Rita—" He stepped toward her.

"No, you listen." She did not say it rudely, but more like someone sharing an idea. She pointed toward the ceiling, and her expression was no-nonsense. "Maybe you've forgotten the Palace is also my home for the time being. Having your car parked outside is bound to stir up some talk."

"Talk? Why?" He laughed. "Nothing illegal or immoral is going on here. I'll drive back to Memphis before dark and make a big show of coming back in broad daylight. Tool straight through the center of town with the top down and the radio blasting just like the old days if that's what it takes."

"Mercy, don't do that! Only an untrained hound sinks his teeth in a decoy." Rita slashed both hands through the air. "And there are no untrained busybodies in Hellon. The harder you try to fool people into thinking you're on the high road, the more down and dirty the gossip is going to get."

"Either way, my car won't stay there overnight. If a few people with nothing better to do think they can spin that into some kind of scandal, let them try."

"This is Hellon, Billygoat. They *will* try." Jillie walked over to Rita, then turned to face him. They both folded their arms forming a would-be wall of feminine solidarity.

He hit his share of walls in his life, one more didn't faze him. "Let them. What do I care about a bunch of idle gossip?"

"I care. I wish to God I didn't." Rita rubbed her forehead and sighed. "But after all I've gone through these last few years, can you blame me if I shy away from offering up one more juicy tidbit to circle town at my expense?"

"I didn't think of that."

"Why would you?" It was a question devoid of

bitterness, and yet it and her expression conveyed every ounce of her disappointment in him, or in something about him that touched the deepest hurt in her. "You'll be out of here in a day or so, with all this left behind and forgotten."

"Don't count on that." He met her gaze and held it, hoping he could convey even an inkling of the esteem he held her in.

She looked away first.

"I don't understand why this is such a problem." He hadn't expected to hear the ring of hardness in his own voice. Still, he pressed on. "I'm here on business, plain and simple."

"Yeah, but it's *my* business." She put her hand above her breasts and shut her eyes. "Your consultation not withstanding, Will, I haven't decided exactly what I want to do with the Palace. I hope to spare myself a few dozen heaping helpings of 'constructive' input mucking up the process while I'm making up my mind."

"Then don't put up with it."

"I have to. Don't you understand that? I live here. Maybe you don't recall what that's like anymore."

"Of course I recall it. Why do you think I live in Memphis?"

"You can take this lightly. It all rolls off you like water off a duck's back. But I'm the one who has to stay and deal with the aftermath." She walked to the counter and began to clean up the dishes from lunch. "Move your car, Will, please, before someone besides Jillie sees it, and—"

"Actually, that's why I'm here." Jillie took a seat on the other side of the lunch counter. She put her hand on Rita's. "Word's out. Pernel is on his way over right now."

Rita's lips silently formed a swear word that he suspected wouldn't faze a Sunday school teacher. "He's the very last person I want to know about my plans for this place. And him hearing I brought another man in to make over his old business? This won't be pretty."

"Of course it won't be pretty." Jillie crinkled up her nose. "We're talking about Pernel here."

Will laughed.

"It's not funny. Pernel will resist my trying to do anything new to his precious palace."

Will felt a double edge to Rita's words. "The place is yours now. What you do with it, or yourself, is none of his concern."

She didn't even look Will's way. "Pernel will take my making changes without consulting him as a personal affront—or worse."

"Worse?" Will scowled.

"He could insist on lending a hand, getting involved with the renovations himself. That's one headache I want to avoid, thank you." Rita scraped the last bit of potato salad off the serving fork.

"Then just tell him to butt out."

"You don't know how he can *get*."

"Let him *get* his panties in a wad. That's not your lookout." Will rounded the lunch counter, took the dishes from Rita, and started for the kitchen. "You don't have to tell him a damn thing, you know. You don't owe him anything anymore."

"I can't just turn a blind eye to the feelings of a friend or family member. I'm not like . . . some people," she called after him.

I'm not like you. She did not have to say it aloud to drive her point home. He stood just inside the kitchen door, his hands full and his spirit drained. He and Rita had always been worlds apart, and, at least to her thinking, they always would be.

"Jillie, are you *sure* he's on his way over?" Even from the kitchen he could hear weariness and worry butting heads for control in Rita's tone.

"I'm sure," Jillie said.

"*How* do you know?"

His sister paused. He could just imagine her drawing this out just to hang on to the attention even a few seconds longer. "Right place, right time."

He flipped the faucet on to let the water run into the deep steel sink as he set the dishes aside.

"Is he coming *alone*?" Rita asked softly.

Again an unwarranted lag in the conversation followed.

It was all he could do not to go back in there and grab his sister by her scrawny neck and make her give Rita the kind of outright answer she deserved.

"I don't think he'd dare bring his new girl-friend around," Jillie finally replied with a soothing tenderness he had forgotten she possessed. "Not here. Not yet."

"I want to meet her at some point. I want him to bring her by sometime soon but under . . . better circumstances. You know?"

"Well, I don't think it'd hurt to have him wonder what's gone on here between you and *Wild Billy*." She all but shouted the hated nickname right at the open kitchen door. "But you're right. You ought to get yourself a little more fixed up before you meet the 'other woman,' so to speak. Or in this case is this the other other woman?"

"Mind your manners, Jillie."

"Ignore her bitterness, Rita. That's just the voice of experience talking." He'd never have sunk so low if his sister hadn't started the low blows with that "get yourself a little more fixed up" crack to Rita. He shut the water off. "I don't think you have a place telling anyone how to act, baby sister, or who they should meet with when, or how they should look when they do it."

"Fine. Then I won't bother to tell you to pull your swelled head out of your behind before Mama gets over here."

"Mama?"

"She's on her way, too."

The plates crashing into the suds covered the worst of his low-from-the-gut cussing. He strode to the doorway between the dining area and kitchen and hit Jillie with a glare, his lips stiff. "How the hell did she find out I was here?"

His sister toyed with the empty napkin holder. "One of her ladies saw your car."

"Round here we call them Miss Peggy's Secret Service." Rita put a hand to her hip. Her dark eyes lit up.

He suspected she felt some sort of affection or some such nonsense for his mother and the Retired Junior League gossip brigade. "They know all the secrets and consider it a service to let your mother in on them."

He cursed again.

Rita laughed.

He gave her a look that made hardened workmen shut their mouths and drop their gazes from his.

"Smile, Will, company's coming!" Her dimples betrayed how much she enjoyed seeing him in the same fix as her.

He clenched his jaw.

"I wouldn't want to be in your shoes now." Jillie cocked her head and aimed her gaze at his feet. "Or ever, for that matter."

"Putting yourself in someone else's shoes has never been your forte, little sister. Putting your scrawny ass in another woman's marriage bed seems to be more your style now."

"Bastard," Jillie hissed.

"Got that right." He braced himself for the slap he so deserved and felt all the more the big jerk when it did not come. "At least I can stand to hear the truth about myself. Can't you?"

"You wouldn't know the truth if . . ."

"Y'all stop it, right now!" Rita stepped between them.

Jillie turned her glaring gaze on her.

Will smiled, just a touch of his practiced wiseass smile.

"We are standing at ground zero of a couple of converging you've-plunged-a-knife-into-my-heart-for-not-telling-me-what-you-were-up-to, walleyed, claws-out hissy fits." A commanding calm came over Rita. A new kind of power seemed to vibrate around her. "We have to decide how to handle this with a minimum of hurt feelings or hair-pulling and without any significant information exchanges, right?"

"Right." Will focused on his sister, his tone threatening her to keep on arguing.

"Yeah, right." Jillie brushed at her collar.

"So, any suggestions on how we go about accomplishing that?"

"Is gunplay absolutely out of the question?" Will narrowed his eyes and grinned.

"Will!"

"Just a couple of warning shots over their heads." He tried to pull off looking innocent but had no illusions that it worked.

"Too bad you don't have tea and cake to serve them." Jillie's wistful gaze made him wonder if she actually meant that ridiculous suggestion or if she had finally gone mad from years of starving herself to stay thin.

But Rita's eyes twinkled like Christmas. "Who says I don't have tea and cake?"

Jillie turned her head so fast her red curls trembled. "You do?"

"How long have you known me?"

"You do!" Jillie grinned. "I don't dare hope that it's . . . ?"

"Yes, indeedy."

"Mother and Pernel are bearing down on this place like two bad-weather fronts about to clash and y'all have started talking in shorthand or code or something." Will leaned his shoulder against the doorframe but kept one eye on the front window.

"I made a Perfect Princess cake." Rita held her hands together and raised her gaze heavenward, all childlike and waiting for a reward of high praise for her actions.

Jillie clapped. "Yes!"

"I was going to serve it to your brother later."

"Oh, Rita, that's just the thing, isn't it? You and Billy sitting here waiting for them all cool and collected like a pair of spiders poised on a web—and with Princess cake to offer no less!"

"I don't . . ." Damn he hated to say this aloud. He cleared his throat and folded his arms. "I don't believe I understand."

"Follow me." Rita snagged his sleeve as she hurried past into the kitchen.

"I'll pull a table and four chairs into the middle of the floor."

"What is going on here, Rita?"

"You know that old song 'If I Knew You Were Coming I'd Have Baked a Cake'?"

"Song?" He tagged along with her to the mammoth steel-doored refrigerator.

"Well, I knew you were coming, so I did bake a cake. My specialty."

"Princess cake?"

"Three layer, red velvet cake with a seven-minute boiled frosting and a crown on top made of drizzled white chocolate and strawberries." She brought out a large plastic container of tea. "Pour that into the nicest pitcher you can find, why don't you? I'll get the cake."

He scanned the shelves until he found the one pitcher that was neither cracked nor stained nor ugly enough to send his mother into a fainting spell. He filled it with ice from the machine. "You were going to serve me something called Princess cake?"

"And you were going to ask for seconds, probably thirds, and a piece to take home for a midnight snack."

Having tasted her cooking already, he did not doubt that. He poured the tea into the new container. "But *Princess* cake?"

"Don't start with me, Will." Both of her arms and most of her upper body disappeared inside the fridge. "I cannot deal with your mother, my ex, and your sexual-ambiguity-in-regard-to-snack-food identity crisis all at the same time."

He didn't even know where to start to address that. "Sexual ambiguity? Snack-food crisis? *Me?* I am not the one here with identity and self-esteem cri . . . Damn."

She held the plate before her, peering at him over the peaks of lacy confection and strawberries dipped in white chocolate. "The Perfect Princess cake."

"This will stop even my mama dead in her tracks."

"Shh. Quick, say a prayer."

"A *what*? Why?"

"Never say *dead* and *mama* in the same sentence if your mother is still living. Don't you have any sense at all?"

"You've as much as told me I don't."

"Shut your eyes and say a prayer, I mean it."

He closed his eyes and muttered under his breath. The message was far from heavenly. When he opened his eyes again Rita was gone, but the sweet aroma of that cake still lingered. So did the feeling that for all his bravado about coming here to help her realize her potential, he might well be the one who ended up learning a thing or two about life and himself in the bargain.

Chapter 5

EVERY DIXIE BELLE DISCOVERS:
What we tell ourselves we are, that's what we become.

"I thought you said they were on their way." Will raised his arm just enough to give Rita a view of his flexed muscles.

He was showing her his wristwatch, no doubt, but what she saw was muscle. Her pulse picked up. When Rita caught the subtle scent on Will's skin and took a deep breath she swore she drew in some kind of electrical charge that sent a shiver through her whole body.

Careful not to jiggle the table where they both sat in wait, she moved closer and pretended to make a note of the time. "Well, you know how it is around here. A body dare not step a toe outside the house without proper attention to hair, clothes, and makeup. Or the next thing you know somebody down at the Belles and Beaux Beauty

Salon will spread the word that you are definitely letting yourself *go!*"

"And Pernel can't afford that kind of bad word of mouth." Jillie never turned her gaze from the row of parking places out front. Still, her satisfaction at making a cutting remark about Rita's ex showed in the faint reflection of her face on the glass door where she stood watch.

"Did anyone ever tell you what a bitch you are, Jillie?"

"About as often as folks tell you what they really think of your brother," she said, not looking back to see how he took it.

"Then I guess you don't hear it often enough." He sat back and curved his hand around the top of Rita's chair now so close to his. "Unless Rita here gets after you now and again."

"Don't involve me in this." She could feel his hand there—*right there*—just a hairbreadth away from her back, and it made her jumpy.

He strummed his fingers once along the wood, so close she felt the vibrations on her back.

She would get up but what would she do? Pace? Pretend to polish the lunch counter? The one they planned to rip out and destroy as soon as they could? She might as well twist around in her seat and blurt out to the man, "You make me so nervous I can't think straight."

Great. Now *that* idea was in her head. What was it Cozette said about "self" talk? She rubbed her eyes. "What we tell ourselves we are, that's what we become."

"Hmm?"

She blinked, suddenly aware she'd spoken aloud. "Nothing, just an approach Cozie tries to get me to use."

Wham. The door slamming at the back of the kitchen cut her off. An odd cadence of footsteps *clack-a-clacking* toward them rivaled the skipping beat of her heart.

Rita braced herself. "Cozie says that what we tell ourselves we are—"

"I am here, and I am fit to be tied," Pernel's cry echoed through the vacant building.

"That's what we become." She followed Will's gaze to her ex-husband stopped in the doorway.

Pernel aimed his fiercest glare at her, then flung the scarf around his throat over one shoulder so that the end swirled downward to accent his backless sundress perfectly.

"I guess not every bit of gossip around Hellon is a gross exaggeration of the truth." Will narrowed his eyes.

Pernel smoothed back his auburn pageboy wig. He anchored his substantial pumps shoulder width apart and proceeded to wrestle with something inside the top of his dress. Pernel shifted his shoulder and one of the lumps in his bodice slipped lower than the other. He set about correcting the problem.

"Of course that depends on your definition of gross." Will shook his head.

"He hasn't decided which is the best cup size for his frame, and I'm sure that halter bra is giving him fits." Why Rita felt compelled to offer that tidbit was beyond her.

"Are they evened up now?" Pernel held his arms out and offered himself for their inspection.

"Not quite." She motioned to him. "Come over here and let me help you out."

"Wait. Hell's hobnobs, one of my press-on nails has come off inside here." He pulled the front of his dress out and began to shimmy and shake.

She thought of reminding him he might have some impediment that would keep the fake fingernail from falling clean through to the floor but stopped herself. She did not know how or if he had alleviated that problem and did not want to give him the opportunity to tell her. She might have come to accept the man's eccentricities, but there are some things an ex-wife just doesn't want to know. Whether the father of her child tucks or tapes to create a . . . streamlined silhouette falls in that category.

"Does he have to do that here?" Will winced.

"You don't have to be afraid of him, you know." Again she had no idea why she responded the way she did. That dang nerves thing, she suspected, or maybe her need to keep everything on an even keel. Whatever the reason, she went on trying to make lemonade out of . . . who was she kidding? Good old loyal Rita was actually trying to make lemonade out of those oversize grapefruits strapped to Pernel's chest. "Dressing like that doesn't mean he's an unfit father."

"Did I say I thought he was?"

"It obviously bothers you. And he's not gay; even if he were, he won't hit on you and as far as his taste in clothes—well, it's not contagious."

"That's twice now you've made a reference to me having some kind of gender hang-up." He held up two fingers, then raised his eyebrows at her. "It isn't because you think I'm intimidated by my mama is it?"

"I never said anything about—"

"Because I'm not."

"Not? Not what?"

"Intimidated by my mama *or* hung up about gender or sexual preferences." He angled his shoulder down so that he could speak into her ear, the clear hint of mischief in his deep, glittering eyes. "I welcome an opportunity to prove as much to you."

"You mean about your mother?"

"If you say so." He jerked his head to the side and grinned.

"Oh." Rita covered her mouth.

He chuckled, then glanced across the room at Pernel and scowled. "I know you don't hold me in the highest regard, but I do want you to know I am not homophobic. And surely you realize after the life I've led, I could care less what other consenting adults get up to in private."

After the life he'd led? Rita dared not speculate on that. "Then why does it bug you so much that Pernel is pursuing an alternative lifestyle?"

"It doesn't."

"Oh please, contempt for that man is written all over your face. How can you—"

"Because he hurt you." His almost black eyes fixed so intensely on her that he honed the world down to just the two of them.

"Got it!" Pernel held his arm up over his head, brandishing the nail between his thumb and forefinger. "I have to get this fixed before I lose it again. Do you have any acrylic glue, Rita?"

"I have some in my purse." Jillie rolled her eyes. "Honestly, Pernel, if you insist on going around town like this, you owe it to whatever personal pride you have left to do it right, not half-assed liked everything else you've ever taken on."

"Half-assed?" He gave her a look worthy of some silent-screen movie vamp and pulled it off stunningly. "Coming from a girl with no ass at all, I take that as a compliment."

"At least what I do have did not come from a mail-order catalog."

"You mean they don't have catalogs at the plastic surgeon's office? What do you do? Cut out pictures from magazines? Because if that's the case, hon, let me recommend you get yourself some new subscriptions."

"High-handed talk for a man with the world's worst case of hooter-scoot I've ever seen. One of those is high enough to put an eye out and the other is about to slip down into your panty hose."

"It is a bit like Big-Busted Bertha now." Rita

held her hands up chest high, then dipped one to waist level. "Big-Busted Bertha thirty years from now."

"I can't believe you just said that." Despite chastising her, Will did laugh. It felt good to hear it.

"Jillie, fix Pernel's nails and his boobies, please." She turned to Will. "I can't believe I just said *that*."

"You are either the nicest woman alive or a damn fool."

"Some people act like those are one and the same."

"I never said that."

"I may not be the kind of sophisticated woman you run into in the 'kind of life' you've led," She made quotation marks in the air. "But I didn't just fall off the turnip truck. I can see what you think of me, of my life and what I've done with it."

"I'm far more interested in what you can do with your life and your future, if you really want to." He almost put his hand on hers, but at the last second he held back and laid it on the table between them.

She didn't care that he hadn't completed the gesture. It felt good to have him beside her, on her team, as it were. It had been a very long time since she'd felt anyone was truly on her side for her sake alone. Though she knew the feeling existed mostly in her mind, she took a second to revel in it.

"Whatever you decide don't let Pernel walk all over you."

"I won't." She gave him a sinful smile. "Especially, not in those heels."

"How can you make jokes about all this after . . . ?"

"After what?" She sat back and watched Jillie work on Pernel. "After nearly fifteen years of him running our lives, me going along trying not to make waves, then him coming home one day and telling me it's over?"

"For starters—"

"Or maybe you mean how can I take things so lightly after he decided to let the world in on his previously private indulgence by showing up at our daughter's graduation in a cocktail dress, wig, and wedgies?"

"Why the bastard is still breathing is beyond me."

"Or how about how can I keep smiling after he sold my home? Made me take him to court to get this dump so I could have something to rebuild with?"

"Take your pick."

"I can be civil to him because . . ." She sighed. Having just recounted the short list of her ex's transgressions, she found herself hard-pressed to explain it adequately. In fact, she had to force the words out through a clenched jaw. "Because he is an important part of my life."

"*Was* an important part," Will amended.

"He is my daughter's daddy." A far reach to justify a lifetime of shabby treatment, but still . . . She raised her shoulders and laced her arms over her chest. She could not meet Will's unwavering gaze. "I can't just discard him or the role he has played in my life simply because he had the poor taste to fall out of love with me."

"Not even if you fell out of love with him right back?" He asked it so quietly she half wondered if she'd imagined it.

Had she fallen out of love with Pernel? Even looking at him now pressing his Plum Patina-glossed lips together while Jillie adjusted his fake bosom she could not go so far as to say she had fallen out of love with the man. That would mean she had been "in love" with him. She had never deluded herself, or him, into believing that. But she did love him in her own way. "I don't think you and I have the same definition of love, Will."

He tensed and looked away from her.

Her head told her to pull back, but the words rushed on. "For me it's a commitment, a promise. You can't just walk away from it when it doesn't suit you any longer. You can't turn it off when it's no longer pleasant or convenient."

His mouth grim, Will sat silent, motionless, his gaze on the elaborate cake in front of them.

She'd gone too far. The urge to pull things back into balance overtook her. "Not that I think you ever did that."

He straightened the forks, smoothed out a napkin with the back of his hand. He did not look at her. His very lack of response told her he had taken her words as an accusation.

"I know I might have implied something like

that in the past, but I don't . . ." In trying to protect her own emotions she'd trod on Will's feelings and reminded him how she had viewed his actions toward Norrie and the baby when they had needed him most. "Maybe we should change the subject." He exhaled, loudly.

"Blow on that nail so it will dry faster, and keep your shoulders straight but relaxed, that's what's making your girly-parts sag in the first place." Jillie pushed here and prodded there until she had Pernel standing like a shop mannequin. As she turned to head to the rest room, she called out over her shoulder. "Mother always told me to think of your spine as a string of pearls and to picture pulling the pearls straight, but not taut."

"Straight but not taut," Pernel echoed.

"Oh, now there's a motto for you if I ever heard one, Pernel," Rita called out, glad for the distraction. "Maybe I'll embroider it on a pillow or have you a bumper sticker made up. 'Straight but not taut.' "

"Stick to cooking and kindly leave the humorous commentary alone, Rita." Pernel started toward them. Oddly he did not look effeminate even in that outfit, but more feminine in a masculine way. Like a woman with mannish features. When he spoke, he went for a soft, raspy whisper instead of trying to raise his voice a register. When he reached the table he tried to swipe some frosting off the perfect cake. "Tackiness does not become you."

"Best to leave that to the experts." Will didn't so much as flinch as he took the cake stand in one hand and lifted it up and away. "Pernel here takes tacky to new heights—or is that lows?"

"I may dress like a lady, Mr. West. But I can still whip your ass man to man."

"I wouldn't want you to lose another nail." Will settled the cake back where it belonged and narrowed one eye at Pernel.

"Don't act all smug and coy with me."

Will grinned. "I wouldn't dream of it."

"I know what you're up to, both of you." He lowered himself into the seat next to Rita, but he completely ignored her and fixed his false-eyelash-framed eyes on the man next to her. "I know why you're here, West, and I am not happy about it."

"What could you possibly know about anything?" Rita bumped his elbow off the table and swept away the pool of magenta silk along with it. Heaven help them all if the man's scarf, which she suspected cost more than her secondhand wedding dress had, should trail across her Princess cake. "And why do you have anything to say about who comes and goes in my life?"

"I have something to say about what happens to the Palace. My name is still on the sign out front."

"But it's not on the legal documents. I am now sole owner of this place. I can do whatever I please with it."

"Rita, you have never done whatever you please. I know you." He licked the tip of his thumb and began cleaning up the tiniest fleck of white chocolate on the neckline of his dress. "Your entire life is about pleasing others, not yourself."

"Then maybe it's time I changed." Mercy! Did she say that? And without so much as a quiver in her voice?

"I know you've brought him in to fix this place up to sell it." Pernel stabbed a finger in Will's direction, his silver charm bracelet almost knocking over a dipped strawberry on the edge of the cake's crown. "Or worse yet to show me up. I won't have it."

"That not your call, bud . . . uh, lady?" Will scratched his ear and grimaced. "Is there something particular that people call you?"

"Is that a crack?" Pernel shifted in his seat so fast the cake stand wobbled. "Rita, your hired help is making a crack at my expense."

"He just wants to know how to refer to you," she said.

"And I'm not the *hired help.*"

"Tell your handyman that I haven't chosen my new name but do lean toward Starla."

Rita put her head in her hands.

"Starla Stark. It has an air about it." He raised his hand elegantly. "Don't you think?"

"All I can think about is keeping this cake nice until Miss Peggy arrives."

Pernel sat up straighter than an arrow. "Miss Peggy is coming *here*?"

"Any minute."

"I like that Miss Peggy." Pernel shook the hair off his face. "She has a lot of class. Person with that much class can hold her head up despite the occasional disappointment handed her."

Will grunted.

"Style. Class." Pernel sighed. "That's something a person is born with. You wouldn't understand, of course, Rita. You totally missed the boat on that count."

"I . . . I what?" She lifted her head, unable to believe her ears.

"Face it. You're middle-of-the-road, middle-class, fair-to-middling, muddling along through life."

Up until she'd heard it spill out of her ex-husband's glossed-within-an-inch-of-an-oil-slick lips, she had thought those were totally acceptable traits. Admirable even. Not the way she dreamed of living her life, but nothing to feel ashamed of, either. Her cheeks grew hot.

"And no amount of small-town social butt-kissing, no too-tacky-for-words tea party you stage, no meathead brought in from Memphis, can alter that simple fact." Pernel said it so matter-of-factly, not haughty or mean.

That only made it sound all the more scathing as a description in Rita's ears.

"You are what you are, Rita. Darling in your own way but deliberate and dull. Dull, dull, dull. And I forbid you to take on changing anything in my restaurant on your own."

Will's chair creaked. Hostility rose from his body like steam from a pot about to bubble over.

Rita beat him to the boiling point. "You forbid me? You *forbid*? Oh, that takes the cake, Pernel."

"No, Rita, he's not worth it." Will must have read her mind, or maybe in her anger she had telegraphed her intent a little too clearly. Either way, he got to the Princess cake a half second before she could grab the stand by the pedestal and dump all three layers down Pernel's dress.

"You're right, of course, Will." She threw back her shoulders. "My cake deserves better, and so do I."

"Yes, you do," Will agreed.

"So listen to me, Starla and/or Pernel Stark. You cannot forbid me to do anything."

Pernel crossed his legs like he'd grown bored with her attempted outburst already.

Rita ground her back teeth together. "I *will* renovate the Palace."

"I'll believe it when I see it," her ex muttered.

She pulled her shoulders up and raised her chin. If she had her crown handy, she might have plunked that on her head to add the proper air to her pronouncements. "Maybe I'll get myself a makeover while I'm at it."

Pernel scoffed.

"I may even overhaul the way I live my very life if I damn well please." *Was that me talking?* Rita recognized the voice, but the fire underneath the words was new and exciting in ways she couldn't fully grasp. "Whatever I do, whenever I do it, and whomever I do it with, that's my business, and *you* have nothing to say about it."

Pernel rose. "All I'm saying, sweetie, is that you will need some advice, some guidance."

"I have that." She put her hand on Will's shoulder. "From someone I trust and look up to." She glanced down at Will. For one fleeting instant she wondered what emotion she saw glinting in those dark, deep eyes, then it disappeared.

With a nod he urged her to go on.

"And furthermore . . ." She faced Pernel again. "I will not take any more lectures in style and class from a man who doesn't have any more taste than to wear red shoes with a magenta scarf and trowel on more makeup than a two-dollar whore on half-price night."

"Oh puhl-eese, Rita. You are never going to follow through on this. I know you. You can't endure any upheaval in your life."

"I've already endured plenty of that. Now I find I can endure anything I have to in order to get what I want."

"What you *want*? I don't think you know what that is!"

Damn but it was hard to argue with the truth. She folded her arms. "Right now I want to stand up for myself and maybe just once in my life meet whatever is coming without fear for how it might throw everything off kilter."

"Careful what you wish for." Will pushed back his chair and stood slowly.

Pernel's resentment softened, and he offered

a genuinely warm glimpse of the kind man— person—he could be when not on the defensive. "Now, that's the only sound piece of counsel you're bound to get from your—"

Outside the Palace, brakes squealed. A *whumpa-whump-thud* announced that a tank of a car had swerved too fast into the pitted parking lot, hitting every pothole and rut possible along the way.

"She's headed straight for the window!" Rita didn't know whether to dive behind the counter or sacrifice herself to protect her cake.

"Relax, she won't—" Before Will could complete his assurance, the cruise ship of a Caddy came sailing up onto the sidewalk and glided to a halt just inches shy of the picture window.

"Jillie!" Will called in the general direction of the powder room. "Get your skinny ass out here pronto! Mama has arrived."

Rita took a few steps toward the door.

Will held her back with a touch. "If you'll excuse me."

She pressed her hand to her heart and tried to force her breathing into some kind of normal rhythm. She had not asked for any of this. Not for Pernel's intrusion, or for Miss Peggy and whatever turmoil she would most certainly bring. She had not even asked for Will's help, had she? She hardly knew anymore. Hardly recognized her own life.

Careful what you wish for? Up until now she'd been careful with everything. Now she was making speeches about letting things come into her life without fear? Maybe Pernel was right and she—

"Miss Peggy's in on this?" Pernel tucked his too-obviously synthetic hair behind one ear and bent over the table, inhaling the aroma of the perfect cake sitting there. "That's some comfort. She'll set things straight right away."

"I don't need anyone to set things straight for me, Pernel."

"Oh, Rita, that's cute." He laughed, and though he did not seem to intend it to hurt, it did. "Admit it, you are in way over your head. I tell you, you are simply not equipped to handle the unexpected. You're just too predict—"

She never would have guessed how good it would feel to push anyone into one of her prized creations. But, oh, as Pernel went facefirst into the three layers of blood-red cake with creamy white frosting, sending the carefully dipped strawberries bouncing off the nasty Palace floor, she sighed in utter delight and relief.

"Predictable, huh?" She wiped the last bits of boiled frosting onto Pernel's skirt. "Bet you didn't see that coming."

He pulled up and began wiping the mess away with both hands. "Rita, you are going to regret this."

She already did, she thought, as she heard the door open and Miss Peggy scold, "Great Caesar's ghost! Honey, that is no way for a lady of quality to behave!"

Chapter 6

EVERY DIXIE BELLE SHOULD REMEMBER:
*A lady of good taste and breeding serves her guests first,
then she pushes her ex-husband's face into the cake.*

Will had planned to help his sixty-seven-year-old mother out of her six-month-old Cadillac, but she'd beat him to the punch—and to the Palace front door. Of course he had the excuse of getting distracted by Rita's sudden burst of independence and her unexpected decision to help Pernel to some Princess cake.

"Miss Peggy! I never intended for you to see . . ." Rita tucked her hands behind her back. "You caught me at my worst, I'm afraid."

"Worst my ass, I'd say she caught you at your very best." Will laughed as he leaned in to kiss his mother on the cheek. "Afternoon, Mother. If you've come for cake, you're too damn late."

Margaret Curtis Morgan West breezed right past him. She'd get to him later. He had no doubt of that. Right now she had her priorities. "Rita, I won't pretend. I am disappointed to see so blatant a breakdown of those most gracious conventions that define us as people of good taste and breeding."

"I know, Miss Peggy." Rita hung her head.

Seeing her humbled like that, in the wake of her first real attempt at standing up for herself, just hit Will the wrong way. "Mother, you have no call to—"

"A lady of good taste and breeding serves her guests first." His mother hobbled by, aided by nothing but her brass-handled cane and more nerve than one tiny, pale-haired woman had a right to possess. "*Then* she pushes her ex-husband's face into the cake. Good manners before bad temper always, Rita-sugar."

"I . . ." Rita blinked.

"At all times, good manners, first and foremost."

"I'll keep that in mind, thank you."

"I know you will, sugar." She tipped her head ever-so-demurely to the right. "Unlike my own ungrateful offspring, you listen and pay heed when I try to share the benefit of my experience."

"That's because, unlike your own undaunted offspring, she doesn't realize that half of what comes out of your mouth skims the shady side of the truth." It only took Will one stride to reach his mother. He tried to take her elbow to assist her, but she slipped it from his hand and tapped her cane as though she intended to use it for more than support. "The other half is pure orneriness for nothing but orneriness's sake."

"Is there a window open in here, Rita-sugar?"

"No, ma'am. Do you need some fresh air?"

"No, darling, thank you for your concern. I just felt a draft of hot air a moment ago and heard a lot of senseless buzzing." She pulled a hankie from inside her jacket sleeve and waved it around, shooing away invisible gnats.

Will raised an eyebrow. "Comparing your only son to a pest, Mama?"

She did not acknowledge his presence with so much as a bat of her eyelashes. "Well, it can't be my son. My son is in Memphis. He would never come to town without telling his precious mother he was here. I raised him better than that."

"Me?" Will burst out laughing. "Mama, since when has how you raised me been an indicator of how I'd act?"

She tipped her nose up and sniffed, waved her hankie about again. She took a few steps and handed the crisp white cloth to the man dripping bits of red cake onto his size-eleven pumps. "And how're you doing, Pernel?"

Pernel dabbed the handkerchief to his face, careful not to smear food on the delicate monogram. "I'm hurt, Miss Peggy. Hurt and beleaguered."

"That's nice." She smiled and gestured toward the door like she was scooting away a sulking child. "I think it's best if you go on home now. This doesn't concern you anymore."

"It never did concern him," Will muttered, moving closer to Rita.

"What did I miss?" Jillie emerged from the bathroom just in time to cut him off before he got to Rita's side.

"Nothing." Rita had the composure to appear as if that were the Gospel truth.

"Trouble mastering the complexities of silverware, Pernel?" Jillie took a spot between Will and Rita, leaning close to share a snicker with her old friend.

His sister pushing her way in to take Rita's side only pissed Will off. It shouldn't have. He understood that. But ever since Pernel paraded into the Palace, Will had gone on primal-male-as-protector mode. It was the same kind of thus far untapped feeling in him that had led him to volunteer to help Rita entirely against her wishes, he supposed. Whatever it was, it sure as hell kicked in around that woman with her hopeful eyes, bountiful sexy body, fabulous dimples, and a life sorely in need of a rescuer.

A rescuer? Him? Man, he got in deeper and deeper with every breath, didn't he? He looked over Jillie's head at Rita and had the odd but not unpleasant sensation of sinking in quicksand.

Pernel folded the handkerchief and wiped his chin. "I just don't know what to do about all this, Miss Peggy."

"I told you what to do, darling. Go home."

For a split second, it looked like Pernel might challenge the imp of a lady dressed in an impossibly unwrinkled pink-linen suit. Then he threw back his head and with the weight of the icing on one side of his wig causing it to slowly slide lop-sided, he said, "Yes, ma'am."

"Looks like your mama's wishes even hold sway over men daring enough to wear rhinestones in the afternoon."

"Rhinestones?" Will dragged his knuckle over the beginnings of a five o'clock shadow on his jaw and chuckled. "That sure does explain a lot. Men with real stones are neither bullied nor beguiled by her, I assure you."

Rita leaned forward. Her hair swung against her cheek, and her shirt fell open to show as much of her magnificent breasts as a man dared see with his mother so nearby. She grinned at him, her voice soft, "You adore her, and I know it."

"You aren't actually accusing me of giving a damn about someone besides myself, are you?"

"Y'all pipe down, I'm trying to listen." Jillie tipped her head toward the Peggy and Pernel floor show being served up a few feet away.

Pernel offered to return her handkerchief, but the Dixiefied pixie of a woman shook her head. "Oh, and Pernel, darling, before I forget—did you pick yourself out a pretty new name yet?"

Mother was in rare form today. Every inch the woman Will often described to his friends as "Scarlett O'Helmsley."

"I'm leaning toward Starla, Miss Peggy, but nothing definite yet."

"That's fine. Just don't forget to send 'round

notecards when you make your final decision, you hear?"

"I will, Miss Peggy."

"Now hurry along, or stains will set in that attractive new dress of yours."

"I will." He nodded a good-bye and, with the awful magenta scarf trailing behind him, headed for the door. He paused only long enough to give Rita a surprisingly tender look. "I do want what's best for you, you know."

"That's not for you to decide," Rita whispered.

"Regardless of what direction my life takes, I will always care about what happens to you."

"I know."

"Asking me to stay completely out of your life, after all we've gone through together, after all the years we've invested in our child and each other? It's like asking me not to breathe."

"Now there's an attractive proposition." Will shifted his feet, both hands in his pockets and his shoulders deceptively relaxed.

"This is not for you to mix into, Will." Even with her head bent Rita's voice carried an aching uncertainty that gripped Will by the emotional throat and left him speechless.

How could she still harbor feelings for the man? If someone had treated him the way Pernel had Rita, Will would be gone so fast and so far . . .

"You'll always be a part of my life, too." She took her ex's hand and gave it a squeeze. "I do understand that."

She'd ruin everything. She felt bad about the

way she'd acted and, with one pointlessly sympathetic gesture, was going to undo the small stride she had made by standing up to Pernel.

Will raked his hand through his hair. "This is not happening."

Both Rita and Pernel looked at him.

Had he said that aloud? No matter. He'd meant it, and he'd stand behind it. He folded his arms. "Well, not while I'm around it's not."

"You may have a reputation as a hound but you won't be playing watchdog here for long, and we *all* know it." *In other words Rita's life will go back to the way it was in a day or so.* Pernel didn't have to say it to communicate his meaning.

He told the truth. Will could not play watchdog indefinitely. However, maybe he could stay on the job just long enough to help her find her own voice. Coax her toward claiming her strengths so she could stand up to anyone who would play on her fears of stepping beyond the boundaries of her present life. Anyone who would keep her from reaching for something more.

She had done as much for him once by being the only person who would tell him the truth, who would not let him coast, who pushed him to be the kind of man that even he had not known he could be. He wanted to do the same for her.

He came up behind Rita, ready to speak.

"One other thing, Pernel," Rita cut Will off before he opened his mouth.

"What?"

"Next time you come by, have the common courtesy to call first and don't bother trying to let yourself in with your keys. I will have had all the locks changed."

Pernel did not look back.

"Yes!" Will jerked his fisted hand back like his team had just scored big-time.

"Don't let the door hit your padded behind on the way out, you hear, sugar?" Jillie called out.

The door slammed shut, and suddenly a deathly silence fell over the room. Rita had sent her worries packing—if only for the short haul. Will, on the other hand, had not yet even made full eye contact with his troubles.

"Isn't anyone going to offer to get me a chair?" The tip of a cane tapped on the dirty floor. "Or do I have to do everything for myself?"

"Mother, I promise you, no one here wants you to do everything. In fact, I'd lay odds no one here wants you to do anything . . ." He pulled the best of the wooden chairs out from the table and took her arm, firmly at first, then backing off until he scarcely touched more than her sleeve. When had Mama's bones started to feel as fragile as bird wings? He settled her into the chair, then bent low to plant a kiss on her cool, perfectly rouged cheek. "No one wants you to do anything but sit down, rest your feet, and have a nice glass of cold tea."

"Nice save," Rita murmured behind his back as she hurried around to grab up the pitcher of once-strong tea now diluted by melted ice. "Sweet tea, Miss Peggy?"

"I don't dare, sugar. I have my social calls to make this afternoon and at my age if I drink too much tea I'm likely to leave a trail of piddle up and down the finest walkways of Hellon. And God spare us from the consequences if I'd have to sneeze!"

"Mama!" Jillie shut her eyes.

Will laughed.

Rita clunked the pitcher down so hard the table wobbled.

"Well, that's the way of things. Why act prissi-fied about it?" She laid her purse in her lap and folded her hands. "I am officially too old to mince words and too highly placed in the com-munity for anyone to tell me to straighten up and act better."

Will took the seat next to hers and motioned for Rita to join them. "And what do your *'ladies'* have to say about this new attitude?"

"They have decided . . ."

Rita sat on the very edge of her chair.

"To find it charming."

"Well, of course they do." Rita brushed some dark red crumbs off the white tablecloth. "I wish I had your poise, Miss Peggy. I'm afraid I'm some-thing of a charm-school dropout."

"Well, I can't hold that against you, sweet-heart." She patted Rita's hand, but her gaze swept over her two children. "Look at the company you keep."

If the insult got under Jillie's pale, polished skin, she did not let it show. "Will's here on business, Mother. He isn't keeping company with Rita."

"Then he's a bigger fool than even I thought he was."

"What? You *want* me to keep company with Rita?" He didn't realize until it went tumbling out of his mouth how harsh that must have sounded. "Whatever you want to say, Mother, just come out with it."

"I will. Leave Rita alone. Her life here is hard enough without the likes of a careless gust of wind like you blowing through." She slapped her hand flat on the unsteady table. "She's too nice to say it to you, but I don't have that problem."

"Mama, I don't see that being any of your business. And since I'm too big to whup and too damn cute to holler at, you better just spare the rod and save your breath."

Finally, somebody on her side! Rita plunged her hands into the lukewarm, soapy water and sighed. Who'd have thought that the feisty old gal, who at this very minute had both her children's undivided attention as they helped her back to her car, would become the voice of reason in all this?

Merciful heavens! She pulled one of the heavy gray-white lunch plates out of the water to scrape at a stubborn bit of pimento with her fingernail. Miss Peggy, the voice of reason? When had her life gotten *that* far off kilter?

She'd tried so hard for so long to keep everything in balance. Then one day she surrendered to a totally irrational flash of empathy for a man who swore he needed to help her, and what had it gotten her? A seemingly endless parade of folks intent on telling her what to do, when to do it, and even whom to do it with.

Or was that whom *not* to do it with? Either way the person every buttinski had in mind remained the same—Wild Billy.

Just thinking the man's name gave her goose pimples. Even to imagine that she had some kind of choice over whether or not the two of them did or did not do . . . well, anything, made her heart rate kick up. She took a deep breath to quiet it.

"To do it or not to do it, that is the question," she joked to her blurred reflection in the plate. As soon as the pitiful paraphrase left her lips she pressed them shut. Standing so still she swore she could feel the moist lemon-soap-scented air sinking into her blazing cheeks, she waited and listened.

A muffled round of good-byes carried in from the next room.

A bead of sweat trickled down the back of her neck, and she sighed. No chance of a smart-mouth Jillie or an incorrigible Will listening in and misinterpreting that whole "do it or not" thing. She'd meant do the work, not do *it* in the giant orgasmic break-the-bed-and-make-me-forget-my-manners way, of course but . . .

"*. . . don't kid yourself . . . this is about sex.*" Again Cozie's admonition rang in her head. *Sex.* She exhaled in a long blast of breath that blew her bangs back off her forehead. How long had it been?

She dunked the plate into the dishwater and scrubbed the surface in hard, swirling motions. What did it matter how long she'd gone without sex? Not like she had much hope of breaking the streak anytime soon, Cozie's earlier observation notwithstanding. After all, there was nothing to say Will would even be interested.

"Okay, y'all take care." Will's warm tone carried into the kitchen. "I won't. I won't. I *might*—but don't expect I'd tell *you* about it."

The front door fell shut, and the lock ticked into place.

Rita rinsed the last plate without checking to see if she'd actually cleaned it. She sensed as much as heard the muffled footsteps approach. She held her breath, and they stopped.

"Alone at last."

Alone. With Will. Her stomach lurched like the first time she ever rode the Zippin Pippin at Libertyland over in Memphis. "Where's Jillie?"

"She took off. Not much for her to do here. She'd only get in the way."

Three *is* a crowd. Rita thought about saying something like that and wondered if she dared try using the low, sultry tone she heard in her head.

Will stepped fully into the kitchen. "What can I do to help you finish up in there so we can get back to work?"

Quit acting so stupid. Work, that was his only objective, his only reason for being here at all.

Something in the man needed to perform a good deed, and she was his pitiable project. She wasn't a carefree young girl on a wooden roller coaster anymore. She was over thirty, overweight, and overdue for a reality check.

"What more do you need to see around here before you make your recommendations?" She pulled the plug. The sink glugged, and the water began to drain. The only way to the other side of this situation was straight through it.

She shook the suds from her hands and tossed the dish towel over the edge of the drainer. She'd go along with Will's planning sessions, send him on his way, then deal with Pernel and whatever fallout her choices might create. "If you're almost done poking around, you could just tell me your ideas and we could have you on the road to Memphis in no time."

"That anxious to get rid of me?"

"No, I—"

"Then come out here a minute. I want to talk to you."

"About the renovation ideas?"

"Just come here." He held out his hand.

She looked to the stairway that led to the safety of her apartment. Finally, she dried off the last of the soap and water, then slipped her hand into his.

His palms were rough. She had expected the soft, pampered hands of a man who gave orders and let others do the dirty work. His fingers closed around hers, and her whole being felt enveloped in safety.

How could such an insignificant gesture do that? More importantly how could she protect against it? A lifetime of yearning for security and never finding it had taught her a thing or two. She had learned the hard way that false security was worse than none at all. And a man like Wild Billy?

His nickname told the tale. Wild, restless, adhering to no one else's rules and belonging to no one. To put her faith in him was grabbing on to false security with both hands. She must never let herself forget that.

She tugged her fingers free and curled them into a fist against her chest. "Well?"

"Can we sit?" He pulled a chair out for her.

She hesitated.

He brushed the last bit of cake crumbs from the seat and offered it again.

She perched on the edge, one hand braced against the back.

He took the chair next to her, his broad shoulders relaxed, his legs open so that his foot touched the side of her tennis shoe. "So, is it always this . . . um, interesting around here?"

"Is that what you brought me out here to ask?"

"No. Just trying to lay some groundwork. Trying to understand what you're up against."

"Oh, please. Can we skip over the part where you play amateur social worker so you can earn your wings?"

"Wings?"

"Wings, halo, Scout badge, whatever lame thing it is you think you're getting out of this project you've made of me."

"I thought we were long past that." He leaned forward, his forearms on his thighs.

She crossed her legs. "If you have something to ask me, Will, ask it outright."

"Humor me."

It was not a request. Anyone else came on with that kind of arrogance she'd have humored him right through the roof. She gritted her teeth. "You have eyes. Both times you've been here you've pretty much seen how it is. Jillie, Cozie, Pernel, folks around town like your mother, there's always somebody handy with an opinion for me."

"And?"

"And what? Some try to push me one direction. Some pull me in another. I just try to stay—"

"In the middle."

Coming out of his mouth it sounded so sad. She bit her lip to keep from saying so out loud.

"Don't you want more?"

"More? I have just about all I can handle as it is."

"Don't you have dreams and hopes? Ambitions? Aspirations beyond living alone above a greasy spoon, working your ass off to make everybody happy but yourself?"

She laughed. "Working my ass off? Anyone with eyes knows that's not happening."

"Don't do that."

"What?"

"Run yourself down like that. I think you have a damn fine ass."

"And so much of it, too."

"You are a very attractive woman, Rita."

"Don't patronize me."

"Me? Patronize anybody?" He laughed. A wonderful, throw-your-head-back-and-cut-loose laugh that startled her at first, then made her join in. "Did you totally forget who you were talking to?"

"Oh, don't play that game with me. I know you are not the unredeemable jerk you want everyone to think you are."

"How can you know that, Rita?"

She started to tell him exactly why, but somewhere between the thought and her open mouth the old fears welled up. It had been a full enough day without making a complete fool of herself in front of this man. She exhaled hard and shook back her hair. "Because."

"Oh, yeah, that's the kind of multifaceted million-dollar answer I was looking for."

"Does that mean the question-and-answer period of the afternoon is over?"

He shrugged. "It was a stupid idea anyway."

"What? What was a stupid idea?"

"I thought . . . well, if it's always like this around here, I thought that my coming around for just a day or two probably only added to your headaches."

"You had to put me through all this to come to

the same conclusion I came to the day you first suggested getting involved?"

"What can I say? I'm a thickheaded bastard."

"I never said—"

"If you knew it would only make your life more crazy, why did you agree to take my help?"

"You asked. You said you needed to do it."

"But still . . ."

She wet her lips and when she spoke, it came out in a heartfelt whisper. "Because of what I saw when you took your sunglasses off that day."

He suddenly seemed fascinated by his hands in his lap. "What? Bloodshot from too much tequila the night before?"

"No."

He looked up, his expression weary and his heart in his eyes.

"That." She smiled, just barely.

"What?"

"That somewhere underneath all the bravado of Wild Billy West is a decent man who wants something different for his life."

"I never said that."

"You had the gall to talk to me about *my* hopes and dreams. Assuming, I guess, that a plain, plump girl like me would have plain, puny dreams."

He dragged one bent knuckle along his lower lip.

"What did you think, Will?" Her voice came out more steady than she felt. "That you could come here for a day, flirt with me a little? Make me feel better about myself? Then show me how to fix up this dive and go on your way hoping the effort moved you closer to realizing your own dreams?"

"You don't know my dreams."

"I'll bet they're the same dreams everyone else has, Will."

He narrowed his eyes at her.

She'd never learn, would she? This man tapped something inside her that she could not fully control. It scared her. And yet, she felt perfectly safe going on. "We all share some of the same hopes, you know. Whether we are handsome small-town heroes, successful big-city businessmen, or the girl who lives over the Pig Rib Palace with her books and music to keep her company."

"If you know my hopes, Rita, I wish you'd tell them to me."

"You want for your life to have meaning."

He nodded.

"You want someone to miss you when you're away and mourn you when you've passed on."

His gaze fell to the floor for only a moment, then he looked to her again. "Go on."

"You want to be really good at something, to hear praise for your work and know it's earned."

He huffed out the sort of hard laugh that told her that one had really hit the mark.

"You want . . ." She held her breath. She'd probably regret this just as she had regretted the last time she'd dared to tell this man the whole unvarnished truth about himself. That did not stop her. "You want to be loved."

He bent his knees, putting his feet flat. His jaw tightened, and he dipped his chin just enough to really drive his dark gaze home. "You still don't pull any punches, do you?"

She raised her chin. "Am I off base?"

"More like out of line."

"Me?" She smiled her best innocent smile. "The girl who always keeps things in the middle?"

He smiled back. "Just goes to prove that you have what it takes to fly in the face of other people's expectations."

"It proves I'm foolish enough to spit into the wind."

"I can't walk away until I know you can do either one of those things, or both, but that you do them because you want to, not because it's the path of least resistance."

"Then grab those walking papers, pal, because this lady of quality won't spit anywhere."

"What about flying in the face of expectations?"

"I'm afraid to fly."

"You're afraid of too damn many things, Rita."

"Right now I'm afraid this conversation is over."

"You can stop talking to me, but that won't change things."

"What things?"

"That I can't leave until I know you won't let the people you care about pout, cajole, bully, or bad-mouth you into not going after your . . . not-so-plain dreams."

"Why?"

"Let's just say I have a debt to pay."

Payback. Yes, it certainly felt like that was the principle at work. "What exactly are you saying, Will?"

"That I'm staying in town until we get these renovations under way and you have the foundation to move on with your life, wherever you want it to go, whatever you want to do with it."

"Staying? At your mothers'?"

"I'm willing to make some sacrifice for all this, darling, but not *human* sacrifice." He pushed away from the table and took a long, steady look around the room. "How 'bout I bring in a rollaway and bunk in the restaurant?"

"How 'bout I put a red light outside and open this up as Fat Rita's Pleasure Palace?"

"If you don't mind the gossip it would stir up, I sure don't."

"I don't give a flying fig about gossip."

"But you said . . ."

"I said I didn't want the talk to start around town."

"What *talk*?"

"Where all the people who have watched over and wagged their tongues about me for all these years start spreading the word that Rita has finally started acting like her mama." She put her hand to her temple and shut her eyes. "I would rather not give them the satisfaction, if you don't mind."

"Then, if I promise to park in the church lot and come through the back door under cover of darkness, will you let me stay here?"

She could see how that could work. She still didn't fully understand why he would want to go to such lengths on her behalf. But if he could do it without anyone knowing . . .

Of course *she'd* know. Will, sleeping under her roof. She'd know down to the very deepest fiber of her being. She could feel the sweet tension winding tighter and tighter in her even now. But she would never try to act on those feelings.

Cozette was wrong. This was not about sex. And Will was wrong. It was not about flying in the face of anyone's expectations or standing up to people who meddled in her life. This was about showing herself she was not her mother. In a situation like this, in any situation that came along after that damned tornado, Tammy Stark wouldn't have given a rip what the other person wanted or needed, would she?

Well, Rita did not go any way the wind carried her, and she would never abandon the people she cared about on a whim. Will had come to help her out of that personal sense of honor of his. Nothing more. There was no reason for him not to stay here if that's what he needed to do.

"You can come and go without anyone seeing you?"

He grinned.

She felt his satisfaction down to the pit of her stomach. She folded her arms. *But this was not about sex.* "I thought you said you didn't want to spend a single night in Hellon."

"But I won't be." He stood.

She tipped her head back and wet her lips. *This was about her acting as the Anti-Tammy.* "You won't?"

"No."

Not about sex. "You won't be staying?"

"I won't be single." He moved in close enough that his breath tickled her ear as he whispered, "I'll be with you."

"Oh." Okay, it *was* about sex. *Heart-stopping, mind-blowing, I-didn't-know-my-body-could-still-do-that, sex.* Not between her and Will tonight under this roof, of course, but in her dreams night after night from now on . . .

"Great." He straightened away from her and stepped back. "Meantime, we've got lots of daylight left. What do you think? Shall we get to it?"

"It?"

"Yeah, *it*. Work. I came here to work on the renovation, remember?"

"How could I forget?" She raised her hands and smiled like an idiot. "Let's get to it."

He nodded, then turned to gather his tools to get back to the real job at hand.

Rita stood there, admiring the view for a last few moments before she sighed and headed into the kitchen. Someday, somehow she would repay her friends for stepping in when they did. She just wasn't sure right now if that payment would come as a reward for giving her a breath of fresh air or a retaliation for thrusting her into the heart of an irresistible whirlwind.

Chapter 7

"Think you've taken enough precautions against being seen around town with me?" Will looked down on Rita as she slid into a low-slung child's swing.

"Let's see. I forced your sister to drive us over to the next county, made her buy us each a Rainbow Snowball Bliss while you and I cowered in the car outside Angel's Shaved Ice Shack. Then insisted she drive us to the playground behind this elementary school at least a dozen miles from anyone we know. I think we might be safe."

"Go long, and I'll throw you the bullet." The tallest of a mutt pack of skinny young boys called out as he cocked his arm, then hurled a football into the air.

"For now. But I have my eye on those kids." Rita made a big production of scoping out the ragtag huddle of shirtless boys. "Somebody in there probably has a neighbor with a cousin whose daddy used to date a girl whose old gran plays gin with your mother."

Will chuckled. "Plays gin or drinks it?"

"People know people." Rita nodded with an air of wisdom that seemed at least two parts tongue in cheek. "And people talk."

"I don't know why you went to all this trouble." Jillie sat pigeon-toed in the swing, next to Rita, shoes dragging in the soft dirt. "You could walk through the heart of Hellon naked, but if you had Will along no one would so much as notice you."

"I have put on a few pounds, but I doubt if I'd totally obliterate anyone walking beside me from view." He gave Rita a wink to include her in his fun.

"You don't. But your reputation does. You're the golden boy. You're Rhett Butler, Troy Aikman, and Elvis all rolled into one."

"That many people?" He patted his stomach. "I must have put on even more weight than I thought."

"You can joke, but you know it's true." Candor more than anger colored his sister's words.

"And I hate every minute of it." He responded in kind.

"Oh, yeah. I see how much you hate Mama doting on your every move and word."

"Apart from Daddy and her social standing, Mama never doted on anyone or anything in her entire life."

"Least of all me." His sister looked all of about five years old again, sitting in that swing with tears in her eyes.

"Then why do you stay with her?" he asked, his own voice tight and faint.

She laid her head against the swing's thick, tarnished chain.

"Where would she go?" Rita set her cup aside and smoothed her hand down Jillie's curved back.

"Anywhere." Damn he hated to see her like this. Hated it most because Jillie brought it all on herself with her thoughtless choices. He couldn't fix it, and she wouldn't.

In that way she was much like Rita. That thought only turned his anger up a notch. Jillie didn't just hurt herself by her actions and attitudes, and she didn't even seem to see that. "Maybe she could move in with her lover . . ."

"Will, stop," Rita hissed.

"And his wife." He clenched his jaw.

"What the hell is wrong with you?" The chains clanked and clattered as Rita leapt up from the swing. "This is your only sister."

Jillie held her hand up. "It's all right, Rita. I had that coming. I hope you'll both be glad to learn, too, that it's over."

"What's over?"

"You and Paul?" Rita brushed back the heavy curls that hid Jillie's profile. "When? What happened?"

"He lied to me."

"Oh, an adulterer who is also a liar. What are the chances?"

"Paul is not an adulterer, Will. Neither am I, for that matter."

"But you said . . ."

"I said relationships are impossible. Borrowing from the thinking that all the good men at our age are either gay or married, I said I might have to start dating the married ones."

Will crumpled his empty cup and eyed the trash can. "And lo and behold right about the time you announced this you met an adorable professor who just happened to be . . ."

"Single."

"What?" Will froze with the balled-up paper in his fingers.

"He *told* me he was separated—actually. But there's no wife at all."

Rita bent down, trying to force Jillie to make eye contact. "Why would he do that?"

"I might have . . . I think I . . . I shot my mouth off about my theories."

"You told him how disenchanted you'd become with his sex?"

"In detail. Well, I didn't tell him exactly." She huffed out a sigh. "I got to class early that first night and started yakking with the other women. The whole class was women. Most thought extension college courses might be a good place to meet men."

"You met one there." He threw the paper ball into the can.

"One who came in the room in time to hear me proclaim I had no interest in any man who hadn't already proven he could make that walk down the aisle."

"So he told you he was married?"

"Separated. It wasn't a bad idea from his end—he said it gave him the chance to go out with me with a built-in escape route should I prove as hard and jaded as I sounded that first night."

Any smart-mouthed response died on Will's lips when he saw the genuine pain in his baby sister's eyes.

Thuds and grunts from the boys roughhousing on the flat grassy play yard filled the silence around them.

"He swears he never intended to let me keep thinking that for so long but after a while he wondered if the truth would scare me off. He said he wanted to be sure I cared for him enough before he ratted himself out."

" 'Rat' being the operative word," Rita grumbled.

"For which one of them?" Will sniffed.

Rita folded her arms. "Do you have to be ugly about this?"

"How is it ugly to point out that she took up with this guy thinking he was legally married?" He spoke softly but did not hide his contempt entirely. For once he wanted to hear his sister take responsibility for her thoughtlessness. Not blame her mother, or him, or men in general.

"We went out. That's all. Museums in Memphis,

dinners, visiting some clubs on Beale Street. I never slept with him. And he wasn't legally married."

"You didn't know that." Cruel to be kind. He'd never grasped that concept until this moment. He could not back off and excuse himself from caring how Jillie worked through her pain and problem. That was Rita's influence for certain. So he pressed on. "When you found out the man was single that's when you broke it off with him."

"I broke it off with him because he lied to me."

"Any married man seeing another woman on the side is going to be lying to somebody, Jillie."

"You're missing the point, Will." Rita's warm hand fit flat against the knotted muscles between his shoulders. She stepped in close, creating a welcome buffer between him and his sister.

"See?" Jillie tossed her hair back. "Rita knows."

"I know, but I doubt you do." She bumped Jillie's shoulder with her own. "You didn't break up with Paul because of any lie. You broke up with him because of the truth."

"I think I know why—"

"Paul saw the worst about you. He even went to great lengths to protect himself from the hurt he suspected you were capable of inflicting."

"I thought you were on my side, Rita."

"I am always on your side, honey. But never mistake that for always approving of what you're up to."

Will chuckled softly.

"You'd do well to remember that, too," she said, with a sideways glance his way.

"Yes, ma'am." He grinned.

"You broke up with that man because he got rid of the only impediment to you two furthering your relationship. What Paul did must have scared the life out of you."

Her brow pinched above the bridge of her nose. "What did he do?"

"He loved you. Not just the idea of you or the you he thought he could make you over into. He really, really loved you, all of you. Now, didn't he?"

Rita's smile came slowly, but her eyes lit up all at once. "Must have scared her half out of her wits."

He looked from Rita's warm, encouraging eyes to Jillie, with her shoulders slumped and head bowed. "I can well imagine."

"You can well imagine? Scared witless by somebody caring about you?" Rita rubbed her hand over her forehead like she had the mother of all migraines. "What is wrong with you two?"

"Anyone who knows our mother knows the answer to that." He would have said it himself. He almost did. But now hearing the words wrung out between Jillie's tight lips, Will cringed.

"Oh grow up, the two of you!" Rita took a couple of long strides away from them, then stopped and turned, her hands on her hips. "At least you *have* a mother around. At least you still have the home you grew up in. You have looks and talent and money and all those things lots of folks count as important."

Jillie rubbed her upper arm. "Maybe those

aren't worth a whole hell of a lot if you don't have someone to share——"

"You have each other!" She didn't stomp her foot, but attitude accomplished the same thing. "And you have friends. Damn good friends. Better than you deserve on any given day of the week."

"You're right about that," he muttered.

"That a snipe at me?" Jillie's head jerked up.

"I swear, you two bucktoothed, backbiting mules have got so much and yet you appreciate so little."

"I don't know that that's a fair characterization, Rita. I may be a mule, but there are things in this life I appreciate more than I have words to tell about." Will stepped forward. "You, for instance."

"I appreciate Rita, too." Jillie turned from him to her old friend. "I do, Rita. Way more than I ever say."

"I know. I never should have talked like that." Rita put her hands to her cheeks and sighed. "It's just that you two have both had so many opportunities to move beyond your upbringing and difficulties. I don't understand what holds you back."

"Listen to this." Jillie jabbed her thumb in Rita's direction, smiling a put-her-in-her-place but still sly smile. "A lecture on how we must start moving on from the woman famous for refusing to budge an inch."

Before Rita could dig in for a really good comeback, the football the boys had been playing with came sailing in from the field and landed with a thud at Will's feet.

"Hey, mister, will you throw us the ball?"

He turned to Rita. "Do I dare interact with those boys without first finding out all about their neighbors, cousins, and gin-guzzling grannies?"

She bent down, picked up the ball, and pressed it into his hand. "I think we can risk it, this time."

"Wow, Rita, those are words I never thought I'd hear coming out of your mouth."

"See? I'm not as inflexible as y'all think I am. I have the ability to change, too."

As he fired the ball off to the waiting boys, Will muttered under his breath, "Risk? Change? I'll believe that when I see it, Rita."

Rita tucked her hand under her cheek and stretched her legs between the cool bedsheets. She stared at the rhinestones of her tiara without seeing them in sharp detail. She let her gaze drift to the mirror. The dark but familiar trappings of her apartment reflected there held no interest for her. Her gaze fixed on the door leading to the staircase.

For two nights now she'd lain motionless in bed hour after hour hardly sleeping. Fearing that if she so much as got up and turned on the lights to read, *he* would hear her stirring overhead. Would that tip him off to the unsettling effect his presence had on her? She didn't want to find out. The saying goes that knowledge is power, and she was not about to hand him any kind of power over her.

Of course she didn't have to *hand* him a dad-gummed thing. Any fool could see that he already had some kind of power over her, and Will was no fool. She managed a cheerless laugh at the way she'd deluded herself into thinking she'd stayed aloof. Oh, yeah, she was so cool and in control around the man. How could he ever suspect that just watching him across the room turned her to a mass of quivering jelly?

She sat slowly up in bed and fanned her hair off her face. Two days working around him. Two nights knowing he was sleeping on a rollaway just one flight of creaky stairs away.

If he *was* sleeping. She raised her head to peer out the window at the big summer moon, pale in the midnight sky. The sight spoke to her of solitude and distance. It left a cold sensation in the pit of her stomach.

She only warmed again when she wondered if Will might be looking up there, too. Or maybe he'd gotten up to fix a late-night snack or to go over the pages of notes he'd made about the renovations.

The man had not skimped on either his time, generosity, or expertise. He'd measured and figured, paced things off, and knocked on every inch of wood in the place. She'd watched in awe not because the work was so hard or so important but because Will did it so well. What on earth was more intriguing, exciting, and downright sexy than watching a man doing what he did best?

He'd placed phone calls to old friends and called in favors from cohorts. No one turned him down, and most offered to go above and beyond his requests for no other reason than it was Will doing the asking. That in itself said something about him.

Goose bumps rose on her bare arm. She let her breath out in a low, moaning sigh.

She could see him in her mind's eye, head bent over the yellow pads, a pencil in his thick, strong fingers. See him toss that pencil aside and tip his head back until the black waves fell to brush his tight, broad shoulders.

She flexed her fingers. How many times in the past two days had she wanted to go up behind him and sink her hands into those knotted muscles? To knead and rub and work until he let go of the day's tensions—and she had chased away whatever ghosts had caused him to take on her pointless cause in the first place. Just to help him.

No, that was a bald-faced lie. What she had wanted was to touch him. To put her hands on the man who had rekindled a fire in her she had long forgotten. The fire of a woman wanting a man, to be sure, but so much more than that.

A fire for life, for believing things could change even for a woman like her, even in a place like Hellon. He had given her a glimpse at hope. His presence had roused the girl she used to be from a very long, safe-but-empty sleep.

And tomorrow, after he went over his recommendations in detail with her, he would go back to Memphis for good.

She ran her hand up her bare arm and shivered, though with the aging air-conditioning system in the apartment, she felt anything but chilled. She pulled her knees up to her chest. She curled her toes into the sheet. She rested her chin on the cool satin of the snowy white nightgown Cozie had given her as an if-you-don't-pamper-yourself-who-will? gift. One spaghetti-thin strap fell off her shoulder.

She supposed she should feel ridiculous for wearing the thing. It had stayed untouched in the gift box since the day after her divorce. Why bring it out now? On the last day for her last chance to . . .

"Last chance to what?" She couldn't finish the sentence. She didn't dare. The old single bed groaned as she lay back down but the sound did not still the echo of remembered words.

"Last chance."

"It is about sex."

"I think you have a damn fine ass."

"I'm not as inflexible as y'all think I am. I have the ability to change, too."

She sat up like a bolt of lightning had just coursed through the bedpost. Her skin felt all afire, and her pulse fluttered like a kid caught knee deep in no-good.

"Rita, you are a damn fool," she murmured, knowing that as "self" talk went, she could have chosen a better message.

Before she could think or say another word that might talk her out of it, her feet hit the floor. The same instant she snagged up the old hospital gown she used as a bathrobe. Halfway to the stairwell door she thought of going back to root around through the stacks of still-packed moving boxes for her one and only frilly robe.

"No." If she did that, she might as well climb back in that single bed and pull the covers over her head. She'd never get the nerve up twice to head for the door and start down those steps and . . .

"What?" She only wanted to see Will. To thank him in some small way for what he'd done for her. To look into his eyes and feel alive one more time.

The soft cotton slid over her arms, and two seconds later she paused with her hand on the knob. Last chance or not, she couldn't go barging down there wrapped in nothing but her nightgown and her need to spend just a little more time with Will. She had to have a backup. Some reason for her to go down there besides her silly fantasies about a man who, for all she knew, was snoring up a storm dreaming of the women he would have when he went back home again.

"Cake." Of course. It was absolutely the perfect cover.

Guilt had gotten the better of her sometime in the late afternoon and she had done up some single layer, small red velvet cakes. One to appease Pernel. One to send over as a courtesy to Miss Peggy. One for Will to take back with him to Memphis. And the fourth and final one for medicinal purposes to use like a poultice on her heart full of regrets once he'd gone.

No white-chocolate crowns, no hand-dipped

strawberries. That's how she convinced herself it was no big deal to do it. To tell the recipients that she expected nothing from the gracious, but insignificant, gesture.

If she could pull off explaining that with a straight face, she could certainly get herself downstairs on the pretext of a midnight snack. She crept down the steps, her hand trailing along the wall so that she wouldn't have to flip on the light.

She could do this, she told herself in the bravest bout of "self" talk ever. She could do anything. She could even change . . . a little . . . for a while . . . and still find her way back to her cherished secure lifestyle.

Her foot hit the cold, bare floor of the kitchen. She would be all right. She would pull this off. She was, after all, so very, very hungry, and down in this dingy shell of a restaurant was the only thing that could satisfy her.

"Looking for something?" Will nudged the refrigerator door open just enough to catch Rita in its light.

"Oh! I . . . I came for . . ." She lurched to one side, a flash of white, then only an outline in the darkness. "Don't move. Give me a minute and I'll just . . ."

He heard her bump into the big stainless-steel sinks. She let loose a milquetoast swearword, then lurched the other way, toward the wall.

Will immediately sucked in his gut. *Sucked in his gut?* He held back a curse at the sudden attack of vanity. Not like him to fear she would suddenly flip on the overhead light and see him standing there in nothing but a pair of boxers and a smile. Not that he had one of those low-slung beer bellies a lot of other men his age were developing. He didn't have love handles either . . . exactly. However, he did notice this last year or so that he'd begun working on a set of let's-be-friends-and-see-what-happens handles that no amount of morning crunches could dissuade.

His body was still hard and fit, but it wasn't chiseled and lean. He wasn't eighteen anymore. It showed in the mirror and in the way young girls no longer looked at him with worship in their eyes. Hell, young girls hardly looked at him at all these days. That didn't really bother him as much as he thought it would. But dammit, if Rita was going to see him in any kind of state of undress, he wanted her nothing less than awestruck.

So he sucked in his gut. He squared his shoulders. And he let the fridge door fall shut. That put them both in the silvery, forgiving light of the moon shining in the window. "What did you come down here for?"

His question stopped her in her tracks. She stood, a silhouette against the window with her outstretched hand a hairbreadth from the light switch.

"I didn't . . . you see I . . ." She pulled her arms in close to her body, her hands clasped in front of her.

Her inability to come right out and say what she wanted, the way she left the possibilities lingering in the air, and her sudden shyness only notched up his anticipation.

"I . . . well, I . . ."

"Yes?" He hoped that did not sound as snake-oily to her as it did to him. He took a deep breath and let it out slowly. "You what, Rita? You wanted something?"

Framed in moonlight, she nodded.

Of course she'd come down here wanting something. He'd wanted *something* himself. Wanted it for a time now if he'd admit the truth of it. But he'd told himself it wasn't right.

Rita deserved better than a quick roll in the hay brought on by the normal prickling of male hormones from sharing close quarters with a woman. She deserved better than a man who could only give her a night now and again, nothing more. Nothing permanent. He knew that and honored it. Despite his reputation, he still had a very real sense of honor. No one deserved that kind of respect more than Rita.

However, her coming to him changed everything. He'd never sweet-talked her. He'd never promised her anything but what he'd already given her. She could not have any expectation of him beyond whatever he gave her on his last night in town. "What do you want, Rita? Say the word. Just say it."

"Cake."

"I thought s— What? Did you say . . . ?"

"Cake." It came out stronger this time but carried no less impact on his overinflated ego.

"Cake?" He put his hand to his forehead and groaned. What was he thinking? That she had crept down in the middle of the night, when she felt sure he'd be asleep in another room to what? Jump his bones? "Of course. Yes. Cake. You came down for cake. That's . . . that's logical . . . what else? It's a kitchen, isn't it? A kitchen with cake in it. Why wouldn't you want . . ."

"And you."

"Wha—I beg your pardon?"

"In all honesty, cake was the last thing on my mind tonight."

"What was the *first* thing?"

"You. I couldn't sleep for thinking."

"About?"

"About? Mercy, Will, about everything! About the twists my life has taken and the turns on every road ahead. Mostly about all these unsettling urges that having you around these last few days has put in motion. It's all clash and whirl like a fearful storm, and all I want is to quiet it down so I can get back with my life the way it ought to be."

"How you going to quiet that storm, Rita?"

"I can only think of one way."

"And?"

"I can't believe I am saying this to you, to Wild Billy West."

He started to protest her choice of nickname, but she never gave him the chance.

He heard the whisper of her gown only moments before the cool fabric swirled against the bare part of his legs.

Only her fingertips brushed over his bare chest. Heat and cold swept over his skin all at once.

She tipped her head back to look up at him. "I know I shouldn't even say this. It's not the kind of thing I'd ever dreamed I'd do."

He fit his arm around her and splayed one hand on the small of her back.

She wet her lips.

He moved in close enough to look into her eyes. He wanted there to be no doubt, no misunderstanding when she answered his question. "How you going to quiet that storm? What did you come down here to find, Rita? What?"

"A little taste of heaven, Will."

"Heaven?"

"That's all. A little bite of bliss—nothing more."

"I'm still leaving tomorrow, you know. I will be back in town from time to time, of course, but—"

"You think you have to tell *me* you're not the type to stick around?" She lowered her head for only as long as it took to clear her throat, then she raised her chin and smiled. "Just one night, Will. I know that. I don't want anything more, honest. I just wondered if you would even want *that* much . . . with me, that is?"

He would have laughed at the innocence of that question, but he didn't dare risk making it seem a joke to him. "One night? With you?" He stroked his thumb along her temple and let his fingers tangle in her soft brown hair. "Rita, that *would* be a little taste of heaven."

"Honestly?"

"Honestly." He traced his finger downward from the warm apple of her cheek to the hollow of her neck, where her pulse beat like a hummingbird's wings under his touch.

"But I'm . . . surely I can't be your type."

"My type?"

"The kind of girl you usually . . . I'll bet you've dated some of the most beautiful women around."

"*All* women are beautiful, Rita."

"I've all but offered myself on a platter, here. No need to fall back on cheap, corny lines to try to win me over, you know."

"I'm not the kind of man who has ever had to resort to cheap, corny lines." His fingers moved lower, skimming the lace of her gown over the achingly soft swell of her pale, full breasts.

" 'Course not," she murmured.

"You *are* beautiful to me."

"How can I be?" She tugged at the cloth around her shoulders to pull her makeshift robe closed at the throat. "I'm a mess. A total mess."

"You're unpretentious."

"I don't have buns of steel."

"Who the hell wants to curl up next to steel?"

"My thighs are . . ."

"Goddess thighs."

"Oh, right." She laughed, her hand on her hip. "Like in those old paintings of the goddesses frolicking buck naked in the woods or lounging on fainting couches with their clothes half falling off?"

"No." He took her hand and kissed her palm, then the underside of her wrist. "Goddess thighs—where I long to surrender myself in helpless adoration."

"Oh."

"Rita, there are thinner women than you." He took the front of the hospital gown in both hands.

"Undoubtedly."

"There are women with a whole lot less mouthy attitude." He gently peeled the gown back off her shoulders, down her arms.

"Poor things."

"And there are definitely women with better fashion sense." He released the gown, and it crumpled to the floor. "But they don't have a thing on you."

"I hardly have a thing on myself," she whispered, raising her hand to cover the inviting valley between her breasts.

"You are a banquet to my eyes, woman." He pulled her hand away and kissed her wrist, just where her pulse pounded closest to her soft, fragrant skin. "Just looking at you makes me . . ."

"I think the line here is shut up and kiss me."

He stepped in until not even a shaft of moonlight would fit between them. "I plan to do a lot more than kiss you."

"Then you'd better get started. We only have this one night, and it's already half over."

Chapter 8

EVERY BLUSHING DIXIE BELLE WOULD ADVISE: *Never think while aroused. It's like waiting an hour after you eat to go in swimming. You try using your brains while in this condition, you might just give yourself a cramp.*

He pressed his body to hers, shut his eyes, and sighed like a man come home from hell itself. He kissed her temple, her cheek, then nudged her head to one side and placed a hot, lingering kiss on her neck.

In that moment she surrendered everything. Her fears, her worries, a lifetime of self-doubt and herself—if only for this one extraordinary night.

"I don't . . ." He nuzzled her bare shoulder. "I didn't carry any . . . protection, Rita."

"I have plenty." She tipped her head back and gloried in his attentions. "The key is in the cash drawer."

"If that's a euphemism I don't know it." He pulled away, his eyes dark and his naked chest rising and falling in a hard and heavy rhythm.

"The machine is in the men's room, the key to

it is in the cash drawer." She went up on tiptoe to whisper into his ear, her hands on his shoulders. "*I'll* be waiting in the bed."

A smile made do for his answer.

She hurried away, not looking back. Tonight of all nights there was no looking back.

"Crazy . . ." she sang out the beginning of her favorite Patsy Cline tune.

"Did you say something?" Will called from the nearby men's room.

"Never mind." She finished the verse in a breathy hum, hurrying along to her destination.

She stopped only long enough to grab matches and some candles from behind the lunch counter. She had always loathed the tacky things Pernel had insisted sit at the center of every table. She hated the thick, orange-red glass. She hated the netting that covered the teardrop-shaped globes. And she especially hated the burnished amber glow they gave off because it reminded her of the yellow porch lights meant to chase the bugs away. She lay on the bed and lit the candles surrounding it. One by one they cast the dingy room in forgiving, sultry light, and she decided they were the loveliest things on earth.

Will's footsteps stopped. The bed dipped on one side under the weight of his knee.

"Candles, huh?" He kissed the nape of her neck, then lower still and lower along her spine. His hand reached around to cup her breast in the satin coolness of her clinging gown. "Nice touch."

"I could say the same for you." She blew out

the last match and met his gaze with a backward glance.

He kissed her shoulder, asking only with his eyes if she was sure.

She faced him and slid one strap of her gown off in answer.

He kissed the spot where the strap had held the fabric over her body. He hesitated, let out his breath, then slid the other strap off.

The gown fell to her waist. She did nothing to cover herself. She did not apologize for being so far from the picture of perfection. She felt no need to do either because she saw in his eyes the one thing she always dreamed of being—wanted.

She murmured his name.

He nuzzled under her chin.

She shivered. Urgency welled inside her.

If he shared that drive to rush toward the sweet surrender, he did not show it. He bent farther, slowly kissing, nibbling. When he paused, eyes shut, and laid his cheek against her bare breast she felt cherished in a way she had never known before.

She wound her fingers into the careless waves of his hair and kissed the crown of his head.

He raised his head. He brushed her hair out of her eyes.

She blinked and parted her mouth but had nothing to say.

He rested the pad of this thumb on the center of her lower lip and grazed his fingers along the side of her face. "You are so beautiful."

She flattened her hand to his bare chest, her smile trembling. "*You* are."

He laughed, then leaned forward, his hand still holding her face. He kissed her first on the corner of her mouth. Then, lightly, just on her lower lip. His face to hers, he let out a low, satisfied growling sigh and moved his body over hers. At last he kissed her full and hard, holding back nothing.

Somehow dull, plain Rita found the courage to touch this man's body. To feel and familiarize herself with every plane, every shallow, with the mass of his muscles and the textures of his skin. She sought what made him groan with pleasure and what made his pulse quicken as they explored and enjoyed each other.

She only tensed once, when he whisked the gown from her lower body and she lay there revealed and vulnerable.

"You are amazing . . . amazing," he whispered.

She let her breath out and reached for the waistband of his boxers. She tugged them downward until he sprang out, thick and heavy and ready to find his way inside her. "Let me return the compliment."

He nudged his knees between hers.

She gasped.

"Goddess thighs." He spread his hand high on the inside of her leg. "I knew they would be."

"Will . . ."

"Shhh."

She wet her lips, shut her eyes, and waited.

His weight came over her.

The mattress creaked.

His coarse hair chafed against her legs, stomach and breasts, teasing her with the promise of what would follow. He licked the shell of her ear before whispering, "Now?"

"Now!" The tenderness in her plea surprised her. Had it sounded too desperate?

No. She wanted this. She had wanted it—this act, this sensation, this man for a long time. For once in her life she had gone after what she wanted, and she would not talk herself out of relishing every moment.

"Now," she moaned. "Please, yes. Give it all to me, give me everything—just for now."

He groaned and in that split second joined them.

She raised her hips to take him in, all of him, holding back nothing of herself. "Oh, yes. Yes."

He grunted, moving into her faster, deeper as she urged him on.

"Give it to me. All of you, all of you." Every thrust pushed her farther until finally she let go of every inhibition, every doubt and indecision and surrendered to the man and the marvel of the one fleeting moment.

"Oh, darling, I can't hold back any longer." Braced on his elbows above her, he bent to press his face to her neck.

"Don't. Just let go. Let go. You're safe inside of me," she said against his temple.

He cried out her name, then primal, powerful sounds replaced words, and he drove deep into her one last time, then went quiet.

She had made love with Wild Billy—made love, not just bumped uglies in the night to stave off loneliness and lust. He had been so careful—so *caring*. What did that mean? Had he acted out of pity or . . .

Not tonight. She would not talk herself down from this high. She would not analyze or worry. She would not try to forecast the future or build walls and dams to guard against what tomorrow might bring. Tomorrow Will would go home. She would have plenty of time then for rehashing her every mistake.

His breathing still labored, Will lay atop her, spent. "What now?"

She ran her fingers through his hair and cocked her head to meet his gaze. "Well, there's always cake."

His laughter shook the rickety rollaway. He rolled away and stretching out alongside her, enveloped her in his arms. "You truly are amazing, Rita. Amazing."

"Where . . ." Rita scrunched her eyes shut against the shaft of sunlight aimed right onto her face. That wasn't right. She always slept with her back to the window.

Two months in this tiny apartment and not once had the sun awakened her. She was an alarm-clock kind of gal. Set it faithfully each and every night of her life. Every morning of her life, her eyes popped open five full minutes before the thing went off and she hopped out of bed to face . . .

"Will." His whispered name hummed on her lips.

Light came streaming in through the gaps in the torn curtains and around the painted pig she despised but Pernel had insisted putting on the door. She had to get out of here before Will woke up. She held her breath to keep the bed from squeaking and lifted the sheet.

"Good morning, Rita."

"It is morning, isn't it?" Morning and what they had shared was over.

"Penny for your thoughts."

"I wouldn't give a plugged nickel for my whole brain this morning."

His fingers skimmed along the exposed skin of her back. "Was it that bad?"

She shut her eyes. "It was that *good*. I can hardly think today."

"Excellent."

"Far from it." She pushed his hand away. "I *have* to think today. Your part in all this may be over, but mine has just begun."

"My part doesn't have to be over." He kissed her shoulder.

She wrestled with the covers until she got them almost under her chin. "Let's just leave it at one special night."

"Why? Why only share one night when we could have the summer?"

"Summer? What are you talking about?"

"There's a lot of work here." He edged the sheet lower on her back. "You know how we discussed having to do as much as possible by yourself and with the help of friends."

"With the help of friends, yes. Cozie will pitch in, no problem. Her husband, Mouse, too."

"Cozette's husband's name is Mouse?"

"Not his legal name, no. That's a nickname left over from his hippie commune days."

"I of all people know how a nickname can haunt you, no matter how hard you strive to get shed of it."

"I don't know that he ever tried to get shed of it or felt . . . haunted by it." *Haunted?* She really wanted to ask him to explain but wanted to get out of this current situation more. "Ridiculous nickname or not, he'll be here and work till the cows come home."

"So far you've got Cozie, Mouse, and the cows. Not much of a crew."

"Well, I have two hands."

He fit himself close behind her, reached over and took her fingers in his. "And they are lovely, magical hands, but can they wrap themselves around a hammer and drive a nail home?"

"You tell me."

He laughed.

"So my contribution will mostly be in the food supply end of the business. I've still got Jillie, and even Pernel might come around if he thinks it could give him a chance to put his two cents' worth in on how it's done."

"I can see the pair of them now. Tightening screws with fingernail files, using fake boobs for counterbalances, hissing and spitting at one another like rivals in a 1950s bad-girl lockup movie."

"Don't be tacky."

"How could I be anything but tacky talking about that pair?"

She cocked her head. "Pernel's pair?"

"My sister and your ex-husband."

"Oh, right. Right." She sighed. His nearness created far too big a distraction. "But beggars can't be choosers."

"Rita, you don't have to beg at all. You've got a first-rate carpenter who is right now looking for a reason to find his way back in town now and again until the job is done." He cupped her breast, his breath warming the back of her neck.

She rolled onto her back but did not quite focus her gaze in his. "Are you suggesting working something out in trade?"

"No! No, I . . ." The hollows of his cheeks went red as he must have realized how he had sounded. "I have a light schedule right now. I could clear it with a few phone calls and stay, if you want me to, Rita."

"Stay?"

"Just until the work is done. A month, six weeks at the most."

"And then what?" He was asking too much and too little of her in the very same proposition.

"And then the summer will be over."

"Right." What had she expected? The man wouldn't hang around longer than a weekend for his own family. He'd had one long-term relationship in his life that lasted longer than a football season, including playoffs and a bowl game. He hadn't even made himself available for his own baby until it was almost too late. What made her think he'd change for her? "Go back to Memphis, Will. There's nothing for you here."

"Rita . . ."

"We'd better get moving. Never know who might happen by and peek in the Palace window."

"They'd get an eyeful for sure."

She let her breath out all at once. "They'd get an eyeful, then I'd get an earful of advice, a few lectures on decorum, and more than one attagirl for finally doing something worthy of my bloodline."

"How do you stand all those people mixing into your life?"

"It's just the way it is." She flicked a strand of hair from her eyes and shook her head. "You know that. Life in a small town. Everybody being in your business is the trade-off for everybody being there for you when you need them."

"I just can't stand that they might say things to hurt you."

"Hurt me? How can they hurt me? They love me."

"People who love you are the very ones who can hurt you the most."

"Isn't that a song?"

"You know what I mean, Rita. *You* know."

"Anyway, I can't fathom they'd do much bad-mouthing of me over this—on account of my 'situation.' "

"Situation? That's funny euphemism for ex-husband."

"Ex-husband? No, my dear, the situation I mean is a girl like me having the once-in-a-life-time shot at waking up buck nekkid in bed with a man like you." She raised the sheet to peek beneath. "They'd call me a fool and worse if I'd let that pass me by."

"Well, you couldn't, could you?"

"Because you're so damned irresistible?"

"Because you had to grab your taste of heaven while you could."

She laid her hand on his stubbled cheek. "There is that."

"Funny, huh?"

"Funny ha-ha or funny like *The Twilight Zone*?"

"Somewhere in the middle."

"My favorite place to be." She smiled.

"I came here to work with you thinking some little part of what's special and good about you might rub off on me."

"Well, if it didn't, that's not my fault, I did some of my very best 'part rubbing' for you last night."

"For which my parts are mighty grateful."

"Especially those swollen, throbbing, thrusting parts of you?" She raised her eyebrows. "Right?"

"Do you kiss your mama with that mouth?"

"No, I don't. I don't see my mama. I haven't for years."

He only nodded in acknowledgment of her situation.

Rita sighed and patted his cheek. "Maybe now would be a good time to tell me about that in-the-middle-funny thing."

"The thing is, I came here to *do* something good."

"Help me make plans for the remodeling."

"Yes. But I also thought I'd *get* something good. I didn't know I would *give* something good—or that maybe you'd take it."

"You've lost me."

"Long time ago you took me to task because you thought I should be more like you—to stick by people, to invest myself in them."

"I still think that."

"Ah, but you also have learned to let go. Today when you told me to go back to Memphis I knew a little bit of me had been left with you."

"We took precautions against that happening, remember?"

"Make a joke, Rita, but you know what I mean. These last few days together, they've changed you as much as they changed me."

"Have they changed you, Will? Really?"

He didn't answer, and that was answer enough.

"Maybe I can let you go because that's the only way I can get my life back. Did you ever think of that?"

He started to shake his head, then stopped and just went on gazing into her eyes.

She slid her hand down his cheek until only her fingertips rested on his jaw. "You have thrown things out of kilter since you showed up in my kitchen that morning. Now it's time to set them right again."

"I hate the idea of leaving you here to deal with the meddlers, busybodies—and people betting on when you'll up and start acting like your mother—on your own."

She wanted to believe he meant it. If he did, then he had changed. He had made a connection and felt responsible. She did not dare think it would make him long to settle in and put down roots, but she couldn't help hoping it would make walking away a little harder this time. And next time . . .

Next time it would be another woman, another bed where he hesitated and perhaps finally decided to stay.

"Never you mind what folks will say. They've always been generous with pieces of their minds."

"That certainly explains a lot of the half-witted behavior around here."

"Besides, all things considered, my status in town may well rise a notch or two."

"How so?"

"Did you hear that our Rita got herself bedded

by a certain handsome gentleman caller from Memphis?" She put on a nasal twang, animating her gestures to play up her performance.

He chuckled, just barely.

"None other than *you know who*. She said he'd come to town to take some measurements and give her a 'consultation.' " She made the quotation marks in the air though no one in Hellon would have used the affectation. They'd prefer instead to hit each syllable of the word hard, eyebrows arched and lips pinched white to convey any underlying—and unsympathetic—meaning. "I'll tell you what—reckon that ain't *all* he did."

He laughed outright.

She touched his chin. "I could survive that I think."

"You ought to flaunt it. Have some fun with it. Show them you don't give a Yankee dime about their gossip."

"What? You mean put a plaque on this spot? Local hero slept here?"

"Slept?" He nuzzled her neck. "That hardly tells the tale. I did a hell of a lot more than that."

"I'm not writing *everything* you did here on a plaque." She pulled away. "I wouldn't even know how to begin to describe some of it!"

"You would need a lot of damn big words, maybe even have to make some up."

"Are you flattering yourself?"

"Am I?" He commanded her gaze to meet his.

Meeting his eyes, she recalled his every touch,

kiss, the warmth and wit and the very wildness of him.

She swore she felt a blush work over the length of her whole nude body. "No."

"Besides, why limit your marketing possibilities to this one space? I also used the rest room."

"Maybe we could rename that the William West Junior Memorial Reading Room."

"You can, but you'd be honoring my grandfather, then, not me. I'm a third."

"Shame you're not a fifth, we'd keep a liquor bottle behind the cash register with your picture on it."

"Given my reputation around here folks'd just think it was a saloon keeper's version of the face on the milk carton."

"How about I come up with a whole new menu to commemorate our night together? Start with eggs—over easy, of course."

"You kidding?" He sat fully up. "There was nothing easy about what happened here last night."

"For the lunch special how about fried chicken on a bed . . . of mashed potatoes."

"Kinky, but I like it."

"Nothing but breasts and thighs—"

"Goddess thighs."

"Goddess thighs," she amended without making eye contact.

"And for dessert?" He ran one finger along the edge of the sheet just above the swell of her breasts.

She put her thumbnail between her teeth and smiled. "We never did get around to indulging, did we?"

The sheets rustled and he stretched his long legs out, "Speak for yourself, I felt entirely indulged."

"It does beat the bejeebers out of cake for a late-night treat any day." Rita rolled onto her stomach and laid her cheek on Will's chest, where she felt more than heard him chuckle in response.

"Do people still say 'it rocked my world'?"

"Since when does Wild Billy West care what people say?" He went silent. Not simply grew quiet like he'd gone pensive or something but silent—dead silent—at the mention of his old nickname. His whole body stiffened up tighter than a drum. She wasn't even sure he took a breath for two, three, maybe five whole seconds.

"Doesn't matter anyway." Her words rushed out to fill the vacuum his tension created. "Rocked world or not, it's morning. Time to set everything back the way it was and go on with our lives the way they ought to go on."

"Like nothing ever happened." Some would say a man like Will did not have the capacity to sound wistful. But that's what Rita heard in his barely audible response.

"Maybe more like something happened, but now it's passed, like . . . like a . . ."

"Like a tornado?"

"Like a sweet dream that ends when morning comes. You still have the memory of it, but—"

"The dream was never real. What we had was real, Rita."

"And I'll have the muscle aches for days and days to prove it." She propped herself up on one elbow. "And a faraway look in my eyes and a secretive smile no one can quite explain."

He pushed the feather pillow into a lump and leaned back against it. The sheet, glaring white against his dark skin, slid down to his belly, then lower still. He made no move to catch it.

She had a twinge of regret when it did not slither completely off the bed.

He sighed and looked up at the ceiling. "Technically, this night's not over until we get up."

"Then it must be over." She raked her fingers through the black coils of hair on his chest, while her gaze wandered to a more southerly point on his wonderful, masculine body. "Because you, sir, are definitely *up*."

"Up and rarin' to go, girl." His movements under the sheets confirmed his boast. "What do you say, Rita? One more for the road? Want to try to reheat some of last night's passion?"

"Reheat? You make it sound like leftovers."

"Some things are just plain better the second time."

"Yes, but we've had our second helpings, and our thirds. I'd hate to see us make gluttons of ourselves."

"Not me." He nibbled her neck. "In fact I was thinking . . ."

"You should never think while aroused, Will."

She turned her head so he could kiss the tender spot under her ear.

"Why not?"

"It's like waiting an hour after you eat to go in swimming. You try using your brains while in this condition, you might just give yourself a cramp."

"What a way to go."

"Go any old way you please, but please, just go." She inched away slowly.

"Rita, I never intended for there to be any bitterness between us."

She brushed her knuckle along his chin. "I'm not bitter. I'm . . . just ready to get back to my life. It was great fun while it lasted."

"But it couldn't last, could it?" He said it more to himself than to her outright.

She let it go without further comment.

It took a contortion or two, but she managed to hold the sheet in place both above her breasts and above her behind. Delicately as a charm-school valedictorian balancing a book on her head, she leaned over the edge of the bed to reach for her nightgown. She stretched, ever mindful of her modesty but could not quite get her fingers on the pool of satiny fabric.

"Rita?" The jouncing of the mattress told her Will had started reaching for his boxers. "You might want to get after covering up real quick here."

It flashed through her thoughts that she could just give the bedcover one firm yank and wrap up in it instead, like lovers in the soap operas always did. That would save her having to wear something that had spent the night on the Palace floor. It would also spare her the mortification of wriggling into her gown in broad daylight with her never-going-to-happen-again lover looking on.

And leave Will lying there in his naked glory. Good gravy, how would she ever keep up the pretense of dignified detachment *then*?

She gripped the sheet more tightly in one fist and strained to grasp the gown.

"Rita!" His urgency made her look his way.

She narrowed her eyes. He had his shorts on his body and his eyes on the door. "Man, once you admit something is over, you just can't get away fast enough, can you?"

He leaned over her, his face close. "And you've anchored yourself so firmly in one spot emotionally as well as physically you can't understand there is a time to hang on and a time to let it go. A time for standing and arguing and a time for shutting up and hauling ass."

"Yeah, I think I recall that quote from Sunday school class."

"Good thing, cause here's one of your playmates come to take you to church."

"My . . . ?" She spun around just as Cozette cut off the engine of her truck parked squarely in front of the Palace. "I am so stupid. How could I let this happen?"

"You are not stupid, but you are naked, and you'd better correct that damn quick."

She snatched up her gown and tossed it over her head, arms flailing to find the right holes.

"Do that on your way upstairs. I'll hold her off down here. I won't open the door for her until I hear your footsteps overhead."

"Open the door for her?" The gown smashed down her nose. She had to give an extra jerk to yank it down into place. "You'll never get the chance."

"Why not?"

"She has a key."

"Why?"

"You know, you leave a key with one friend just in case?"

"I thought you gave a key to Jillie. She was the one let me in that first day."

"Okay, so both Cozie and Jillie have keys, they are both my friends and—"

"And Pernel."

"Pernel what?"

"Has a key." He wouldn't if she'd gotten around to changing the locks as she promised, but she decided not to confess that to Will.

"He did used to own this place, you know."

"And I suppose your daughter has one too?"

"So?" She bent her head forward and tried to finger-comb some life back into the morning-head mop.

"So when are you going to wake up and realize that you, Miss thinks-she-has-every-detail-of-her-life-locked-down-safely-under-her-sway that you don't even have control over who comes into your home and when?"

"That could be, but I do have control over who *goes*." She shoved at his shoulder and turned away.

"Fine." The mattress shifted as he dragged the sheet from her hips and got up, leaving Rita cold both inside and out.

Chapter 9

Every Dixie Belle Understands:
*You have the power to go after your heart's desire.
Don't let anyone take that away from you.*

He'd been too harsh with her. Spoken out of turn. The guilt of it weighed on him but not too heavily. He'd been trained in handling guilt, after all, by the masters—his mama, his sister, and the woman they both liked to refer to as his former "common—and, sugar, I do mean *common*—law wife."

So he did not feel any great compulsion to look back to see if Rita was shooting daggers at him with her eyes. He tugged on the jeans he'd left on a nearby chair and put on his T-shirt as he made his way to the front door. "You going to run upstairs or just face your nosy friend as God made you?"

"I've got my gown on and I'm getting my robe," she called out, her bare feet slapping lightly over the floor as she dashed into the kitchen.

Will had his hand on the door handle before

Cozette could fit the key into the lock. He held the bolt in place and cocked his head to peer around the image of the pig on the glass. "Morning, Miss Cozie. We're not open for business, much less breakfast, you know."

"Oh, for land's sake, you big bonehead, let go of that lock and let her in." The hospital gown flapped behind Rita like a cape as she rushed to start the coffee brewing in the machine behind the lunch counter.

"I didn't come for breakfast." Cozette folded her arms over an array of shell-and-stone necklaces that hung low on her chest.

"We aren't open for lunch either. Maybe if you'd call ahead you'd have saved yourself the trip in from Hippie Valley."

"I was already here." She nudged at the door's kickplate with her thick-soled sandal. "I didn't come from the farm, smart-ass. That's why I'm here right now."

"You're here because you were already here. The drive in from town isn't the only trip you've taken today, is it?"

"Rita, are you in there?" She pressed her face to the window. The clash of her long yellow vest, her formless green dress, and the print scarf tied around her waist almost hurt his eyes.

Rita, whose own getup left much to be desired— much, much to be desired from his vantage point—did not even try to tie her pitiful robe shut. She just came charging from behind the counter toward them. "Just open the door."

He motioned to her to cover up better, all the while still buying time with Cozie. "Awful early for a social call. Is Rita expecting you?"

"And you had the nerve to lecture me about letting just anyone stick their noses in my business." Quick as a flash, Rita nudged him aside with her hip. "I do have some say over who comes into my home, and you have no call to try to keep anyone out."

"You don't understand." He kept himself between Rita and her curious caller. "You—"

Cozie beat on the door with the heel of her hand. "I didn't come to see Rita. I came to talk to you, Will."

"Me?" He finally stepped back from the door.

"Him?" Rita pushed past, undid the lock and threw open the door. "Why would you come over here at this hour of the morning to talk to Will? You hardly know him."

"Not as well as you do, it would appear." Cozie jerked the sides of Rita's hospital gown together with the decisiveness of a crook closing his hideout curtains.

"Me? I don't *know* the man! He's only here to give me some suggestions on the Palace overhaul. Nothing else. Nothing at all. I hope you believe that, Cozette."

"I do, sugar. I believe anything you tell me." She tied the neck strings of the improvised robe into a bow. "But before you run that line by anyone else, you might want to make sure you don't have your nightgown on backwards and your boobies about to burst forth like dawn on the mountains."

"My . . ." She flattened her hand to her chest and shut her eyes.

"I tried to warn you."

"Bet that's not all you tried." Cozie lurched a bit to one side to take a peek at the disheveled rollaway. Being a big woman, she did not have to move much.

Will could not have blocked her view short of leaping in the air, nor could he have distracted her determined gaze, he decided, with anything shy of full-frontal nudity. "You said you came by at this unholy hour to see me?"

Her gaze remained pointedly fixed on the bed in the background much longer than good manners would have allowed. When she did turn to him again she took on a air of a member of a royal court speaking to some raggedy dog hanging around the back door. "I came to tell you your mother is feeling poorly and asking for you to come."

"How do you know that?" He scratched under his jaw. Cozette coughed. "I've sort of befriended Miss Peggy the last few . . . well, in recent . . . I go over to her house for coffee a couple mornings a week."

"Why?"

"Does that matter?"

"I suppose not." He crossed his arms. "Just never featured you as one of Miss Peggy's ladies, Cozie."

"Life is chock-full of surprises. You, of all people, should know that."

"Not where my mother is concerned. She's a one-trick pony putting on the same old act year after year. She's only playing sick." He'd seen her hold the whole family hostage with bouts of imaginary illnesses, headaches, and illusive pains no doctor could ever diagnose.

But she hadn't tried it on Will in a very long time and with good reason. The last time anyone summoned him to a sickbed he'd gotten a call at work to come to the hospital where the baby had been born and lived for two months. He'd been unable to get away from the job in time. He had gotten there just as they were unhooking the tubes and machinery that had kept the tiny body alive. For his mother to use a phony illness to force him to pay heed to her wishes went too far. "What the hell is wrong with that woman, anyway?"

"It doesn't matter what's wrong with her." Rita pushed at his back. "You have to go."

"I couldn't have put it better myself, Rita." He glanced at her over his shoulder.

"Good." She held her robe shut at the top.

"So I won't." He turned to Cozie. "It doesn't matter what's wrong with her, like Rita says, I have to go."

"You can't mean . . ." What Rita left unspoken told him she gathered his meaning completely.

He dipped his head to Cozette. "Tell Mother I have to go back to Memphis. I'll call her when I get there."

Rita gripped his arm. "But she's your mother, you have to—"

"It's her old nervous condition all flared up again . . . oh, and her sciatica." Cozie put her hand to the low part of her back like that lent some authenticity to his mother's complaint.

"See? It's her nerves." He gave Rita a slow, ornery grin. "If I go over there, I'll only make things worse. God didn't create the human being who could get on my mama's nerves faster than me."

"God may not have created one, but your parents sure did—Jillie is with her now." Cozie made a sour face. "And she's aggravating her something awful."

"Jillie is aggravating Miss Peggy or Miss Peggy is aggravating Jillie?" Rita's brow creased.

Cozie opened her mouth and looked up for a minute, then she sighed, her head shaking. "Six of one, half a dozen of the other."

Rita clicked her tongue.

Cozie's expression softened. She folded her hands and looked Will square in the eyes. "You really should come."

"My mother, my sister, sciatica, and nerves?" He rubbed his chin. "We'd just need frogs and locusts to have the whole bag of biblical plagues."

Rita did not crack a smile at his joke. "Why won't you go over there and just see that she's all right? Why is that so hard for you to do?"

Because he was a self-involved jackass; he wanted to throw her old opinion of him back at her. Somehow, though, he doubted she would accept it as readily now as she would have before. At least, he hoped she wouldn't. "Don't you get it, Rita? She's manipulating me."

"She's asking you."

"It's a ploy"

"It's a plea."

"For attention."

"For time."

"It's the same thing."

"No, not at all. At her age time becomes her most precious commodity."

"She's not *that* old."

"How can you be so callous?"

"How can you be so gullible?" He strode toward the kitchen door. "There is nothing wrong with my mother. Well, nothing *physically* wrong."

"You can't just leave."

He clenched his jaw. He did not want to say this to her. He did not mean it *for* her. But if he jumped every time his mother pulled some attention-getting stunt, his feet would never touch Tennessee topsoil again. "Can't leave? Watch me."

"I have no intention of watching you." She folded her arms and stood there, her gaze locked on him.

Will could only grab up his keys and wallet and head for the ready escape of his car waiting down the way in the church lot.

"You said you'd changed." Rita's lip trembled. "That a little of what you admired about me had rubbed off on you."

He stopped beside the lunch counter. Guilt twisted like a knife between his shoulder blades. It galled him all the more because he deserved it, and because it was delivered by the one person whose opinion really mattered to him. "Damn it, don't blackmail me into giving into that blue-tint terrorist's demands, Rita. If you did that, I could never . . ."

"Me? The person whose life is such a pathetic mess I can't even manage it. What makes you think I'd even try to run roughshod over yours?"

"I never used the word 'pathetic,' Rita. I would never characterize anything about you that way."

Behind the counter the coffeemaker sputtered, and the dark brew began to drip into the pot.

She met his gaze and acknowledged his round-about compliment with a stiffened lower lip and a concise nod. "I'm only asking you to do what you said you would."

"I always do what I say." That's why he was so very careful about making commitments—usually.

"Then stay."

He should have known that would come back to bite him in the ass. The rules were that promises made while naked and/or lying down did not count. That's the way things played among the people he knew. But this was Rita.

The aroma of rich, strong coffee filled the air.

"You said you could stay until the work on the Palace was done," she said softly.

He had. He had said it plain and clear. She had

not asked him for something he had not already promised to give. She had not put expectations on him other than he live up to the bargain he'd made with her. Standing there fully dressed, looking at her, with her hair a sexy mess, her skin radiant, and her jaw slightly scraped from his whiskers, he did not regret the offer. "I never said I'd stay at my mother's."

"Sleep in your car for all I care, just live up to your word."

"You can't make me go see her."

"I won't have to."

Damn it, she had him pegged—like an insect on a hatpin. "You are going to be the ruination of me, woman."

"Well, to quote a famous local philosopher— what a way to go!"

"Well, well, well." Cozie leaned back on the stairway door until it closed with a undeniable *clack*. She ran her hand down her braid, her chin tucked to her chest. "I'd ask what's gotten into you, but I guess I already know the answer to that."

"You don't *know* anything." Rita marched on through the kitchen.

"I live to learn." Her footsteps pounded a trail behind Rita. "C'mon, girl, out with the juicy details."

"There are no juicy details."

"Liar, liar, pants—Oh my, look at that! You're not wearing any pants—on fire!"

Rita spun around, almost going nose first into

Cozie's low, ample bosom, which was decked with layers of hand-strung necklaces. "Cozie, if I didn't love you so much, I'd give you a pinch that'd leave a mark."

"Do it, then we could compare combat scars." She reached out and brushed the pad of her thumb over Rita's jaw, like a mama spit-cleaning a child. Only, thankfully, without the spit. "That the only place you have whisker burn?"

"This the only place you can be a pain in the rear?"

"You knew I was blunt-honest the day you be-friended me, girl."

"And I did it anyway. Must be some kind of emotional deficiency, the way I gather people into my life that only seem to make it harder." She plunked down on the wobbly arm of the couch.

"You don't mean that." Cozie smoothed one hand over Rita's hair.

"Not about you, I don't."

"But Will, now, he's another story, isn't he?"

"What ill wind blew him into my life I'll never—" She jerked her head up.

"We only meant what was best for you. So, how was it?"

"What?"

"It."

"It?" Maybe if she played it dense, Cozie would tire of the game and just go away.

"The best?"

She smiled before she could catch herself.

"Well, of course it was." Gleeful. Only that

word described Cozie's reaction. "You were only with the one and only Wild Billy—was it actually *wild*?"

"I'm not having this discussion." Rita pushed up off the couch and started for the bedroom.

"Why not?"

"It's too . . . personal. Besides, what went on here last night was moonlight and quicksilver, only a taste of heaven, not the kind of thing a person is meant to hang on to."

"Why not?"

"Can't you say anything else?" She settled at her dressing table, finding Cozie's gaze in her mirror.

"Yeah, I can say that if it was me, I'd hang on with both hands and enjoy the ride while it lasts."

"But that's just it, Cozie, it won't last." The big pink faceted stone at the center of the Dixie Belle Duchess crown looked cloudy and dull in the morning light. "It can't."

"So? Make hay while the sun shines. Or should I say roll in the hay while the sun shines?"

"This is all your fault. Yours and Jillie's. Yours mostly because Jillie only brought him around because she thought Will and I would both benefit."

"Well, did you?"

"What?"

"Benefit?"

Rita sighed as she picked up her hairbrush. "Yes."

"Did you benefit? Simultaneously? Multiple times? I hope he didn't suffer from premature benefaction."

"There is no such word and don't look so smug." She tore the brush through her tangled hair, ignoring the way it tugged her scalp. "You and that kind of talk is what put the idea in my mind to start with. You and your *'this is about sex'* speech."

"Metaphorical sex. Fantasy sex."

"Never going to happen again as long as I live sex."

"Are you kidding?"

"No, I'm not kidding. I'm a happily ever after, roots in a small town, plain, chubby girl with one asset to my name."

"Don't sell yourself short."

"I'm not selling anything, Cozie. Not selling, not buying. I'm trying to get things back the way they were."

"But *why*? The way things were was not all that great, girl." She took Rita by the shoulders and met her gaze in the mirror. "Wouldn't you rather find out about the way things *could* be? Even if it's only a short-term dream?"

"My life is off kilter enough without tossing a temporary lover into the mix."

"Did it ever occur to you that maybe he's not here to be part of the turmoil but to provide you with an anchor?"

"Anchor?" She shut her eyes, her head bowed. "Like so much more deadweight? Yeah, I really could use another person in my life like that."

Cozie patted Rita's shoulder.

Rita did not meet her gaze, even in the mirror.

Finally, Cozie's necklaces rattled quietly as she stepped away. "I ought to go back over to Miss Peggy's and tell her that Will . . . what should I tell her?"

"I don't know, you're her new bosom buddy." Rita toyed with a half-empty bottle of perfume that Pernel had given her almost a decade ago. "What's that about anyway?"

"She's interesting. You ought to get to know her."

"I've known her all my life."

"You see her through Jillie's eyes and probably never looked past her public persona. Have you ever sat down and talked to her?"

"She was in the Palace just a few days ago."

"Not the same. You of all people should understand that passing the time of day, or night, or seventeen years of marriage with someone does not guarantee that you truly know them."

"Well, amen to that."

"So I'll tend to Miss Peggy. Do you have a plan to work on Will?"

"I told you that relationship has no future."

"Work on getting him over to visit his mother?"

"Oh . . . I . . . no. No, that's not my place."

"Then why finagle him into staying here to help you with the Palace?"

"Because he . . ." She sighed.

"If you didn't want to pursue a relationship or hope to convince the man to make peace with his mama, then why not tell him to hightail it back to Memphis?"

Because he made her mad. Because his refusal to make himself available to his family touched a raw nerve in her. Because he was so insistent that her choice never to give up on people you love was foolhardy, and she wanted to show him different. She shrugged.

"Oh, Rita." Her friend pulled her into a hug.

Not the usual girlfriend hug, either, but a long, close, healing embrace. Rita shut her eyes and eased her breath out slowly. For the first time since she'd awakened in bed with Will that morning she felt safe again, like she might just make it back to her old life not too much the worse for wear.

Cozette stepped back, bending at the knees to put them at eye level. "What do you want?"

"What kind of question is that?"

"It's the kind of question you should be asking yourself."

"Yes, well, since you and Jillie saw fit to meddle in my life I haven't had time to talk to myself as much as I used to, much less ask questions."

"You are what you say you are."

"So I've heard."

"And you get what you say you want."

"Not always."

"No, not always. Then again maybe those times when a person doesn't think she got what she asked for, she didn't want it badly enough."

"Cozie, why do conversations with you always end up with my head hurting?"

"Better your head than your heart." She kissed

Rita on the cheek. "Think this through, sugar. You have the power to go after your heart's desire. Don't let anyone—not even yourself—take that away from you."

Chapter 10

EVERY MODERN DIXIE BELLE PONDERS:
Was there a gracious, sophisticated way of dealing with the end of a purely sexual relationship? Perhaps put black sheets on the bed, find a sympathetic doctor to start an IV with fine chocolate and have notecards printed up to send to your friends that announce: Guess who's celibate again?

"No. I don't care. Throw out any excuse you want. Throw down a first-class hissy fit. Hell, throw a friggin' debutante ball and invite real debutantes with real balls." Will covered the mouthpiece of the phone. "No offense, Pernel."

"Offense?" The other man stuffed one hand into a stiff canvas work glove. "I was already dreaming up what to wear."

Will stretched the phone cord into the kitchen, putting his back to the commotion in the dining area of the Palace. "Today is D-day. Demolition day. The biggest single undertaking of the entire renovation."

"Excuse me." Pernel pushed his way into the kitchen and immediately began clanging cabinets and opening drawers.

Will clenched his teeth at the intrusion on the

lone island of privacy he'd had in the three full days since Rita had coerced him into staying on. "Do you have to do that now?"

"Just be a minute," Pernel assured him.

Will hunkered down over the phone and pressed on. "For the past few days we've bickered and bartered, kissed behinds, kicked butt, and bent over backward to accommodate a mostly volunteer workforce. Do you understand that?"

A "humph" followed by measured breathing on the other end was his only answer.

"And finally everyone involved in this mammoth undertaking is, at this very moment, waiting in the next room drinking coffee, flapping their jaws, shuffling their feet, and generally getting restless."

"That's right." Pernel shook his head and kept searching.

"In ten minutes we will start ripping out every booth, every bolt, every fixture and bit of flooring that we can get our hands on in there."

Pernel froze, his eyes shut, and clucked his tongue.

Will kicked at the floorboard with his steel-toed boot, put two fingers to his temple, and forged on talking before his tirade could be interrupted with whatever was on the other man's mind. "Already today the guys hauling in the industrial Dumpster have busted up the sidewalk. All the utilities have been shut off for the day, so we've had to lug in water, had to arrange to use the church for cooking, and we have a big blue Porta-Potti parked two feet away from the front door."

"Four feet away if it's an inch." Pernel went right on rummaging around the kitchen, muttering. "Think a master carpenter would be a better judge of that kind of thing."

Will put his finger in his ear and lowered his voice to a commanding rumble. "That's what I'm dealing with today. I do not have time for frauds, or whiners, or lag-abouts wasting my precious time with a bunch of nonsense."

The slam of the phone in the cradle hung in the air in a way that reminded him of the guilt he felt at lashing out at the innocent caller. Guilt that just as quickly turned to anger and then to frustration. He rubbed his forehead, right between his eyes. "Damn it. When did everyone's problem become *my* problem?"

"How *is* your sweet mama?"

He thought of denying he'd just hung up on his mother, but knew it would do him no good. Rita's ex-husband was on to him. How or why, he could not say. Still, the man standing there in freshly ironed white painter's overalls and an undershirt—the kind usually called a wife-beater of all things—with the creases still in it from the packaging seemed to have him pegged from the git-go. And that fact just plain chapped Will's butt.

"Why aren't you wearing a dress today, Starla, darling?"

"Same reason you aren't in your old football jersey, Wild Billy, baby."

"I haven't worn a football jersey in years."

"Doesn't matter. You don't have to have it on for all the folks in town to see you that way."

He gritted his teeth. "So what? Are you saying that even in that getup people see you in a dress?"

"People see me the way they want to see me. You can't deny that."

He didn't try.

"And people see you the way they want to see you. The only difference is that I'm okay with how they look at me and what they think. It just doesn't bother me anymore."

"But it bothers me? How people in Hellon see me? That your point?"

"Honestly, my point is that clothes do not make the man. Least not in our cases."

He folded his arms and cocked his head. He'd listen to Pernel's theory on this, but he'd be damned if he'd seem receptive.

"In our cases, the man makes himself. In my case that translates to makes himself over. In yours—makes something more of himself than a rich, lucky, son of a bitch—no disrespect to your mama—"

"Understood."

"High-school jock."

Will gave the briefest I'm-following-you nod he could muster.

"The clothes we use to express or downplay

those choices may help us face the world with our illusions, but they don't mean squat here in Hellon."

Pernel made sense, and that made Will want to punch the wall.

"You dress like you don't belong here, West. Like you have no stake in this town. But it will always be a part of who you are. You will always be adored here."

"You've got your share of admirers around and about I'd dare say, Pernel." His mother was one, it seemed. And Rita. Will dug the thumb of his right hand into the palm of his left, like a baseball player working his glove. "What of it?"

"Just seems to me that if a body finds a place where folks accept the person he *wants* to be as much as the person he *seems* to be, well, maybe that ain't the worst place under the sun after all."

"Damn it, Pernel." He gritted his teeth and shut his eyes.

Pernel laughed. "It's killing you, isn't it?"

"What?"

"That I'm not the thoughtless, evil jerk you want me to be?"

"You screwed Rita over royally."

"Word around town is that I'm not the only one."

"If you weren't a lady under those overalls, Pernel, I'd knock you on your butt for saying that."

He folded his arms and puffed his chest out. "And if I *weren't* a lady, I'd do the same to you."

"I'm not the one who sold Rita's home out from under her."

"House." Pernel put both hands in the deep side pockets of his overalls. "That was no home excepting how Rita made it one."

"No surprise. Rita has a way of making something damn fine out of whatever life hands her."

"She tried to do that with our relationship, for sure." He eyed Will in way that left no doubt that, given the opportunity, Rita would apply the same kind of loyalty and compassion to a relationship with Will. "But ours was no marriage except in her desire to stick it out till death do us part. As Lacey Marie got older we had less and less in common and I . . . I just couldn't be the man she needed me to be."

"I'll imagine my own cross-dressing joke and laugh quietly to myself to save time."

"Appreciated." Pernel gave a nod and drew a long breath. "Thing was, I saw us both growing older but not really growing at all, not as a couple or as individuals."

"Yeah. I've had that 'where am I going and how will I know when I get there?' dialogue with myself a few times these last few years, too."

"Finally, I woke up to the fact that I was running out of time to become . . . well, to become myself."

"Okay. Understood." Had he and Pernel actually agreed on something? Will set his jaw and wrapped his knuckles on the burnished stainless-steel countertop. "But you could have made a gentler exit, could have eased your way out and left Rita with—"

"You think I didn't try? Look around you! Why do you think I put a brand-new kitchen in a dump like this?"

"Good business? Improve customer relations?"

"Customer relations? You've gone over this place with a fine-toothed comb—you honestly think the Pig Rib Palace clientele are the type who care about the state of the kitchen? Hell, as long as the beer has a head and the ribs don't have hair, they are one happy crowd."

"Okay, I'll give you that."

"I tried to tell Rita in a million ways I wasn't happy.

When I redid the kitchen she should have seen I was getting ready to change everything."

"Starting with the Palace."

"I hoped to gradually turn this place into something . . . well, that's water under the bridge now because there is no gradual with Rita. There's the way things are, the way things are going to stay, and the only way out is to kick up a hailstorm and force her to deal with the aftermath."

"Sounds harsh."

Pernel shook his head.

"But not just on Rita. You had to consider your daughter."

"Lacey Marie knew I was going to do it, even encouraged me."

"For a fact?"

"She's a smart girl. Has a good heart. That's her mama's doing."

"Rita really could do anything if she wanted."

"You have no idea."

Will wondered at that but knew a direct question would get him nowhere. Coaxing Pernel to keep talking might yield some answers, however. "She could do a damn sight better than ending up a cook in this piss-poor excuse for a roadside restaurant."

"Aren't you going to say 'no offense'?"

"Nope."

"I'll accept that."

"One thing *I* won't accept. If Rita ends up stuck here, instead of following her dreams . . ."

"So, she did tell you."

"Of course, she told me." Will paused, half-expecting to feel the ground begin to shake. That lie had come so fast and so smooth, he figured at least two generations of gentleman Wests had just rolled over in their graves.

"Have you heard her, then?"

Will cleared his throat. "Not exactly heard, more—"

"You have to hear her. Make her drag out that karaoke machine I got her for our last Christmas together."

"Karaoke?"

"Went to the city and got her top of the line, like they use in small bars. Thought it would inspire her to want more for herself and maybe she'd just up and leave me to go start a singing career in Memphis or Nashville."

"She sings?"

"Hmm?"

"Uh, she sings . . . like an angel."

"I guess so—if angels sing torch songs and the blues. But that don't seem right, does it?"

Torch songs and the blues. Sexy, he'd bet, rich and full as the woman who belted them out. He smiled.

Pernel opened one last drawer and muttered under his breath, "Finally."

"Find what you came in for?"

"Yeah." He neither said what it was nor took anything from the drawer. "How about you?"

"I only came in here to have some quiet so I could give my dear sweet little mama the hell of a chewing out she deserved."

"Like everybody in town doesn't know you've checked with her doctors and that you call her every day to make sure she's all right."

"Yeah, well."

"Who'da ever thought me and you would have so much in common, huh?"

"I don't see . . ."

"Like this clean, fancy kitchen behind the doors of that gulp-and-gobble exterior. Things ain't always what they seem with either of us."

"Yeah. Imagine that. We do have *that* in common, I suppose."

"You thought I meant Rita, didn't you?"

"No, why would I?"

"Because she's my ex-wife and she's your . . . What is she to you, West?"

"Friend."

"You are good at it, I'll tell you that."

"Good at what?"

"Keeping the act up. You're so good at it you may have even fooled yourself for a while."

"Not only are you overstepping your bounds, buddy, but you've made a wrong assumption about Rita and me."

"Have I?"

He wouldn't dignify that with an answer, much less another whopping lie.

"Fine. I get it. You think I *don't* get it, but I do. Just because of what I done, don't think I don't appreciate your protecting her good name and keeping the gossips and meddlers from going at her."

"As long as we understand each other."

"Better than you think."

"We have a lot of work waiting."

"That we do." He started for the door. "By the way, if you hurt her, I will forget I'm a lady and come after you. That's a promise."

"I won't hurt Rita." He meant it even if he remained skeptical of the odds on carrying it off. "I can't. We just aren't close enough for that."

"I don't believe that, and neither do you."

"Then believe this, I won't hurt her because I won't have the chance to. We've got two days to tear everything out of the dining room, then a couple days' break while the flooring guys come in. After that, one crew after another to bring in and fit the new fixtures." He snapped his fingers in quick succession to show how fast the work would go. "Then the finishing work. Rita and I won't have a moment alone. That should put an end to any talk or speculation."

"You think talk's the only thing that can hurt Rita? Man, she's weathered a lot more of that than even you could inspire."

"If I don't see her, I can't hurt her."

"You really are a master of denial, you know that?" Pernel headed through the door empty-handed, with the drawer he'd last looked into still hanging open. "And that's coming from one of the best this town ever saw."

Will went over and shut the drawer with a *wham* that made the coffee spoons on the counter rattle and dance. He grumbled a curse, stole a glance at the back door, then to the stairway that led to Rita's apartment.

She'd taken off early that morning, gone to do the grocery shopping to feed her volunteer work crew. She wouldn't be back until she'd finished that and cooked lunch down at the church.

He was glad he wouldn't see her. Glad he had not seen much of her these last few days. That would make it so much easier to take his leave when this job was done.

"Torch songs and the blues?" The hair on the back of his neck prickled. He rubbed his knuckles under his jaw. What he wouldn't give to hear her sing just once before he left.

* * *

"Ooo-ooo-oo-yeah." Rita improvised an ending to an old scorcher of a torch song as she pulled the car to a stop a few feet back from the corner of Winter and Providence.

"The best!" Pernel indulged in an overplayed golf-clap to reward her performance. "As always."

"Your opinion can't be trusted. You're unduly influenced." She looked across the car seat at her ex-husband.

"Me?" He put his hand to the bib of his dusty overalls. "By what?"

She noticed he had on a pale opalescent nail polish that the morning's hard work had not chipped. "By the fact that you think I should get out of Hellon and out of your hair."

Pernel swept his sandy brown bangs to one side with his fingers.

"I know you think I shouldn't waste my talents here. That I should take up singing in smoky lounges for tips and the occasional hotel key. That's just the kind of story you'd love to go around telling about your ex-wife, now, isn't it?"

"I admit, it would make a hell of a conversation starter." He laughed, then crossed his legs at the ankles. "But then I never needed someone else's good stories to start a conversation, Rita."

"True."

"Fact is that despite all the antipathy between us . . ."

"Antipathy," she whispered with a smile, knowing it was just the kind of word Pernel loved to sprinkle into even the most mundane exchange to impress people. Something Will would never do. But then, he didn't have to. What impressed people about Will—what impressed her—often came from what he didn't say.

"Despite our recent unpleasantness," Pernel went on, "I do remain your most devoted fan."

After all they had gone through, she still welcomed the sense of comfort she found in his company. Pernel gave her a sense of things as they once were, of continuity and—heaven help her—of having a safety net. No matter what became of them both she knew she could count on Pernel to be there for her, probably driving her crazy. "You must be pretty devoted to have come walking over to the church in the midday sun just to help me load up the lunch fixings."

"Anything to help. You know that."

"I know anything but that. The minute I saw you walk through the door of the church basement I figured you were up to something." Driving her crazy seemed his long-term ambition. That in itself was a form of continuity, she guessed. "If you came to stir up more trouble . . ."

"I came to help. To maybe make amends a little for how bad I acted when you started all this renovation nonsense."

"Really?"

"No, not really. I just had had enough of 'Wild Willie' ordering everyone around. And frankly, I hated watching people tear down and rip apart what it took most of my adult life to build up."

She thought of mentioning that she had felt the same way when he left her and later sold her house with her still living in it. Instead she patted his shoulder, nodded, and hummed a non-response. "Hmm."

"I know it was a dive. I know it seems at odds with the way I want to live the rest of my life, but I still hate what you're doing to my Palace. I doubt I'll ever fully accept it."

"Continuity, Pernel, honey." She sighed and gripped the wheel. "You do provide me with that."

"And an appreciative audience for your singing."

"Yes, that too."

"Though I do confess if you're sitting here in the middle of the road waiting for me to demand an encore, you had better switch off the motor to save gas. I've had enough entertainment already. I'm hungry, and I'd wager your voice is just about to give out."

"True again." She'd been singing all morning. Sultry numbers of aching sexuality and longing followed by sweeping, sorrowful tunes that all but broke your heart to hear. Singing and cooking.

Cooking because she had to and because it acted like a poultice on her raw emotions. And singing because it tore those emotions wide open again and let them soar. Singing gave them voice and power, and a legitimacy that she only dared to claim in the name of the blues and the ballads.

"It's West, isn't it?"

She looked in the direction of the Palace. Sitting back from the stop sign like this, she could make out the parking lot. She could see who went in and came out perfectly between the rows of trees that hid her car from view.

She'd discovered the vantage point when Pernel had first left her. She'd spent way too much time parked there, hoping to get a glimpse of the goings-on. She'd told herself she wanted to try to understand her then-husband's actions by keeping an eye on him. Mostly she was too scared to let go. So she had sat on the edge of her old life and looked in as often as she could.

It left her a tiny bit weak-stomached to sit there now with Pernel at her side, talking about the man she had made love to in that very building.

"He said he wouldn't hurt you, Rita."

"He . . . said?" She swallowed hard but her weak stomach felt like it had crept into her throat. She blinked at her ex. "You two . . . you talked about me?"

"Only in a roundabout way. Now, don't get mad, Rita. I still care enough to worry what happens to you, you know."

"He didn't *tell* you anything, did he?"

"No, he didn't; but your reaction sure as hell does."

She held her head up and shook her hair back. "What reaction?"

He laughed and rolled his eyes. "If there was nothing between the two of you, then those people providing you with all the volunteer labor would be eating right now instead of starting to wander out into the parking lot, checking their watches. You're holding back here for a reason."

She looked in his eyes and felt nothing more than she would if she were staring at a face in a high-school yearbook. Affection and fond memories, but nothing more. Even so, how could she talk to her ex-husband about Will? He simply would not understand.

It had all been so simple when she and Pernel had stopped having sex. It brought a kind of relief, really, to both of them. Neither of them talked about it, or planned it, but after a time they just seemed to know that that part of their relationship had passed. That sort of took the pressure off the rest of it. They fell into an easy friendship. And they had Lacey Marie to act as a bond between them.

Rita had never *stopped* having sex with anyone else before. She had no idea what a miserable experience it would be. Or how awkward it would make her feel around the person she *wasn't* sleeping with. There had to be a gracious, sophisticated way of dealing with the end of a purely sexual relationship. Perhaps she could put black sheets on the bed, find a sympathetic doctor to start an IV with fine chocolate, and have notecards printed up to send to her friends that would announce "Guess who's celibate again?"

"Rita?"

She was already picturing greeting cards with

adorable woodland animals in chastity belts when Pernel interrupted her daydream. "Hmmm?"

"It's a cowardly thing to sit here while people who have worked hard all morning wait for their lunch," he reminded her like a dog with a bone.

Cowardly. Yes, that described her to a T. Still, she couldn't put her foot to the gas and go.

"You need to get going now, Rita."

"Going? I can't." Her head thudded against the window as she slumped to the side. "Going means facing Will."

"So?"

"Facing Will means facing the ugly truth about myself."

"I refuse to believe there is any such thing," he said with such conviction he almost had her convinced.

"Well, there is in fact such a thing. And you know, Pernel, the one thing my whole life long that I have worked harder at than singing, or cooking, or maintaining impossible relationships is avoiding the ugly truth about myself."

"We all do that to some extent." He slipped his arm over her shoulders, gave her a little shake. "I can't imagine you are any worse than average and a lot better than . . . well, a few people who shall remain nameless but could be found in your innermost circle of friends and family."

She managed a chuckle. "Truth, ugly or not, about anyone else I can handle, you know."

"Given time, yes, I believe that's so."

"But facing up to myself?" She clenched her

jaw and struggled to keep the tears from flooding her eyes. "How could I do that and not have it shake my world to its very foundations?"

"Your world is a lot more solid than you think, Rita."

"You don't understand. It will change my world because it will force me to change. If a person knows the worst about herself, then works up the gumption to admit it but doesn't do anything about it—what kind of a person is that?"

"Damned miserable." He rubbed a fingertip beneath one eye, careful not to smudge his liner and light mascara. "At least I was for a long time."

"Stupid," she whispered. "That's what this makes me." So, she'd come full circle since that first day Jillie brought her brother to the Palace. Now just imagining looking Will in the eye made her feel like a first-class chump. A dumped chump, to boot.

All right, technically *she* had dumped *him*—in a preemptive dump because she had known what was coming. And it gave her no consolation these past few days, as they'd tiptoed around one another, never looking in each other's eyes, talking only about curtains and colors and cushioned versus hardwood chairs.

She should never have maneuvered to make him stay. Stubborn fool of a man had not gone to see his mama and, to hear Cozie tell it, that only dampened Miss Peggy's spirits all the more. He'd done the work he promised, in record time and far better than she ever could have managed on her own. But he had not done the work she had hoped.

Then again, neither had she. That's why she couldn't push on that pedal and go. She pressed her forehead to the steering wheel. "Lord, but I feel awful."

"Are you heartbroken, Rita?"

She eased out a long sigh. "No. Heartbroken implies my heart has gotten involved. It hasn't." Her head, her hopes and, heaven help her, her hips were involved but not her heart. "I'm just so . . . disappointed. And embarrassed. And stupid."

"Now that's not true. I will not allow you to talk that way about yourself."

"I am what I say I am," she whispered. "Then I am . . . a mess."

"You are amazing, Rita. You could do anything you put your mind to."

She took a deep breath, and the smell of ham salad and baked beans, corn-bread muffins, and peach pie filled her senses. "You think I can sneak in and out of the Palace without once crossing paths with old Wild Billy?"

"Oh, Rita." Pernel put his hand to his forehead and looked toward the Palace. "What am I going to do with you?"

"Stay quiet and hang on." She sat up and looked both ways down the street. She urged the car on slowly, negotiated the turn onto Winter, and made a beeline for the Palace. She had to deliver the lunch, but she didn't have to deliver it directly to Will.

She'd just steer clear of him. Judging from the group gathering, it wouldn't be hard to avoid one person. Simple as that. In and out so fast he wouldn't know she'd even been there. She began to hum as she pulled into the lot, a happy tune with words she struggled to remember.

That distraction did her a disservice when her tire hit a chunk of wayward sidewalk cement.

Suddenly, her would-be stealth lunch wagon careened to the right.

She overcompensated by yanking the wheel hard to the left. She jammed her foot on the brake.

Pernel yelped like a scalded pup.

Gears ground. Her brakes squawked.

Every head in the parking lot swiveled just in time to see her big old car coast to a bumpy halt directly against the door of the blue portable toilet a few feet from the building.

Like everything else in her life just then, Rita's plans to keep a low profile had gone up in smoke.

Chapter 11

EVERY DIXIE BELLE ACCEPTS THAT
THERE'S A TIME TO:
Sit tight and don't say anything that might come back to haunt you.

"Are you trying to kill me?" Pernel popped the door open and scrambled out.

"You? What about the people in the parking lot?" she called after him, hoping no one took that to mean she'd wanted to run down her friends instead of killing her passenger. "What if there had been someone on the sidewalk? What if there is someone in the . . ."

Pernel slammed the door.

"No!" She lurched to the side as if she could soften the *wham* of the heavy door.

Too little too late. The car rolled gently forward until the bumper wedged itself just beneath the handle of the rent-a-privy's door.

People in the parking lot gasped.

Rita didn't dare back the car away and risk dragging the bathroom door open or worse. In fact she wasn't sure she should even risk getting out and throwing things off-balance. All she could do was roll down the window and address her appreciative audience. "First one to say this is when the shit hit the fan—"

"More like when it hit the fan belt Rita!" Cozie's husband Mouse looped his arm over his wife's shoulder and grinned.

Everybody laughed.

Great. *Everybody*. She couldn't pull a stupid stunt like this without witnesses, could she? She had to do it when everybody she knew had gathered in one place, standing in the parking lot waiting for her arrival, no less. She scanned the crowd of familiar faces looking for one in particular. "Um, where's . . ."

A muffled curse rose from behind the blue door.

She dropped her head forward onto the steering wheel. The horn blared!

The curses increased in creativity and volume to match her rude blast.

"Tell me the person I have just trapped in that traveling outhouse is *not*—"

"Where the hell you learn to drive? From my mother?" Will stepped over some concrete debris to rest his hand on the side mirror.

She blinked, relieved for only a moment. "If you're not in there, then who is?"

"The Industrial-waste guy."

"Do I know him?"

"No, he rents out this stuff." He motioned to

the long black and rust—real rust, not the color rust—Dumpster in the parking lot, then to the portable toilet tilted against her car. "I called him over to make him take responsibility for busting up your sidewalk. He said it wasn't his fault, and he wasn't paying for it."

"Will it cost a lot?"

"It's not just the cost of the sidewalk. There's the legal responsibility should anyone trip or have an accident because of it."

"Wonderful. I could get sued and lose the rest of what I don't have to begin with."

"Man told me there was almost no chance of this sidewalk causing a problem, by the way." He lowered his head to speak to her through the car window. "Sweet irony, huh?"

"Sweet? Hardly the word I'd use to describe his situation right now."

"You are a wonder, Rita. Even when you don't try to be—maybe especially then." If a man could laugh with his eyes, Will did just that. His smile remained quiet, almost sad, but his eyes . . . "Poor guy doesn't know what hit him."

She had no basis for it, but danged if she didn't believe right to the very depths of her heart that Will was not talking about the man in the outhouse.

"What do we do now?" she asked, well aware that her own response had a double edge to it.

The waste-management fellow bellowed out his own suggestion.

"He's certainly in the right place for that kind

of language." She gripped the wheel and sat back in the seat to better survey the situation. "If I back up slowly enough, can y'all keep that privy from tumbling over?"

"Yes, but why would you want to? Looks to me like you have yourself a prime negotiating stance."

"Negotiating? Oh . . . no. No?"

"Have you looked at the state of your sidewalk here, Rita?"

She came within a breath of saying, *Yes and it's the perfect illustration for my life.* But with Will just inches away and wearing that look—she found herself hard-pressed to see her circumstances as anything but on the upswing. "You are one wicked, wicked man, William West."

"That a complaint?"

She let the squawk of her setting the parking brake be her answer.

He laughed. Then he turned and shouted directions to the group milling around the lot.

Immediately, Cozie and Pernel started unloading the lunch goods while Mouse and a couple of men helped brace up the Porta-Potti.

Will put one foot on her car bumper and began talking to the blue door.

She couldn't hear the exchange word for word; however, Will's tone stayed steady and calm while the man's on the other end of the conversation grew more angry and threatening. Once or twice Will cut loose with a good-ol'-boy belly laugh—the kind any longtime Southerner recognizes as a pure power play and nothing to do with good humor. Still, he didn't come off mean with it, like some men do. He simply sounded confident and unwilling to back down when he was in the right.

In response, a string of vulgarities poured out from behind the door. Curses so imaginative and complex that Cozie—the ultimate queen of many-paths-all-lead-to-the-same-God—made the sign of the cross over herself, her eyes wide.

Boot to the bumper, Will jounced the car once lightly, then again, harder.

Rita hung on to the steering wheel and shut her eyes. All she needed was to get carsick in a parked vehicle to put that crowning jewel in her near-perfect day.

A stillness fell over the whole scene. An eerie stillness, they'd say in books, the kind that came over battlefields when no men stood left to fight. Will not only stood, he strode toward the driver's side of her car, his expression dark.

"Scoot over, I'd better do this."

Will nudged her over to the passenger side so he could take the wheel without so much as a *do you mind if* or a *please*.

"Should I get out?" She scrambled for the other door.

"We're both getting out." He grabbed her by the wrist and slammed the door shut. "Getting the hell out of here."

Her heart raced. *Well, your heart would race*, she told herself. Good gravy, not every day a girl gets herself into a fix like this and has the man of her dreams charging to her rescue.

"Sit tight and don't say anything that might come back to haunt you."

"Always good advice." She gritted her teeth and tried not to dwell on having just thought of Will as the man of her dreams. Instead she focused on how it just figured that her one chance at playing damsel in distress involved outdoor plumbing and strong-arming a stranger with his pants around his ankles.

Will shifted into reverse and eased the car back just a bit, then leaned out the window. "Don't let him out until you see our taillights round the corner."

"Taillights around the corner? Where are you planning on taking me?"

"Doesn't matter, just so he doesn't come out and realize who had him pinned in." He gunned the motor, shifted again, and tore out of the lot. "If he knows it was you, he might claim we set him up."

"Oh, right. Like I could really have planned anything that perfect." She shook her head. "If they took it to a court of law, all I'd ever have to do is submit my life as exhibit A."

He came to a stop at the intersection just north of the Palace—where the road to the left led to Miss Peggy's grand old home and, to the right, headed out of town to the narrow dirt lane that ended in the cemetery. He made a quick glance in either direction. "Exhibit A?"

"Incontrovertible evidence that I no longer have control over anything that goes on with me anymore, at least not since *you* showed up."

"Only since *I* showed up?" He made a right. He didn't look at her, but he didn't have to for her to see that smug expression. *See it?* Hell, she could *hear* dripping snake oil in his voice.

He scrubbed bent fingers along his jawline. "I confess I did aim to have an impact on you."

All right, snake oil was too strong a description. Without stealing so much as a glance his way, she sensed a gentling in his demeanor.

"And not just the impact of . . . making the earth move for both of us the other night."

Merciful heavens, the man was showing understanding and kindness. Trying to reach her on an intimate level to make sure everything between them was all right. That *she* was all right. If he hadn't been driving, she would have strangled him for it.

Her only goal for the day had been to avoid Will. Barring that, she had wished simply not to look a fool in front of him. And if that proved impossible, she did hold out the one last auxiliary, backup, please-Lord-I-never-ask-for-much-but-just-this-once hope that there be not so much as a hint of reference to their lovemaking and subsequent failed good-bye.

"Rita, I—"

"Shut up and drive."

The woman had a point. And if he had a lick of common sense left, he'd do just that. He'd shut his mouth and drive around town in blessed silence until it felt safe to go back. "Rita, don't you think we need to talk?"

"No." She faced straight ahead, one hand braced on the faded green dash. "That's the very essence of the phrase 'shut up.' *No* talking. Shutting up of the entire frontal face area in order to prevent the escape of words or even accidental vocal intonations."

"Got it." He guided the car around a long curve, eyes peeled for a driveway or wide shoulder where he could turn around.

"I should have seen this coming a mile off," she muttered, her face to the passenger window.

"I guess the shutting-up portion of the ride only applies to the driver's side of the vehicle then?"

She exhaled loudly.

"Okay." He could sit and listen. Maybe then he'd learn something about what went on in that amazing mind of hers. He could live with that.

"I took on this day with one objective—feed the people helping me with the Palace without once having to deal with you directly. And by directly, I mean all alone, one on one, no witnesses or buffers. That's the thing I set out to avoid."

"Mmm." It was the only noise he could make while still complying with her orders to keep his mouth shut.

"Was that asking so much? It's all I wanted. But now look at us. A pair of renegade toilet tippers, on our own and on the lam."

"Just trying to . . ."

"Don't say it!"

He raised an eyebrow and finished his justification. ". . . help."

"I told you not to say it. I'm sick of hearing it, you know. Sick of hearing you tell me how you're here to help me—*again*."

"That's bad?"

"Every day I climb out of my bed thinking I am one day closer to the end of this chaos. And every night I fall back into that same bed weighed down with the realization that I am mired even deeper in your debt."

"How can you be in debt to me when I set out to do all this to try to repay you?"

"Repay me?"

"You gave me something very precious."

"I didn't want to talk about *that* either."

"That?"

"That little piece of heaven the other night."

"That *was* precious." More than he could describe without taking his hands off the wheel and his mind off the real subject. "That will always remain precious to me, Rita. But it was the little piece of your mind that you gave me more than six years ago that I'm talking about."

Even with her head bowed, he could see her cheeks redden. "I had no call to talk to you that way."

"Somebody had to." The whole car jostled as the tires rumbled from the pavement to the dirt road. It wasn't the movement that made his pulse pick up or the coldness gripping the pit of his stomach. His eyes on the tree-lined lot up ahead, he whispered, "You gave me a great gift then, Rita."

"I hardly think—"

"Time with my son." He pulled up to the ornate iron gate between two rows of windswept pines.

Rita put her hand on the dash. The kind sadness in her eyes cut away all pretense and in the same instant offered healing and hope. "This is where he's buried, isn't it?"

He could not answer that question without giving away too much of himself, so he only nodded.

"Do you want to get out?"

"No."

"Do you want to talk?"

He nodded again.

She took his hand and waited.

He drew on the strength of her compassion and looked down the gravel lane between the rows of marble headstones. "If you hadn't chewed me out up one side and down the other about my responsibilities to Norrie, the responsibilities of being that baby's father, I might never have gotten the chance to hold that precious boy in my arms."

"Oh, Will, of course you would have."

He shook his head. "You don't know the situation, Rita. The way things were and the way things turned out, if you hadn't had the nerve to give me hell, I might never have looked into that child's eyes and told him that I loved him."

She gripped his hand tighter.

"He was so tiny." He fixed his gaze on the small marker in the distance, the one with the carved white lamb on top. "He couldn't have understood, but it meant the world to me to have even that short time with him."

"I think he understood."

"Yeah?" He wanted to believe her. He looked into her eyes, and he did believe.

"Some people say babies are born knowing everything that's important—like love, trust, and joy. It's only as we grow older that we forget."

He put his hand to her cheek. "You're still giving me comfort, Rita."

She turned her face into his palm. "Then I guess I can let go of the shame I've carried all these years for daring to confront you about the way you were acting."

"You've nothing to feel ashamed of. I was acting a perfect ass. Drinking a little too much, ignoring the person who was counting on me."

"Norrie?"

He nodded. "I didn't care that I'd moved her to Memphis from Nashville and she didn't have any friends—at least not any *girl*friends—there to help her and comfort her."

Rita tipped her head, her eyes already conveying the question he knew she wanted to ask of him.

He did not let her get a word in. "I didn't care about my work or my responsibilities in those days. Just tried to hide from my problems by reliving my past glories in a place where all every-body ever expected of me was that I be Wild Billy."

"I'm sure that was a full-time job in itself." She caressed his arm.

"You have no idea. That expectation pressed down on me like a yoke. I know everyone dreams of being the hero, but in a town this small after a time it becomes a kind of curse. People want to be Wild Billy's friend, not *my* friend necessarily, but Wild Billy's."

"I can see that."

"There was always this pressure that came with it, these expectations. And because they weren't unpleasant expectations, how could I re-sent them?" He shook his head, his chest tight. "It's hard to explain."

She nodded. "I understand."

"As long as I stayed in Hellon nobody wanted me to grow up, nobody wanted me to get serious about my life. And nobody had the gumption to say 'boo' to me when I become a selfish donkey-headed bastard."

"Except me."

"Except you."

"In this town half-fueled by gossip, I have never heard a harsh word over my behavior dur-ing that period."

"You lost your son, Will. It's not a town with-out a heart."

"I wouldn't have been there for him—or

Norrie—when he was born if you hadn't spoken up."

"But you did go before it was too late. That matters, Will. You got to see him and hold him."

"Norrie and I had broken up before . . ." No, he could not tell everything, not even to Rita. "Before she even knew she was pregnant."

"You and she were together a long time, right?"

He nodded. "Lived together for almost three years. My longest-standing relationship outside family and folks in Hellon. Guess that sounds pretty pathetic to a person like you, doesn't it?"

"No more pathetic than I figure my choices and relationships seem to you."

"Not pathetic, just . . . we're so different, aren't we?"

"Like sunshine and rain."

"Still, I thank you, Rita. It changed my life."

"Maybe it changed that one eternal moment for you, Will. Not your whole life."

"You can't possibly make that judgment."

"We are known by the fruits we bear. You gather a bushel of pecans and bake a pie, it won't taste like apple no matter how much you tell people it does."

"I don't follow you."

"If what happened with your son changed your *life*, Will, then your life would be different."

"It is different."

She didn't say a thing to that.

"What you really think is that if my life had really changed, that *we* wouldn't be so different. If I were a changed man, I'd be more like you now, right?"

"You've been in town all this time and you still haven't gone to see your mother. Does that sound like a man changed in his heart toward his family?"

He could tell her about the calls, about the checking with his mother's doctors and getting reports from Jillie. He could tell her that if his mother had used any other ploy but a phony deathbed summons, he would have given in by now. He could tell her, but having to tell her something so obvious, something that even her ex-husband had known? It galled him more than a plain old-fashioned slap in the face.

He started the car. "We'd better get back to the Palace."

"Yes, we should. You haven't even had your lunch."

He jerked the car into reverse. "It's you I'm think-ing of."

"Don't worry about me." She put on the phoni-est smile he'd ever seen. "I can afford to skip a meal now and again."

"As can I." He laid his hand on the back of the seat. Twisting around he looked out the back win-dow. "But I was thinking about the talk."

She wound her fingers together in her lap. "The talk we just had?"

"The talk around town." The brakes squeaked.

He faced forward without even meeting her gaze. "You and I take off in your car and stay away too long. It's bound to start tongues wagging."

"I think it'd be hard to top the real big story of the day—me lending a new meaning to the idea of a portable toilet."

"Either way they'll talk about you, and I know you hate that."

"I'll live."

He clenched his jaw. "Why do you do it, Rita?"

"Live?" She purposely evaded his meaning. "Because I'm not ready for the alternative."

The car surged forward. "Yeah, you're a regular survivor."

"I pretty much have had to be."

"But you don't have to be one *here*. Rita, you could do so much more than survive, you could flourish if you'd get out of this town and—"

"Now it's my turn to change the subject."

"We're a pair, aren't we? Both thinking we know what's best for each other, each too stubborn even to consider we might be right?"

"Right about each other or right about what's best for ourselves?"

"If I answered that honestly, you'd shove me out of this car and make me walk the rest of the way." He slowed to ease the car back onto the paved road.

"Let me guess, you think you're right about what's best for me *and* that you know best about what's right for you."

"Spoken as a woman who shares the sentiment."

"Oh, how pleasant things would be if only peo-ple behaved the way I want them to." She laid her head back and gazed at the ceiling.

"Pleasant but not very interesting."

"Did you just call me dull?"

"I know you're anything but dull." He stopped the car a few feet back from the intersection. From there they could see the corner of the Palace's parking lot through the trees, but no one milling around there could see them. "I just wonder sometimes if you know it."

"I know that with all our talk of late of life changing, of renovating and following dreams, that when it comes right down to it, neither of us can do that work for each other. I'll make my choices, and you'll make yours."

"We can be inspired to make better choices."

"Translation: *you*, the wise William West, can inspire *me*, the girl with the goddess thighs, to make better choices."

"You have so much potential, Rita."

"So do you, Will." She put her hand to his face.

He wanted to argue that with his business suc-cess and a home in the most coveted part of Mem-phis he had realized his potential years ago. But material gain wouldn't amount to a hill of beans with this woman if she thought he had missed achieving his fullest human potential. How had she put it?

For his life to have meaning. For someone to miss him when he was away and mourn him when he'd passed on. To be really good at something, to hear praise for his work and know it was earned. . . . to be loved. Will had no grounds to argue he had lived up to that.

"In a week or so, when you've gone and the dust has settled, there's every chance things will look and feel almost like you never came to Hellon at all. Except, of course, people will be able actually to eat in the Palace without breaking half a dozen health codes and a couple of the Ten Commandments."

"Is that all, Rita?"

"That's a lot more than most people have given me in my life, Will. It's more than I expected or ever deserved, and I'm grateful." She leaned in to give him a kiss on the cheek.

He turned just enough for their lips to brush at the corners. Just like that his mouth found hers. At first he thought she would protest, or make a pretense of it for appearances' sake. When she didn't, he cupped the back of her head in one hand and deepened the kiss.

He slid his tongue between her lips.

She sucked at the tip, her fingers curling into the tight muscles of his neck.

He groaned and wrapped his arms around her, pulling her almost into his lap.

He'd given her more than she expected, more than she deserved? He had given her so little and had so much more to offer. One stolen kiss could not begin to convey how much. He pulled away, whispering her name as he did.

She cleared her throat and fussed over her collar, and then over the neat row of tightly fastened shirt buttons. "Well, what do you know? You were right."

"That goes without saying." He stroked one finger under her chin as she slid away, back to her side of the seat. "But just so I don't gloat over the wrong thing, what was I right about?"

She shot him a sly look that did nothing to cool the fire she'd ignited in him. "You said if you and I stayed away too long, that tongues would start wagging."

He laughed though what he truly longed to do was take her in his arms and kiss her all over— over and *all over*—again.

"And now you'd better get me back to the Palace. I have to collect the lunch things, get that all cleaned up, and start on dinner for the crew. Y'all will still be there at suppertime, won't you?"

He nodded. "We'll work till we lose the daylight."

"That's right you don't have electricity. Or water."

"Just the electricity from the portable generator and the water we've brought in. You have a place to stay tonight?"

"Jillie invited me out to your mother's."

"Good."

"Will I see you there?"

"You don't give up, do you?" He took the car out of park and pulled up to the intersection.

She smiled, then fixed her gaze on the Palace as

they drove up to it. "Looks like they are about done with lunch."

"I'm going to camp out on-site tonight. Don't want to risk vandals or anyone helping themselves to the tools, do we?"

"There've been enough people helping themselves around this place already, I think."

"Maybe you can come by later after everyone's left and . . ."

"I'll see you at *supper*." She hopped out of the car and began collecting the dishes and the lavish compliments of those who had just eaten her meal.

Rita was something special. A man only had to watch her like this to see it. If that man were lucky enough to get closer still . . .

She thought he'd given her more than she should expect? Maybe, but more than she *deserved*? Not by a long shot. And he wasn't through yet.

Chapter 12

EVERY STARRY-EYED DIXIE BELLE WILL VERIFY:
*A woman doesn't need a man to find happiness and ful-
fillment. But my, how they do come in handy on a warm
moonlit night.*

"What Rita is saying, Mother, is that she never does *anything* to her hair." Jillie curled into the corner of the overstuffed couch. When she tucked her bare legs up under her nightshirt she put Rita in mind of a twiggy-limbed bird crouching on a nest. "No dyes, no permanents, no extensions, she didn't even try a bad do-at-home frost job in high school."

"Remarkable." Miss Peggy settled back in the enormous leather chair, which sat framed by the open arching doorway in what she called "the receiving room."

She alone called it that. Everyone else, unbeknownst to the regal imp of a family matriarch, called it the "throne room." Here she welcomed family and close personal friends only. That differed from the parlor—where she served afternoon tea or hosted casual parties—and the more formal "salon" where she greeted those not in her inner circle.

For all her years of being Jillie West's nearest and dearest bosom buddy—with Rita supplying all the bosom and more than her share of the buddy bonding—it was the first time Rita had ever been invited to this room. She sat on the floor in her short-sleeved pajamas with the coffeepot, bacon, and egg motif on them and took in her surroundings with unabashed awe.

"Not that your hair isn't perfectly lovely, dear, but haven't you ever had the urge to . . ." Miss Peggy waved her hand with a cavalier air of majesty. Her rose-colored satin robe billowed around her tiny body, and her actions sent a handful of long, thin marabou feathers somersaulting through the air. ". . . experiment?"

Rita sank her fingers into the stick-straight, baby-soft hair falling against her neck. "I've had it cut before and, you know, curled it. But, well, I guess I just never gave it that much thought."

"Oh, but you should."

Rita cocked her head. "Dye it?"

"What have I told you for years?" Jillie coiled her finger in her flawless red curls.

"When you said diet, I thought you meant to lose weight. To think all these years, you only wanted me to go blond."

"Don't you dare!" Miss Peggy clucked her tongue.

"Absolutely not!" Jillie pinched a strand of

Rita's hair between her thumb and forefinger. She studied it like a bug under a microscope for a second before she released it and announced, "Blond is not your color."

"Diet!" Miss Peggy snapped her fingers. "Don't you dare go on a *diet*, Rita, honey. Not unless you really want to or your health is a concern."

"My health is excellent, thank you."

"Mother, don't encourage her. You can't appreciate how hard I've pushed these past few years for her to drop a good fifty pounds."

"Fifty! *Fifty*? Have you lost your very last bit of sense, child? How could she ever do that?"

"I could drop Jillie; she weighs almost that much." Rita narrowed her eyes at her narrow-hipped and tight-lipped pal, and grinned.

"You are fine the way you are, Rita." Miss Peggy held up both hands as if she were issuing a decree. Then she cast a scathing glare at her daughter. "Rita doesn't have fifty pounds to spare unless she cares to walk around skin to bones like this one of mine."

Jillie huffed. The second Miss Peggy looked away she sneered and rolled her eyes.

"Don't you make a face behind my back, young lady." Miss Peggy did not look at her daughter, but Rita wished she had. For once if the pair of them would look at each other, really see the pain they inflicted on one another, it might shake loose a little of that stubborn pride that stood between them.

But Miss Peggy never glanced Jillie's way as

she went on, "If you cared what other people value instead of walking around all put-upon because they don't value *you* as much as you think you deserve, you might learn a thing or two."

Jillie picked at her nail polish.

"Rita, don't you fall for that baloney about having to be rail-thin and dumb as a post to attract a man." If she realized she had just challenged her daughter's intelligence, her expression did not show it. Her face all but glowed with the benevolent liberality of an old Southern matriarch doling out her worldly wisdom "Men don't like that. They want something to grab ahold of in bed."

"Mother! We have guests."

"Oh, that didn't shock Rita, Jillian. Rita was married a good many years. She knows about men and what they want in bed, don't you, darling?"

"Uh, I . . ." It felt like someone had just held a candle too close to her cheeks and that her heart had hiked up too high in her chest. She couldn't form any coherent thought except that Miss Peggy must know she had done unthinkable—incredible, all-consuming, left-you-satisfied-but-begging-for-more—things with Will. But how could she know? Was Rita that obvious? Rita hadn't told a soul but had Will blabbed? She felt certain he hadn't. Of course, there was one person who had her suspicions about what went on that night. Had Cozie said something?

As if on cue, Cozie swept into the room. "Mouse is exhausted and sends his regrets, Miss

Peggy. But he prefers to go on to bed and let us girls gab a while on our own."

She searched her friend's guileless expression and eased any qualms away with a sigh. Not only would Cozie not tell, she probably had put the whole event aside. What with cultivating her new friendship with Miss Peggy, tending her husband and home, and now pitching in to tear up the Palace, Cozie hardly had time to spread speculation about Rita's one piddly indiscretion.

Cozie plopped onto the end of the couch nearest Miss Peggy's chair like she felt at home there.

Rita didn't know what prickled her more about her friend's ease in this house—that it underscored how Cozie had a life beyond the small box everyone normally put her in, or that Rita did not.

"Tell your Mr. Mouse how much I missed his company, won't you?" Miss Peggy coyly patted her teased and sprayed-to-stay-perfect poodle-permed curls.

"After all that work today he'd have been a misery to endure, Miss Peggy, I assure you. Time was he could have worked like an ox on the farm then come home to help with the kids. Later, he'd have gotten out his guitar and serenaded a houseful of friends to the wee hours of the night."

"I didn't know Mouse played the guitar and sang." She'd known Cozie almost a decade and marveled how she was always learning something about that woman's life.

"He doesn't much anymore, only around the house and just for my ears."

"My, isn't that romantic?" Miss Peggy laid her hand to her cheek. "Many, many years ago, I had a gentleman caller who serenaded me out on the veranda."

"Oh, Mother, you sound like some corny Southern story where the innocent flower of womanhood gets her heart broken by the scoundrel drifter."

"Now, that's no way to talk about your daddy, darling." Miss Peggy's eyes twinkled.

Jillie's brow wrinkled, her lower lip went positively pouty. "Daddy used to sing to you?"

"I had many gentleman callers and beaux who brought flowers and took me out dancing in white dinner jackets. But your daddy was the only one who sang to me." She smiled at Jillie in the way Rita always imagined a mother should smile at her child.

Jillie had her head bent.

Miss Peggy sighed. "Oh, my but there was no feeling like that in the whole world. To be young and lovely and adored on a moonlit night."

"Amen to that." Rita sighed, too, but her memory was hardly of serenades and verandas. "Moonlight, summer, no care for the future, and the right man . . ."

Cozie gave her foot a nudge and reeled Rita back in before she said too much. "It's a shame when we get older we sometimes let those sorts of experiences fall by the wayside. It's a smart person who gets the chance to feel that way again and doesn't talk themselves out of going for it."

Rita wriggled the toes of her white socks against the arch of Cozie's bare foot. "But it's a danged fool who thinks she can make that fleeting feeling last longer than the moonlight, wouldn't you say?"

Cozie started to laugh, but the minute she opened her mouth it transformed into a long, face-contorting yawn.

Which, upon seeing it, sent Rita into one of her own.

With her head bowed, Jillie seemed immune, but no sooner did Rita close her mouth and mutter an "excuse me" than Cozie let out another yawn.

"My, but y'all must have put in a full day over at Rita's place." Miss Peggy put her hand to her mouth to stifle her own response to the contagious yawnfest. "What time did you finally finish up?"

"Around nine." Cozie stretched and shifted, then settled down deeper into her seat. "That made for a fourteen-hour day if you don't count the time out for Rita's wonderful meals."

"That's right, because Rita never misses a meal." Jillie folded her arms.

Most people would have been hurt by the jab, but Rita saw the pain behind it. It was a pain she knew all too well. She readily identified with the need to have your mama's affection, to feel that as her daughter you came first in her thoughts and heart. Whenever Miss Peggy extended uncommon kindness to Rita, Cozie, why, even to Pernel, it had to twist the knife for Jillie just a bit. So Jillie took a shot at a safe target to draw her mother's fire. Because when you're starved enough for your mama's attention even anger and reproach will feed your need.

"For such a pretty girl, you have a very ugly mouth on you, young lady." Miss Peggy folded her arms as well, ignoring the feathers it sent cascading around her. "Rita, I don't know why you put up with her at all."

Rita put one hand on Jillie's angular knee. "I put up with her because she puts up with me. She's stuck with me when fair-weather friends went their merry way. She always uses her own brand of candor on me, and she can always trust me to hear the real truth beneath her words and love her as my friend, because of—and some times in spite of—it."

"Damn it, Rita." Jillie sniffed and slapped the hand off her knee but not before she gave it a squeeze. Then she dabbed her knuckle under one eye. "If you make this new mascara run, I will hate you for life."

"You should be proud of your daughter, Miss Peggy, because she may be a pill—and a sour old diet pill, at that—but she is one of the finest friends anyone could ever want to have."

Miss Peggy lowered her head and adjusted the robe over her elaborate pegnoir. The marabou trim flew upward with each movement like it was charged with static electricity.

"Well, maybe you only have to lose forty-five pounds." Jillie pressed her lips into a thin line but still managed to convey a genuinely warm and teasing smile to her friend.

A chilling silence fell over them after that.

Jillie picked at an invisible chip in her nail polish.

Miss Peggy fanned feathers away from her coral-tint lipstick.

Rita tapped her foot, but between the thickness of the Oriental rug and the thin cotton of her white ankle socks, it did not make a sound.

"Oh!" Cozette sat up straight as if she needed to make her body a visual aid to her exclamation of having thought of something to break the quiet. "Thank you again, Miss Peggy, for putting us up for the night."

"Oh, yes, thank you very much. Very, very much." Rita realized she was gushing, but the urgency to make some kind of noise superseded her usual restraint. "What with the electricity out at my place and all. I can sure cook the meals for the crew over at the church, but I can't hardly sleep there, can I? So your invitation is just so . . . it's . . . well . . . what can I say?"

Jillie leaned down to whisper for only Rita to hear, "Well, you could announce you think you just had an embolism, that might explain the sudden brain burp that made that nonsense fall out of your mouth."

"Thank you so much for your support," Rita grumbled back.

Cozie sprang to the rescue again with a well-placed laugh and a tilt of her head that rivaled the acting of any sixties sitcom mom. "I know it's only a thirty-minute drive out to our place. But what with Will asking everybody to show up at the crack of dawn tomorrow so we can finish up the last bit before the flooring men come at ten . . ."

"Don't say another word, child. It's all right." Miss Peggy spoke to Cozie as if Rita and Jillie had become part of the furniture. "I don't envy you young people, all that hard physical labor. You should tell my son not to push everyone so hard."

Rita feigned a sudden fascination with the rug. The last thing she wanted was to be dragged into a discussion about Will.

"He doesn't push anyone half as hard as he does himself." Cozie slid off the fat woven band at the end of her braid and began undoing her hair. "That's what we should tell him, to cut himself a little slack now and again."

"*I* can't tell the boy a thing."

"That's because he's not a boy, Mother, he's a man."

Rita had to grin at Jillie standing up for her brother. Some good might have come of his staying in town after all.

"He's an intelligent, capable, fully operational—without his mother's puppet strings—adult male." Jillie whipped her head around. "Right, Rita?"

"Righ . . . uh . . ." Correction. The *last thing* she wanted was to be dragged into a discussion of Will's manhood. "Yeah, well, he . . . uh . . ."

"If anyone should tell the man anything, it should be Rita. For some reason he listens to her." The sparkle in Cozie's eyes said she understood exactly why and that she had not forgotten finding them together "Why do you think that is, Rita?"

In her own way, Cozie probably thought she was helping along a wonderful romance with her gentle teasing, despite her assumption that Rita held any kind of power over Will.

Quick distraction. That's what Rita needed. Fortunately, that was not a difficult task where Will's mother was concerned. "You know, Miss Peggy, Cozie is one of those all-natural earth-mother types. I'll bet she's never done anything to her hair, either.

"Is that so, Cozette, darling?"

"Don't count on it. My hair started turning gray in my twenties. Not exactly the right image for a youth-culture-promoting, free-love-advocating, living-on-a-commune, going-to-change-the-world type, is it?"

Jillie put her chin on her arm. "So, like, thirty years ago you and Mouse actually lived on a real commune, Cozie?"

"Eight of us started it, and we had maybe twenty at the height of it."

"Twenty people all . . . together?"

"We shared responsibilities for upkeep of the gardens, cooking, raising kids if that's what you mean." The shift of her eyes and the tilt of her lips said she knew well and good that wasn't at all what Jillie wanted to know. "And we also ran a farmers' market, held craft fairs, music festivals . . ."

"Danced naked in the moonlight." Rita held her hands up in a circle like the waxing moon.

Jillie leaned forward. "And no one in Hellon objected?"

"Not as long as they could get a good view." Cozie held her arms out, gave a shimmy, and winked at Rita.

Miss Peggy giggled.

"You're kidding me about that part, right?" Before Jillie could get an answer the phone rang.

"Would you get that, sweetheart?" Miss Peggy waved her hand in no particular direction as if she had no idea where the sound had come from.

Jillie excused herself, jumped up, and left the room.

Rita looked back at Cozette. "Now it's just you and Mouse out there on all that property . . ."

"It *is* ours, you know," Cozie sat ramrod straight. "We stayed on and one by one bought the others out so it belongs to us to do with as we please."

"I was going to say just you and Mouse left to dance naked in the moonlight." Rita cocked one eyebrow. "But the part about you buying everyone else out is interesting, too."

"Oh, well, it's not . . . that's not important really. Just thought I'd throw that in." She jiggled her fingers through her hair to loosen it more.

"There have got to be far more fascinating things to talk about tonight."

"Especially for Rita." Jillie walked into the room with the portable phone held high. "It's Will."

"Will?" The name nearly knocked the wind right out of her.

"*My* Will?" Miss Peggy's chin angled upward. "Did you tell him that I will no longer take his calls?"

"Will's been calling his mother?" Rita whispered to Cozie because she dared not put herself in the middle of the West family conflicts.

"At least once a day. Didn't you know?"

"He . . . he never told me."

"But didn't you *know*?"

She should have known. Will was no villain. He was not heartless.

"This phone call is not for you, Mother."

"Not for me?" She cocked her head. If she wore a hearing aid, she'd probably have tested it to see if it had failed her. "That boy calls every day, and when I finally tell him I won't speak to him again until it's face-to-face he calls anyway, then says it's not for me?"

Will had refused to respond to his mother's royal summons on principle. She should have realized he would never simply ignore someone he cared about, especially if he thought they might need him.

"Oh, I am such a dope." Rita put her face in her hands.

"Dopey enough to talk to my brother?" Jillie held the phone down to her.

Rita shut her eyes tight. If not for Miss Peggy sitting so close, she'd have sworn right out loud. Instead she kept it under her breath and held her hand out.

Jillie slid the phone into Rita's grasp. "If you want to take it out of the room, we'll understand."

"We'll hate you for not letting us listen in." Cozie bent to speak into her ear. "But we will understand."

"No. I can take it in here. I'm sure this is just business."

Their muttering and stifled laughter said they did not believe a word of it.

"I'm sure this is just business," she said into the receiver as she put it to her ear.

"Monkey business," the deep voice murmured on the other end. "Come over, Rita. I'd like some company."

She'd like to know how he expected her to talk when his unvarnished enticing request had turned her mind to mush. "I . . . I'm already in my nightclothes."

"I don't mind."

"Well . . . I . . ."

"I'll get ready for bed myself if that would put you more at ease."

"You said that to achieve the exact opposite effect and I know it."

"He's always been contrary like that," Miss Peggy announced.

"Is that my mother?" Will snapped. "You didn't go somewhere private to take this call?"

"Why would I go anywhere private to take a *business* call?" She tipped her head down and lowered her voice. "That is the only kind of call you would make to me at this late an hour, isn't it?"

"You asking if this is a booty call?"

"Don't you say the sweetest things?" She forced out a laugh as airy as a cream puff, then pressed her lips closer to the mouthpiece. "Damn straight that's what I'm asking."

"Rita, I only want to spend some time with you. No obligations. No expectations. Just . . . to talk."

She wondered if she should tell him that did not make her feel better.

"What do you say?"

"I say . . ." She sensed the intensity of the gazes boring down on her. "I say I'll see you tomorrow."

"But I want to see *you* tonight."

"It wouldn't be . . . good business."

"Business?" He made a sound between a chuckle and a groan. "You're killing me, girl. Do you know that?"

"I'll bring breakfast by for the crew bright and early. If you have anything else to say to me, you can tell me then."

"If you change your mind . . ."

"Me? Change?"

"I'll be here."

"Good-bye."

"See you later, Rita."

She hung up and handed the phone back to Jillie.

"Well?" Cozie smirked.

"Well?" Rita smirked right back. "You heard. I'll see him tomorrow."

"You won't go over then?" Cozie shook her head, and a long strand of hair fell over her shoulder.

"Of course, she won't go over." The delicate knickknacks on the end table rattled as Jillie clunked the phone down. "She has her pride. She has her priorities. She puts a price on herself, and that price is respect, and she wouldn't lower herself to be with any man who did not understand that."

"Yeah." Rita had not thought it through as thoroughly as Jillie obviously had, but what her friend said made sense. "What kind of woman do you think I am?"

"A woman without a man." Cozie brushed her hair back.

"A woman doesn't need a man to find happiness and fulfillment," Jillie said.

"That's certainly true." Rita could confirm that coming and going. "I had a man at my side for many years, and that didn't bring me happiness and fulfillment. They didn't come flying in the window for me as he headed out the door, either. Those things don't come from who you are with, they come from who you are—you gotta find that out for yourself."

"Can't argue with that." Cozie hugged herself and sighed. "Still, once you do find yourself, it sure is nice to have someone to share with."

"Not if it's the wrong person." Jillie hit each word with a cold edge. "Things have changed since the days of communes and times when a girl had gentlemen callers. Right, Rita?"

"Well, those are rather quaint notions, I suppose."

"A woman today doesn't dare let a man think of her as vulnerable, and she certainly doesn't give in to meaningless gestures and sweet talk. She needs something more concrete before she risks any emotional energy. Right, Rita?"

Concrete. Solid. Dependable. That certainly had its appeal. Whereas the phrase risking emotional anything made her squirm. And yet hearing the kind of woman Jillie described, the demands she would make of a man before expending any energy, discouraged Rita. Did she really want to be that kind of woman?

"Rita? I said, right?" Jillie bumped her shoulder with one knee. "Right?"

"I . . . uh . . ."

"Wrong!" Miss Peggy pounded her tiny hand on the arm of the chair. Rita swore if the old gal had owned a gavel she'd have banged with a vengeance to command the floor. "Wrong, wrong, and wrong."

"Oh, Mother, what do you know about romantic relationships today?"

"I know you girls think you have all the answers. That you think your way of handling men is so far and away superior to the way it's been done by generation after generation of women before you."

"The old rules don't apply anymore, Mother. It's a new ball game."

"Still played with balls, isn't it? Still using the same equipment we had in my day, child."

"Mother!"

Rita coughed to disguise her laugh.

"Good one, Miss Peggy." Cozie gave a thumbs-up.

"As for us older ones not knowing about romantic entanglements, well, women must have done something right all this time. Else there wouldn't have been generation after generation leading right down to you."

"Not the same." Jillie shook her head.

"What? Do you think your generation invented sex?"

"*Re*invented it, maybe—with a whole new set of rules and problems, Mother. Your approach to love simply isn't relevant today."

"Oh, and yours is working out so well for the pair of you?" Miss Peggy gave them both long, searing looks. "Is that why you're sitting here with a cantankerous widow and charming married woman with an adorable husband waiting in bed for her?"

Jillie looked at her hands.

Rita glanced over at the portable phone lying on the end table.

"What's gotten into you tonight, Mother?"

"Tonight?" Cozie said. "Honey, your mama is always full of piss and vinegar."

"It's true. I'm going to have to get me some of them bladder-control underpants if it keeps up, too."

Cozie hooted a laugh as she reached out to put her hand on Miss Peggy's wrist. "But she is usually a pure fount of inspiration and insight if you'd only listen."

"Yes, them underpants might take care of one end but there's nothing invented yet going to keep me from speaking my mind."

"Commitment papers come to mind." Jillie batted her lashes and shook back her red curls.

"Commitment?" Miss Peggy turned an icy glare on her child. "What do you know about that? You show more commitment to your hairdresser than you ever have with any young man you've dated."

"I can *depend* on my hairdresser. Men these days? A woman doesn't dare get reckless in the relationship department anymore. She has to guard her heart."

Does she? Rita wondered. *Does a woman have to guard her heart so well that nothing ever penetrates her defenses?*

"I swan, you young things have it all back ass-wards." When she pulled her back up straight Miss Peggy looked a good six inches taller and maybe a few years younger. "Here you are careless with your hair, careless with your self-esteem, even with your bodies, but cautious to a fault with your hearts."

"I am not careless with my hair." Jillie glowered.

"You've had more new shades on your head than a table lamp in a lighting-store window."

Rita tried not to giggle at that. Tried but didn't succeed.

"That's funny?" Miss Peggy aimed the spotlight on Rita now. "Well, how about you? You haven't done a thing but run a brush through once a day and trot down to the Swift Klip for a ten-dollar cut now and again. It's careless. Careless of you both. There's no other word for it. And if it were just the hair, well, I suppose I could bite my tongue."

"Don't you do it." Cozie lent her support like a zealous churchgoer urging on the preacher at a hot revival. "You tell them, Miss Peggy."

"But it's those other things I can't abide in silence."

"Mother, isn't it a bit ironic for you to criticize my . . . careless self-esteem?"

"I have made plenty of mistakes as a parent, honey. I wasn't always right, or patient, or even particularly kind, but I did give you one of the damndest examples of high self-esteem I could to follow."

That made even Jillie laugh, though she looked down when she did it.

"Instead you let strangers in magazines tell

you if you are too fat or too thin. You let the media tell you if you are too old or not sexy enough. You listen to the wrong voices and let them drown out what you know—that you are just *fine* the way you are. Better than fine, you are wonderful, wonderful girls."

Jillie jerked her head up, tears in her eyes. "Mama, you really think that?"

"I do."

Rita sniffled and blinked the dampness from her lashes.

"But you *are* careless. You've been throwing away your youth and beauty on men who don't amount to a hill of beans."

Rita could hardly argue that.

Jillie looked like she wanted to try, but she couldn't manage a sound.

"What do you think as you cast off one man or another for not measuring up? That when the last of your youth is spent, your bosom sags and your eggs are about to expire, when you get desperate enough *then* you can finally take a chance on a less-than-perfect man? Then you can let the walls down around your heart?"

"Doesn't sound like a very good plan." Rita toyed with the top button of her pajamas and thought of Will's offer for her to come by and talk.

"You are protecting the wrong things, my darlings. You are careless with yourselves but holding in an iron fist the one part of you that can't survive without risk and freedom—your hearts."

"Hearts get broken, Mother."

"And grow stronger for it, child. And if the man you risk your heart on isn't *the one,* you'll be all right. Because a smart gal once told me, you don't need a man to find happiness and fulfillment."

"That's right," Rita said softly.

Miss Peggy tipped her head to one side and fanned her feathered lapel dreamily. "But my, how they do come in handy on a warm moonlit night like this."

Rita chewed at her lower lip. She checked the grandfather clock. Will would probably still be awake.

The room fell silent for what seemed forever until Jillie spoke up. "Y'all feel a chill in here?"

"A chill?" Cozie frowned. "But it's June in Tennessee."

"I know." Jillie got up and walked across the room, stopping alongside Miss Peggy's big chair. "But my mother just paid me a compliment and said something that made a whole lot of sense. I figured hell must have just frozen over."

"You're welcome." Miss Peggy held her frail hand out to her daughter.

Jillie leaned down and gave her mother a kiss on the cheek. When she stood she took a deep breath. "Now, I have a phone call to make, and Rita?"

"Hmmm?"

"I have a feeling that if you pretended to be terribly sleepy and excused yourself nobody here would even notice if you slipped out of the house instead. If you were so inclined to do that."

Rita smiled to her companions. "I think I'll call it a night, if y'all don't mind."

In less than ten minutes, she slipped out the front door and headed for her car.

Chapter 13

EVERY DIXIE BELLE EXPERIMENTS:
. . . dare to change, even if it's just for an evening.

What had he thought? One phone call from him and Rita would come-a-runnin'? He must have, or he'd never have gone to so much trouble.

He switched off the karaoke machine he'd dragged down from Rita's apartment and stared up at the tiny white Christmas lights he'd strung across the exposed brick of the back wall. His footsteps echoed in the shell of the room.

A halo of light from a workshop lamp focused on a single stool at the center of his makeshift stage.

The small generator that powered it all hummed in the background.

At least he'd hadn't deluded himself into thinking that she would come at his calling because no woman could refuse him. His ego was not entirely *that* big. But his faith in Rita was.

He never thought she'd turn down a heartfelt invitation from a . . . from a *friend*. Maybe he and his keep-everyone-at-a-distance philosophy had influenced her more than he suspected.

He pushed his fingertips down through his shower-damp hair and rubbed his scalp. The roll-away shoved in the corner called to him. It had been a hard day of work and now a hard lesson learned. If he could put the latter out of his mind, he'd probably fall fast into a deadened sleep.

Thanks to the generator he'd have a fan to provide some relief from the heat of a Tennessee summer night. But not the real relief he needed. To see Rita, to be alone with her one more time. He'd have to do without that for tonight and for the rest of his life. It surprised him how heavy that weighed on his mind.

He reached for the plug on the twinkling lights.

"Don't tell me you're giving up on me that easily?" Rita stood in the doorway, one hand flat against the painted pig, the other holding a large wicker picnic basket.

"You came."

"After all you've done for me I thought the least I could do was come over and bring you a late-night snack." She held the basket up.

"Thank you but I wasn't hungry"—he folded his arms over his bare chest—"for food."

"Too bad." She lifted the top on one side of the green-and-yellow basket to show a change of clothes, a makeup bag, and something under a layer of cling wrap. "I have cake."

"Rita . . ." He stepped toward her.

"Don't screw this up with the standard disclaimer about not offering me anything beyond this evening." She let the basket lid drop shut.

"I wouldn't dream of it."

"Or how you're not a long-term kind of guy."

He cocked his head. "Long-term enough to get the job done, I hope."

"Or how you can't be pinned down."

He stroked his jaw. "But how I do love the thrill of the match."

"Or that as soon as the Palace is done you'll be out of town faster than a sudden storm on a summer afternoon."

He took another step in her direction. "I don't believe I ever used those words."

She held her hand up. "Promise me you won't resort to any of that."

"Come in and close the door."

"Not until you promise not to sacrifice a single second of whatever time we have together worrying about talk around town, expectations of others, or the future."

He raised his hands in surrender.

She pressed her back to the still-half-opened door. "That you will embrace me and the moment and nothing more."

"That doesn't sound like you, Rita." If she caught the hint of sadness in his tone, her expression did not betray it.

"Promise."

"If I don't?"

"Quit being such an impossible bastard, Will!"

He'd been called worse and under less-promising circumstances.

"You've got what you wanted all along. Why question it now?"

Because somewhere "all along" what I want became a little less important to me than what you want, Rita. The words rushed into his thoughts, but somehow he found the presence of mind to keep them from gushing out of his mouth. True as the sentiment might be, it came with a proviso that she already said she did not need to hear. "I just hope you know what you're really getting into. When I head back down the road to Memphis—and I will head back to Memphis soon and to stay, Rita—that you will have no regrets."

"I'll survive, Will. I'll be all right no matter what happens."

"But are you *sure* this is what you want?"

The back of her head bumped the glass door as she looked heavenward. The pig looked down benevolently on her. "Please! Save me from people who continually ask me what I want."

"Why is that?"

She leveled her gaze at him. "Because they ask, but when I tell them they almost never believe me."

"I'll believe you, Rita, just tell me."

"I want another taste of heaven, Will." She let the door swing shut a fraction as she moved a step inside the room. "I want a song on the veranda and to dance naked in the moonlight."

"Those can be arranged."

"I want to have tonight and just once in my life to let tomorrow take care of itself. I want . . ." Her voice faltered. She laid her hand above her breast. ". . . to be careless with my heart."

"I don't understand."

"Then let me make it perfectly clear—I want you . . ."

He grinned his best aw-shucks-come-and-get-me grin.

". . . to knock off the knight in shining armor crap and give me that promise so we can enjoy ourselves, and each other. Period. No strings. No guilt. Can you do that?"

"Can I? I've only spent the better part of my life doing that exact thing." He opened his arms to her.

The door fell shut, and she came to him.

It wasn't until he held her in his arms that he truly understood, though. If everything up until now had been the better part of his life—then his life had amounted to very little indeed.

He wanted to tell Rita that very thing in that very instant, but he didn't. He couldn't and hope to keep her in his arms even for a little while longer.

"Will, I've hung on to everything in my life with both fists, and still it's all slipped through my fingers—my marriage, my daughter, my precious time to make something special of my life. Well, tonight I'm saying 'no more.' I'm letting go of what doesn't matter anymore and opening myself up to . . . whatever happens next."

"It's whatever happens after 'next' that has me worried, Rita. I can't help but think how our throwing caution to the winds for the sake of a few hours of pleasure could have a lasting effect on you."

"On *me.*" *But not you.* She did not have to say it for it to hang in the air between them. She still believed he could walk away from any entanglements he made here without a backward glance.

In all honesty, he could not deny or confirm that suspicion for her. "My hope was to leave you in a better place—and I don't mean a nicer diner."

"The bottom line is that you will *leave me*, Will, better place—*including* better diner—or not. And that's all right. I don't need you to do a major overhaul on my life. In fact for you to think that you *can* do that..." She took a deep breath. "I guess it's sweet in its own caveman way but just not necessary."

"Okay."

She let out a long, world-weary sigh. "Thank you."

"I didn't do anything."

"Exactly." She dropped the picnic basket. "Don't do or say anything more, Will. Just let tonight unfold without any thoughts of yesterday or tomorrow clouding our perspectives."

"But, Rita . . ."

"Damn it, Will, give a girl one shot at a proper seduction, won't you?" She moved close, her hands spreading across his chest.

"If I don't do or say anything more, how will you know if your seduction is working?"

"You'll give me a sign, I'm sure." Her fingers worked lower on his body. "Maybe send up a flare."

"I'll do my best."

"That's all I ask."

"Though it's not nearly as much as you deserve." He bent his head to nibble on her neck.

She pushed him away playfully but with enough relish to back up her warning. "Don't talk."

"Yes, ma'am," he murmured just as his mouth covered hers and he pulled her full, yearning body into his embrace.

They had raided the stash of condoms Will had dumped into his duffel bag the night before and had torn their clothes off before they hit the mattress. Laughing and tumbling over each other, they nibbled and licked and even bit at each other until Rita finally rolled him onto his back and straddled his hips.

Catching her breath, she threw her head back and shook her hair off her face. "You haven't tasted my red velvet yet, have you?"

"Not the cake . . . no." He rose up to try to kiss her.

She pushed him back down. "Then you are in for a rare treat."

"Yes, I know, then later, after we're done, we can indulge in some cake." He traced one finger down between her breasts.

"Why wait?" She had to lie on top of him to reach the picnic basket but considered that a delightful bonus.

He slid his hands down to caress her hips and wriggled beneath her. "Why wait indeed."

"Why wait to indulge?" She moved the small round cake onto the table.

He rolled his head to the side and eyed her handiwork. "I've heard of eating crackers in bed, but cake?"

"Maybe not cake, but how about a little icing?"

"You don't need anything to sweeten our lovemaking but, uh, I have to admit I'm intrigued."

"I can tell. I feel your . . . *intrigue* straining at the sheets under me." She snaked her fingers down his belly.

He groaned.

She leaned forward just enough to trail one fingertip across the thick peaks of frosting on the cake, then held the confection up for him to see.

He licked his lips.

She waved the icing over him, taunting.

He lay back, waiting.

"Where should I start?" She studied his dark, appealing body. "I could dab bits of sweetness along my neck and places . . . south, then let you lick them off—slowly."

"Oh yeah."

"Or I could blindfold you, then feed you while I savor the sight of your naked, aroused body."

"I hope you have the same definition of savor as I do, there."

"Or maybe I could place this glistening glob of creamy satisfaction in one very strategic place on you." She pointed her finger at him, drawing out the word "you" so that her lips stayed round and pouty as long as possible.

"Rita? Do something. The waiting is making me crazy."

"You want this?" She held the icing within an inch of his nose.

"Give it to me," he whispered.

She dipped her hand forward but in the split second before the treat could touch his lips, she popped it in her own mouth.

He started to protest until she slid her finger out and proceeded to painstakingly lap away the wet white covering.

"Oooh, yeah." He exhaled and half shut his eyes. "Is that good?"

"Want to taste for yourself?"

"You know I do."

She leaned down and pressed her lips to his. Her tongue darted out and infused the whole kiss with lush sweetness.

Never had she acted so boldly. Never had she dared so much without fear of the consequences. Suddenly a kiss did not seem deep enough. She tugged the sheet free from between them and took him inside her in one white-hot movement.

He growled, and his upper body lifted from the bed.

She hesitated, even jostled gracelessly, before

she found his rhythm. Then it all seemed so right and natural.

He buried his face between her breasts.

She kissed the top of his head and spread her hands over his shoulder blades. Back arched, she let him pleasure her.

They sighed and moaned and moved in their own moonlit dance as old as time itself.

She closed her eyes and let the sensations wash over her, building, building until the tension peaked. Then she let go, and even as everything went whirling and tumbling out of control inside her, she knew the peace at the eye of the storm.

Will dug his fingers deeper into the supple flesh at her hips and cried out. Then he collapsed back to the mattress, dragging her down on top of him.

When she raised her head from where it lay on his shoulder she could only smile.

"That was very hot." He put his finger to the center of her lips. "And unmercifully sweet. But I admit to a little disappointment that there wasn't more cake in it for me."

"I might, just this once, have dared to be careless with my heart." She kissed his cheek, his nose, then sat up, her thighs still over his. "But I am never, ever, ever careless with my cooking."

He entwined his fingers with hers. "What is this new expression you've taken up? Careless with your heart? I don't recall your having said that before."

"Don't worry. It isn't a euphemism for falling in love. It's not secret code for 'I'm putting my heart on the line hoping for love' or any of those other kinds of sentiments that strike fear in the hearts of even the most manly men."

"Tell me more."

"I'd rather eat cake." She scrambled off him, keeping the sheet pulled up above her comfort zone. As she sat on the edge of the bed she gave him a sly glance over her shoulder. "It's my specialty."

"I've already tasted your specialty." He sat up and kissed her ear. "But I wouldn't mind a bite of cake, too."

"Okay, here." She got out the silverware she'd brought in the basket, carefully sliced each of them a forkful, then handed him his. "To people who dare to change, even if it's just for an evening."

Their fork tines clinked.

"To being naked in the moonlight." Will put the cake in his mouth and almost instantly groaned with pure contentment.

She reveled in his enjoyment so much she offered him her bite as well and laughed when crumbs fell onto his bare chest.

"Don't let those crumbs get in this bed or I won't sleep on these sheets," she warned.

"You planned on sleeping?"

"I didn't plan on anything, Will. That's the magic of this evening for me."

"Would it ruin it all if I said I did have a plan when I invited you over?"

"I don't see how it could since we've already carried out your plan in vivid detail." She brushed away a tiny fleck of red cake with her damp fingertip.

He hissed in his breath at her touch, then stilled her hand with a firm grasp. Much as he craved her hands on him, he had other things in mind for the evening. "Not exactly. Believe it or not, my plan had nothing to do with getting you in bed again."

"Dang it!" She snapped her fingers. "I could have gotten away with just talking."

"Not *just* talking." He nodded his head toward the lights and the karaoke machine by the brick wall. "I kind of hoped the night might involve some singing, too."

"I saw that when I came in and wondered what you'd gotten up to all alone in this gutted place."

"Think I was setting a trap for the ghost of Elvis?"

"Hmmm. No, maybe more like practicing your act so you could take it on the road."

On the road. That was how she saw him. How she would always see him. A man on the move, always with an eye on the clock and mindful of never overstaying his welcome. It was not an unfair characterization. He was not going to stay in Hellon.

The bed creaked as he maneuvered around to sit beside her. "Truth is, I heard a rumor about you."

"Only *one*?"

"Only one that mattered to me." He laid his head against hers and angled his face so he could whisper in her ear. "I heard from a reliable source—well, a source—that you have an incredible singing voice. I'd love to hear it for myself."

"I couldn't." She gnawed at her thumbnail.

"Of course you can. I have it all set up."

"I'm not warmed up."

"After what we did? I'd think cooling down would be the issue."

"Vocally."

"How long would it take to get warmed up?"

Her gaze shifted to the stage. She wet her lips. She looked down. "I . . . I'm not dressed for it."

"Okay. I got it. You're making excuses." He had no right to feel as bad as he did at her refusal. "You don't want to sing for me."

"I don't want to sing *for* anyone, Will."

"You sang for Pernel."

"I sang, and Pernel heard me. Seventeen years under the same roof he was bound to overhear me now and again. Lullabies and the occasional return engagement to the World-famous Shower a Go-go."

"Hey, I could be persuaded to share a shower with you." Though it galled him to the pit of his gut to think that any other man ever had or would do the same. "If that's what it takes to hear you sing."

"Not a bad idea." She pursed her lips. "Except that—dang—wouldn't you know it? We don't have any water here tonight."

"Who needs water?"

"For a shower? I do."

"For singing. C'mon, Rita. There are people who have heard you sing. I know it."

"Okay, I confess, I will sing in front of Pernel. Him and Lacey Marie. Because I know they won't ever think I'm foolish."

He ran the back of his hand along her cheek. "I won't ever think you're foolish, Rita."

"Really?"

"I promise."

"I sing a short solo in the church choir every Christmas and Easter. Maybe you could come around and hear me then. If you're not afraid that your presence would shake the walls to their very foundations."

"I'm not afraid." He kept his face close to hers.

"No?"

"It's not the kind of thing I usually discuss in such a casual state." He made a show of checking that both of them had all the right parts covered by the shared sheet, then lowered his voice to a conspiratorial whisper. "But it so happens I attend church regularly in Memphis."

"You do?"

"I'm not Wild Billy West anymore, Rita. I haven't been . . ." He looked at his hands. He bowed his head and rubbed the pad of his thumb above the bridge of his nose. "I never was. I *never* was. I did some crazy shit. Hell, yes, all us boys on the team did. But everyone had their eyes on me, so I got the nickname. I hated that nickname."

"But all this time you said you didn't care about gossip or what people said."

"I don't. I didn't. But it's the name . . . *Wild Billy*." He clenched his fist. "Wild like I didn't belong to anyone, like I was some kind of mutt they took in and had to tame to make acceptable."

"As I recall all the girls thought it was a very sexy nickname."

"Not for a pretender to the throne of the oldest family in Hellon." He shrugged his shoulders. "Not for a bastard boy expected to play the part of the only son, the only hope to carry on his father's name."

"What are you saying, Will?"

"Don't think worse of my mama." He laid it down like a command, not a plea. He would not beg for anyone to show respect to the woman who had earned more than her share of it over her lifetime.

"I don't think anything, better or worse, Will. I don't understand exactly what you're saying."

"I'm saying . . ." When had this gotten to be about him and his lame-ass problems? Tonight was about Rita. He turned to her and his heart just felt lighter again. "I'm saying I want you to sing to me, Rita."

She never could have planned that the way she tipped her head then sent the moonlight spilling over her cheeks. Or that her parted lips made him ache to draw her to him again.

He put his hands on either side of her neck like he could capture that look, that feeling, that moment forever. "You said we'd just think about this night. If it's all we have, let's not waste it. Sing for me, Rita. Please?"

And she did.

They lay in the bed looking into each other's eyes and she crooned a languid, bluesy ballad just for him. He did not hear every word but somehow every note and nuance penetrated his being. When Rita sang, it was like she was inside of him and it felt . . . like home.

If that thought had wormed its way into his consciousness with any other women, he'd have been gone before the last note stopped vibrating in the air. With Rita? He was safe, wasn't he? She would not twist his deepest hurts or fears to manipulate him. She would not make demands he could never fulfill.

"Wonderful." He swept back her hair as she ended the serenade.

"Going to ask for an encore?"

"Sing as much as you like. I could listen to you all night."

"Okay, but I wasn't talking about singing." She slicked the tip of her tongue over her lower lip.

"All right." He rose up on his elbow to coax her onto her back beneath him. "But this time, I'm in charge of the frosting."

Chapter 14

EVERY WISE DIXIE BELLE BEARS IN MIND:
You do not have to hold the world together all by your-self. You can let go a little sometimes, and life will go on.

The world had not caved in. She had acted carelessly, recklessly, joyfully with her heart, and the world had not come screeching to a halt. As far as Rita could tell, giving in to the whirlwind choice to go for that once-in-a-lifetime event—twice—had not left everything she cared about in a shambles.

For only a second, not even a full second, she thought of how her mother must have felt the day after the tornado. *Freedom.* Awesome, overwhelming, elation-inducing and terrifying all at once freedom, that's what good old Tammy must have known.

For the first time ever Rita understood. Judgment fell away. She even managed a pang of sympathy for Tammy Butcher Stark waking up one day having faced her fears and survived. To realize she could keep right on surviving and facing anything that came her way.

"Wow," she whispered. That morning Rita had had a taste of that power, that wonder, that hopefulness that had moved her mother to action at last. It humbled her as much as it gave her strength.

But she was not her mama. People said Rita had her mother's blood, and so she must have her mother's courage and spirit. She had fought against any comparison or tendency, fearing that if she ever acted like her mother in one way, she might do it in others. She might have it in her to walk away not just from the hard, ugly parts of her life, but from the good ones as well.

After all this time she felt the deep, yearning, lonely ache of wishing her mother would just come to her again. That she hadn't forgotten to include Rita when she fashioned herself a bold new life. No, Rita could never be like a woman who would do that to a child, even a grown child. If she were a clever girl, maybe, she could find a way to draw on her mother's strengths without succumbing to her shortcomings. But what if she failed? The people that meant the world to Rita would pay the price.

She had taken her wild ride and come out no worse for wear. That was enough. She had no intention of uprooting her comfortable existence or abandoning any relationships—save one.

"Mmeenda," Will mumbled, rolling his head to one side.

She sat up in bed and gently worked enough of the sheet out from under him to cover herself. She looked down at the man sprawled out in the most contented sleep she'd ever had the occasion to observe in another human. She feathered her fingers through the black waves of hair tumbling against his temple.

He rolled onto his side, mumbling again, and his lips curved into just a hint of a smile.

She thought of rousing him from his sleep, but on the very real chance that would actually *rouse* him, she decided against it. In less than an hour the work crew would arrive, and while finding her and Wild Billy in bed together would provide more of a jolt than strong-brewed coffee, she opted not to risk it.

The sheet rustled as she eased toward the edge of the bed. From the corner of her eye she caught the flicker of a light. Seeing the stage he had set up for her so he could hear her sing gave her a warmth that stretched way down to her toes.

What a decent guy. More decent than most folks, including himself, gave him credit for being. That decency had brought out things in her she had long forgotten she possessed. And he had helped her see that she did not have to hold the world together all by herself, that she could let go a little sometimes, and life would go on.

Shutting her eyes, she memorized the smell of his hair, the weight of his body on one side of the bed, the sound of his breathing. He would go, and she'd probably rarely, if ever, see him again.

Her memories were all she would have left, so she wanted to get them right down to the smallest detail. She leaned down to place the softest possible kiss on his head. "Thank you."

"Hmmm," he shifted toward her.

She opened her eyes, slid from the bed, kissed her fingertips, and touched them to his cheek. "Thank you, for being my tornado, Wild Billy."

And she was gone.

Wild Billy. Even in his sleep the name struck a raw nerve. His shoulders knotted. His back teeth ground together. He turned his face toward the lump of a pillow to keep from letting the hated specter pull him from a truly wonderful dream. A dream that only built upon an already amazing reality the night before.

The thought of Rita banished all tension. He groaned, a feral, lusty sound made bigger by the bareness of the room, and reached for her. His fingers grasped only rumpled sheets.

"Rita?" He sat up, rubbing his eyes.

No answer.

"Rita, you in the kitchen?" He took a deep breath, sure he'd catch a whiff of coffee just beginning to brew. His nose twitched to fight off a sneeze from the smell of dust and dankness churned up in yesterday's work.

He was alone. He studied the sparse string of lights sagging against the nicked brick wall. Alone in a place where he had expected at least companionship.

The bed creaked as he shifted his body slowly

to face the dirty window with the first light of day breaking in. Pink-and-orange clouds streaked across the gray sky. Will exhaled and put his head in his hands.

Rita had come to him, and now she had left him. She had learned well this business of not getting too attached, of not hanging on to anything long enough to let it become important, much less cherished.

"You there?" He would have cherished one last morning waking up next to her. "Rita?"

For that reason he should be glad she'd gone. But sitting there with the cool sheets pooled in his lap and the harsh light of day creeping slowly into his consciousness, he was not glad. Was this, he wondered, how women felt after a night of no-future-in-this sex with him?

No. To feel as empty as he did right then the women he had bedded would first have to have had the fulfillment he experienced with Rita. He would have had to have created a place in their lives for his going to leave a void. He never allowed any of them close enough really to care about him. And he had never let himself care deeply enough about them to make their partings anything more than a fond good-bye. Only two women had ever left a hole in his heart—the one who had betrayed him and Rita, who had befriended him.

Friendship was at the root of this emotion. He liked and admired Rita. If letting go of that didn't come harder to him, then he really was beyond all

hope. He had passed beyond the precious redemption his sister had promised he'd find in the
Pig Rib Palace. He put his feet to the icy floor. He
looked around and huffed out a dismal laugh.

He had not found there what he needed most
to move his life forward, but maybe somewhere
along the way, Rita had. That gave him more satisfaction than anything he'd done in a very long
time.

"Mom? I tried to reach you all day yesterday!
When I couldn't get you I called Daddy, and he
didn't answer, either. What's going on? Where
have you been?"

"It's a long story, honey." Rita tried to hold the
impossibly small cell phone she'd borrowed from
Jillie against her shoulder. "That's why I called
you."

"Are you at home now?"

"No, I'm in the basement of the Baptist church."

"Oh? That does sound like a long story."

The cell phone slipped, and she had only her
chin to grab it. She let out a curse.

"You sure you're in the Baptist church?"

"It's this stupid phone. I borrowed the thing to
keep from tying up the church phone if I needed
anything. Jillie insists everyone needs one as a
matter of personal convenience." Rita found it
anything but convenient as she tried to talk and
stir corn-bread batter at the same time.

"Mom? You're scaring me. Why are you cussing
on a cell in the basement of the Baptist church?"

"I'm not cussing in the basement. I'm cooking. Making up a lunch for the folks working over at the Palace."

"Cooking? For the people working at the Palace? Has the food gotten so bad that even the staff won't eat it?"

"One thing you could say for the people your daddy hired for his place. They were not stupid, nor did they have a death wish." All of Pernel's employees had been bright enough to find new jobs weeks before Rita even knew her ex was fixing to abdicate his pig rib throneship "The cook and waitresses brown-bagged it for a year or so until they shamed your daddy into putting in that new kitchen."

"Don't be silly, Mom. Daddy didn't change the kitchen for the staff."

"Well, he certainly didn't do it for the customers." She mashed a lump of corn-bread batter against the side of the big stainless-steel bowl on the table before her. "I don't think a one of them noticed they no longer had to skim a layer of grease off the barbeque sauce or that their onion rings actually took on the almost perceptible taste of onions."

"Mama, what does the world look like from where you are?"

"What, honey?"

"Is it all rose-colored and rainbows, happy bunnies hopping by and, I don't know, marshmallow toadstools? Or do you sometimes, just

every now and again, catch a glimpse of reality?"
The soft-humored tenderness in her baby girl's
tone took the hard edge off the sarcasm.

"Lacey Marie . . ."

"Daddy redoing that kitchen was just his first
step toward redoing himself."

"Was it?" Of course it was. How stupid of her
not to have seen it then—not to understand it until someone shoved it in her face.

"And it didn't hurt that the new kitchen set
you in good stead for taking over if it came to
that. Didn't you see that? Can't you see it now?"

"Well, *now*, yes. Now that you spell it out for
me more than two years after the fact." Rita put
her hand to the phone to hold it in place. "But
then I've never been especially good at seeing
things that I don't want to see."

"Oh, Mom."

"I know. I'm such a mess."

"You're anything but a mess, and you know it."

"Really? You think so?"

"I know so. That's the problem." She sighed.

Rita could imagine the expert level of eye-
rolling going on at the other end of the conversation.

"Everything in your life has to stay just so,
Mom. You don't take chances. You never step out
of line."

"You don't know what you're talking about."
Rita gripped the edge of the mixing bowl. Corn-
bread batter sloshed up onto her fingers. She'd

have cussed if she didn't have her child on the other end. "That is to say, I'm not as predictable as you think I am."

"Oh, yeah? So you say you've got people working at the Palace? Let me guess. A cleaning crew so you can reopen the dump?"

"We happen to be remodeling." So there, she might have added if her tone hadn't made that point on its own.

"Remodeling? Isn't that like trying to make a silk purse out of a pig-rib eatery?"

"Not *just* remodeling."

"Oh?"

"Replacing old things that need to go, too."

"And?"

"Refitting. Refining."

"And?"

And rendezvousing with my lover—nyah nyah. If Jillie or Cozie had been on the line, she just might have said it. She adored her daughter more than she could possibly describe. But no other person on earth could make her feel like such a mousy old stick in the mud as that smart, gorgeous child. It was a mother/daughter thing that Rita prayed they would someday both grow out of, but for now . . .

"Listen to yourself, Mom. Remodeling? Refitting? How is that new and challenging?"

She stammered but that hardly qualified as an answer.

"I'll tell you how—it's not. It's exactly what everyone expects you to do."

"Not *exactly* what everyone expects." *Especially the taking Wild Billy as a lover part.*

"And when the remodeling is finished, what then?"

Then Will would leave, and her nights would take on a haunting stillness deeper than she had ever known before. "Then this will be a whole new restaurant."

"New how? New menu?"

"Oh . . . no . . . no, honey." Rita tipped her head to hold the phone in place again as she lifted the bowl and began pouring the batter into the first of three cast-iron skillets. "It wouldn't be smart to start monkeying around with the menu just now."

"A new name then?"

"A new name . . . yes, eventually. Perhaps. When there's enough money to pay for new signs and advertising and all that."

"Then nothing will actually be new about the place but the furnishings?"

"No. No, not really." She chewed at her lower lip, trying to come up with some silver lining to the dark cloud her daughter had unleashed. Finally, she forced out the best thing she could, "But there will be a new owner."

"You're selling? Oh, Mom, that's so . . ."

"*I'll* be the new owner!" She set the bowl aside, then lifted one of the skillets an inch off the counter and let it drop.

"That you pounding your head against a brick wall?"

"I'm getting the air bubbles out of the corn bread."

"I wish it were that easy to get the air bubbles out of your thinking, Mom."

"My thinking is sound as ever."

"Of course it is. Everything about you is as sound and as near to totally unchanged as ever. And where has that gotten you?"

She dropped the second skillet with a dead-weight *clunk*.

"You could do so much, Mom. You could go to college."

"College? At my age?"

"Are you kidding? Something like half of all college students are nontraditional these days."

"That let's me out. I'm about as traditional as they get."

Lacey giggled. "Oh, Mom, nontraditional is PC-speak for *old*."

"I'm not *old* either."

"You love to learn, and you know it." She said it the way you'd talk to a kitten while dangling a catnip-filled toy in front of it. "You could move to Memphis and . . ."

Memphis? Where Will lived? Where nobody else knew her and she'd have to start over from nothing? The thought of it took her very breath away. "I can't, baby. Not Memphis."

"Why not?"

For starters because she'd look a big-ass fool, like she'd trotted off after a man whose main goal in life was to keep his distance. "I think for now I should just work on making things better here."

"Better how? Better for you or better for everyone who relies on you to ease their way in life?"

"Better at the Palace for starters. If I can improve things there, then maybe I can build on that momentum and . . ."

"How can you make things better at the Palace? Start providing decaf coffee?"

"That'd cause a riot."

"Bottled water?"

"Oh, yes, big demand for that in Hellon, I imagine."

"Maybe put little packets of wet napkins on every table? Better how?"

"Just better." Though she did like that wet-napkin idea and made a note to look into it. "I'll do what I can, and you'll see."

"What, Mom? What amazing new innovation could you have come up with to use in the Palace?"

Amazing innovations in the Palace? She and Will had come up with so many—and not a one of them fit to describe to her daughter. Rita put the back of her hand to her cheek and sighed. She dared not let herself get carried too far away with thoughts of making love last night in the dreamy lights from the makeshift stage. "Oh."

"Oh what?"

"I just remembered. That is, I just came up with a terrific idea for something absolutely new and challenging I can bring to the Palace."

"How about bringing in a new owner?" Her sweet voice rang with hope, not harassment.

"How about karaoke?"

Lacey Marie groaned.

"What? What's wrong with that?"

"Have you ever seen people doing that?"

"Only on TV and movies where they play it up all hokey and horrible."

"They are being kind."

"How do you know?"

"There are at least half a dozen bars around Memphis that have those machines, Mom."

"And when were you in a bar?"

"I . . . uh . . . well, there's one in the hotel lounge—you know the one where you stayed when you brought me down for registration."

"Uh-huh." The girl is intelligent, independent, and in another city, she reminded herself. Beyond expressing disapproval there wasn't much Rita could do. "Lacey, I don't want you going to bars."

"It was a hotel, Mom. Anyone walking through could hear it."

"I don't want you going to hotels either!"

"Mom, I'm not running buck wild in the city." The sincerity of her laugh went a long way toward convincing Rita of her daughter's honesty. "You raised me right. I will make good choices."

That gave her some comfort.

"Though how I learned to make good choices with parents like mine . . . Karaoke, Mom? It's just too hokey."

"Then it should be perfect for Hellon. And for me."

"Please! Hellon maybe—it must have its share of frustrated wanna be singers like every other Tennessee town. But you? Mom, you would never get up in front of a crowd and sing."

"Would too."

Her daughter made a sound that in polite company would have been followed by a red face and a heartfelt apology.

"Sweetie, I didn't call you to get into another argument about your wanting me to break out of my rut."

"At this point I'd be happy if you'd just poke your nose up over the edge of that rut and see that there is a whole wide wonderful world out there."

Last night she had dared to peek out of that nice cozy, comfy rut of hers, and the sun and the stars and the moon and her life had not gone careening out of control. Maybe her child had a point. Maybe she could break free of all the expectations and . . . and what? What could Rita Stark do? How could she survive without her roots? "Too big a world, Lacey, for a small-town nobody like me."

"A world that's yours for the taking, Mom. You could do or be anything, you know that, don't you?"

No. She did not know that. "Right now I'm going to *do* the corn bread, or I will *be* late. Bye-bye, honey."

"You know if I thought you would really get up in front of a crowd and sing, even if it was just some silly karaoke, that would be something. A start."

"You just wait and see then." She felt no confidence at all, even in such a purposefully vague promise. She bent to open the oven door, then reached for the first skillet. "Okay, now, I have to hang up. It takes both hands for me to climb back down into my rut."

"Not funny, Mom."

"Talk to you later. I love you high as my heart," Rita whispered, her hand to her chest.

"I love you high as my nose," Lacey Marie came back without a hesitation.

Rita could picture her little girl as a bright-eyed toddler putting a tiny hand to the tip of her nose to go through the motions of the silly poem they'd made up so long ago.

"I love you higher than heaven." Rita lifted her open hands.

"And right down to my toes," Lacey chimed in to say the last words with her mother.

Rita crossed her arms in the sweet memory of hugging her child. "Be careful, honey."

"I will. And you could try being a little less careful for a change."

Less careful? She shut her eyes to savor the sweet, terrifying thought, then murmured to her daughter, "Bye, now."

"Bye."

They hung up and, with tears in her eyes, Rita

set the small cell phone aside. She did not have time for fear or nostalgia. There were hungry people working their butts off on her behalf. She still had to bake the corn bread, tend to the honey-glazed ham, and hope the dessert had set before she had to haul it over to the Palace.

"Less careful?" She slid the pans in the oven and banged the door shut with her knee.

This morning she had indulged in the exhilaration of breaking free of even her own narrow expectations. The feeling had not lasted long, but, like her brief and fiery time with Will, it would leave its mark on her. Maybe, just maybe, they both would finally give her the courage to face down her fears and step out into a new, better way of life.

Maybe . . .

Chapter 15

EVERY DISCERNING DIXIE BELLE REALIZES:
Absence might make the heart grow fonder, but distance makes resolve grow stronger.

Rita placed plastic containers and covered glass pans one after another into Will's waiting grasp as she unloaded the lunch fixings from the back of her car.

"Looks like you brought a whole spread." He passed each serving dish off to the next set of helping hands among the crew waiting to eat.

"I wouldn't usually go to this kind of trouble. Oh!" Wind lifted the hem of her floral sundress just enough to show a flash of her tanned thigh.

A proper Southern gentleman might have snatched the serving dish from her straight off so she could take care of that. For once Will relished the fact that he had never earned a reputation as any kind of gentleman, proper or other. He lifted the food from her hands at his leisure.

"Like I said, I wouldn't normally have done so

much for a group so hungry they'd wolf down ham salad sandwiches and make over them more than lunch at the Peabody." Rita did not blink or scold him for not rushing to her aid. She did not even stop long enough to do more than catch her flaring dress in one hand, hold it down, and get out more food. "But I had a burst of energy today."

"I noticed." He paused to inhale the aroma of hot, fresh corn bread, while moving in close to murmur for her ears only, "You must have broken the sound barrier getting out of here this morning."

"Shhh." She glanced around, pulled a second batch of corn bread from the car, and shoved it toward him, her voice booming as she said, "Why, yes, Will. Y'all did get a lot of work done this morning."

"We have a great work crew," he matched her volume, then used taking the plate of food as an excuse to lean in close. "It's just that you left without saying anything."

"What was there to say? It's been fun? Have a good life?"

Thank you. He didn't realize until he *didn't* hear it that those were the words he'd expected from her. Expected? He'd wanted her gratitude like a scrawny dog hankers for a table scrap. Not like him. Not like him at all. He had helped her for helping's sake alone, not to win her admiration. He wondered if he should take her lack of response as a sign that he hadn't accomplished either?

"So what do we do now?" she asked loudly, her eyes on the crowd.

"Now we get out of the way," he said, not for the people around them and not for her ears alone. Though his words carried a double meaning, he decided not to try to impose that on her. This was the getting-on-with-it phase of whatever they had shared. The time where they slowly went their separate ways. Where Rita found her footing, and he did not rush in to try to prop her up. If he truly had made a difference to her, she would do that just fine.

"Get out of whose way?" she asked.

"The flooring people." He pushed his hands out like he was rolling dough because he didn't know how else to demonstrate it. "We can't do a thing until they lay the new floor."

"How long will that take?"

"Be at least another thirty-six hours before we can even get back into the place, much less go back to work." He took the last tray of corn bread and delivered it into the first pair of hands he found behind him.

"But I can still stay in my apartment?" Rita stepped away from her open car door.

"Oh, Rita, why would you want to? Here." Jillie held the cloth-covered corn bread Will had just given her out at arm's length like it was a pot of snakes. "One of you take this. I just came by to get my cell phone back."

"Your arms and legs ain't broken, girl. Walk a few steps and put it on the table yourself." Will crossed his arms and fixed his heated gaze on his sister. "Everyone here has been busting their asses pitching in, and the least you could do—"

"I'll take it." It seemed like Rita, but it didn't sound like Rita. He pivoted to see a scrappy fellow with pitch-black greased-back hair swoop in. "Glad to help you, Ms. West. Count on me, Billy."

"Um, you know I made so much, why don't I put this batch back in the car so the flies won't get it?" Rita took the tray from Jillie and slid it into the backseat with the grace of a prima ballerina.

"Okay, then." The small man wiped his nose with the back of his hand, then made his good-byes, calling out, "See you Ms. Stark, Ms. West. Holler if you need anything, Billy. Proud to be of service."

"Thanks." Will winced. "That wasn't the infamous Professor Paul, was it?"

Jillie sneered.

"He runs Wally Love's gas station on weekends and holidays, and he eats lunch in the Palace every day he's not working." Rita waved and grinned and kept waving as the stringy little fellow backed away, bobbing his good-bye with his whole upper body. "I don't even know his name. He sure seemed to know you, though."

Will wrung a sigh through his gritted teeth and looked around at the crowd of helpers. He hardly knew a person there, but more than one of them, when they caught him scanning the gathering, gave out a hearty wave. "Everyone here seems to know me."

"Of course they do." Jillie slapped him in the chest with the back of her hand. "When people found out their hero was spearheading this project, they turned out in droves."

"I am nobody's hero. I have never done anything heroic in my entire life."

"Don't sell yourself short." Rita said it so quietly he had to whip around to see if he'd only imagined it. But by then she stood frowning at Jillie. "Now I know I had your phone at the church because I talked to Lacey Marie so . . ."

"Think where you put it. I need to be by a phone or have a phone with me at all times."

"Why?" He snarled at Jillie because she was rude and bossy and useless for not helping her best friend. And she was keeping him from talking privately to Rita, even if they had nothing more to say. "You on some kind of donor list? Waiting for a personality transplant?"

"Grow up," she growled. "I left a message last night for Paul to please call me. The fact that he hasn't yet has me worried sick."

"Oh." Didn't he feel a perfect jerk? He patted Jillie on the back. "Well, don't get worked up. He'll call."

"You think?"

Her face beamed with such hope. How could he lie to his baby sister looking up at him like that? "I have no idea."

"I'm sure he'll call." Rita gave her a hug. "Just like I'm sure your phone is still at the church with the rest of my things."

"Really?"

"Come back with me to the church after lunch and I'll show you. The phone will be there and Paul will call."

"I hadn't planned on staying for lunch." Jillie had the front of Will's T-shirt wadded in her fist before he could open his mouth. "And spare me any jokes about my never staying for lunch anywhere."

"Believe me, if I had made a joke about your eating habits, it woulda been a damn sight funnier than that."

She added a harmless punch in the belly as she released his shirt.

"Y'all go ahead and dig in that lunch, now. Don't wait on us." Rita braced one hand on her car's fender and used the other hand to shade her eyes from the summer sun. She swept her fingers back through her shiny hair when she angled her shoulders toward Jillie again. "I could bring the phone by your mother's later."

"No thank you. I am avoiding my mother today."

Will raised an eyebrow. "Only today?"

"They actually shared a tender moment last night." Rita straightened the collar of Jillie's brilliant blue top. "The experience must have drained the poor little thing."

"Which one? The West family is vastly overstocked in the poor little thing department."

"That's really more information than a girl wants to have about her brother, Will." Jillie put her hands to her cheeks. "Still, your shortcomings have not seemed to have affected your love life much."

"Very funny," he grumbled.

"If you're avoiding your mother, sugar, you can always stay with me in my apartment tonight. I'd love the company."

"With you?" Jillie swung her gaze from Rita to Will, who dodged it with a sudden interest in a piece of broken parking lot. "Maybe I spoke too soon about that love-life thing."

Will grunted his opinion of his sister's jest.

The clatter of forks on plastic plates and the waves of good-humored conversation rolled their way. The aroma of delicious food mingled with the rich smell of summer greenery. Will took it all in, and despite how much he hated the way this town behaved toward him, he felt a solid, awesome sense of contentment well up within him.

"Oh, please, Jillie. Come over and stay with me."

Of course the surroundings might have had very little to do with those new, compelling emotions.

Rita wrinkled her nose and gave no mind to the way the wind kicked up the skirt of her dress. "It'll be fun."

"What demented dictionary are you using to define the word 'fun,' honey?" Jillie tipped her head back to survey the building, her focus on the row of windows above the electric Pig Rib Palace sign. "You've been granted a reprieve from all this. Thirty-six whole hours where you are excused from being anywhere near here. I say enjoy it. Take advantage of it."

"Much as it pains me not to make a crack about Jillie encouraging others to take advantage of every excuse to indulge themselves, this time I have to agree with her." For Rita to take some time away fit his plans perfectly. Absence might make the heart grow fonder, but distance made resolve grow stronger.

"Perhaps I should reconsider my suggestion, then. If Will supports this, it must have a big old flaw in it."

"The flaw is I have no place to go. I don't want to impose myself on your mother another night."

"Another night?" Jillie flicked her wrist like she could dispose of that notion with a half-hearted gesture. "Rita, you didn't even impose on her more than a couple hours last night."

Rita lifted her shoulders. Her dress rustled over her body. She did not look at Will. "All the more reason I'd rather not hang around her house for a whole day and a half."

"Smart." Will nodded.

"I'd ask Cozie if I could stay out there, but she's at your mother's more than she's at home these days."

"I can't tell you how many times I have come down to breakfast the last few weeks to find Cozie already there. She and Mama, coffee in their hands, their heads together over some scheme or another."

Rita laughed. "Oh, sure your mother and Cozette—covert masterminds at work."

"I don't know what they go on about. But it was Cozie being around so much that got me and her talking about *you*, and that's when we decided . . ."

"Cozette's is out." Rita's look could have blistered paint. "Besides, she's gotten awfully strange lately—"

"Lately?"

"About her property," Rita finished.

"Well, you don't want to go out to her old property anyway. If the point is to get away, then you should actually get *away*, don't you think?"

"Where would I go?"

"Where could you go? Where? Where?" Jillie wet her lips and toyed with a strand of her hair. She might just as well have had tiny gears whirring and churning in a side view right into her head—her plotting was that obvious. That obvious to anyone but Rita. "How about over to see Lacey Marie?"

"In Memphis?"

"Memphis, huh?" He stroked his chin in a move even more conspicuous than his sister's. "Isn't that where Professor Paul lives?"

"How could I just up and go see Lacey?" Rita fingered the bow on her sundress strap. "She's in a dormitory. I couldn't stay with her."

Jillie shot him a near deadly shut-your-big-mouth glare.

"Well, we wouldn't have to *stay* with Lacey Marie."

"She has classes and—Well, when you were young the last thing you wanted was your mother showing up on a fine summer afternoon with her overnight bag under one arm and a lifetime of baggage on her mind."

"What does age have to do with *that*?" Jillie shuddered. "Okay, so we won't stay with Lacey."

"We?" Rita's eyes narrowed.

"We'll stay at Will's house!"

"My house?"

Heads turned. The buzzing parking lot went silent.

All Will could think to do was smile and wave. When the conversation level picked up again, he nabbed Jillie by the arm. "*My* house? What gives you the right to volunteer my house?"

"You want Rita to have the best, don't you?"

The best? Damn right he wanted her to have the best, but not *his* best. How could he ever ease himself back from this . . . this . . . nonrelationship of theirs if when he returned to his home he would know that Rita had been there? That she had touched his things, read his books, sat at his table, and slept in his bed?

His body grew hard at the simple thought of her head on his pillow, her naked body between his sheets. He wiped a few beads of sweat off the back of his neck and cleared his throat. She had already forever altered the way he'd look at Hellon, his family, and even cake. How could he let her do the same in his own home? "Of course, I want Rita to have the best. And that's why . . ."

"No." Rita laid two fingers over his mouth to keep him from finishing. "It's a generous offer. Too generous, really. And besides, I think I know where I want to stay."

Jillie grabbed Rita's hand. "Then you'll go?"

"Well, I'd hate to look like a rat abandoning ship." Her chin low, she raised just her gaze to Will's, saying so much more than her words ever could.

"Go. It's not a problem." Not now that she decided to stay anywhere but his house. "I'll stay here and supervise and you and . . . you and Jillie can go to Memphis and whoop it up."

"Whoop it up?" Jillie fanned her neck with her hand. "I have never whooped anything in my life, Billy, that is your department."

"Is there more corn bread Rita? Folks are asking." Pernel poked his head over Rita's shoulder.

"Never whooped in your life? Don't you go all badass Princess Barbie on me, little sister." Will tapped the most prominent feature on his face. "I know where you bought that nose you're sticking up in the air."

"Leave my nose out of this, kindly."

"Oooh. What have I missed here?" Pernel whispered none-too-quietly in the general direction of Rita's ear.

Rita ignored her ex. "Don't let this get ugly, you two. Will, stop picking on your sister."

"Where's that corn bread, Pernel?" Cozie

strolled up, an empty plate in her hand. "What's going on?"

"I'm not sure, but I think it's something about picking Jillie's nose, Rita thinking Will is ugly, topped off with sacrilege spoken against the pinnacle of all womanhood, Saint Barbie."

Will turned to Rita. "Don't tell me hearing that doesn't make you long to get the hell out of town."

"Actually, I could use the break. And there *is* something in Memphis I'd like to see about."

"If you're going to go to Memphis, you really ought to take me." Pernel wagged his finger in Rita's face. "I want to see Lacey Marie as much as you do."

"Memphis?" Cozie pushed in closer. "Rita you aren't seriously . . ."

"The corn bread is in the backseat." Will gave the tall woman a friendly push in the right direction. "Why don't you get the door for her, Pernel?"

"And slam your head in it," Jillie muttered. "I'm not going if *he's* going, you know."

"He's not going," Will assured his sister. "But Rita is. Let these characters take care of themselves for a change and take that careless heart out for a spin."

"Of course that would mean somebody would have to stay with your mother." Rita gave him a Cheshire cat grin, her eyes all innocence and flirtation.

"Perhaps Cozie could . . ."

The older woman took the tray of corn bread in

one hand and put her free arm around Rita, placing a kiss on her cheek. "Great food, sweetie. It's been fun to pull together for a common cause with a large group again, but Mouse and I are looking forward to heading home and sleeping for four days straight."

"Or Pernel?"

"Pernel?" Jillie dipped her head to speak to only Will. "You really want the man who knows all there is to tell and then some about Rita staying alone with Mama for thirty-six hours?"

Will groaned. What had he gotten himself into? He'd avoided his mother all this time only to have painted himself into a corner. "Like they say, no good deed goes unpunished."

"Don't you talk about Miss Peggy that way. Staying with her is anything but a punishment." Pernel stole a slice of golden corn bread. "I'd offer to do it myself, but what with both of us being single and her own son in town? People would talk. Yes, they would."

"And I shudder to think what they might say," Will muttered.

"That thoughtless Wild Billy up to his old ways." Cozie peeled back the cloth covering the bread and offered everyone in the small circle a piece. "He's breaking his mama's heart."

"Uh-huh." Pernel took a second slice of the moist yellow bread. "They would for a fact."

"What?" From the moment he heard the old name, his head began to throb, and he couldn't make heads or tails of the conversation.

"That's what people would say." Rita nudged him.

"Oh."

"But you be the bigger person," she went on. "You go over to take care of your mother even though the whole town knows you were trying to teach her a lesson about not crying wolf or carrying on like who knows what."

He squinted at Rita. "What?"

"Then do you know what they'd say?"

"I don't even know what *you* said."

"They'd say, 'That Will, he's turned out a fine man.' An upright citizen who looks after his neighbor—me—and is kind to his mama."

Pernel let out a low whistle. "Do you have any idea the mileage you can get around here out of that? Kind to his mama? Hell, around here they'll take their hats off and hold a moment of silence the day they sentence an ax murder if the boy was kind to his mama."

"Is that how you get away with so much?"

"I am kind to everyone's mama." Pernel winked. "It's the self-important, unenlightened kind of mothers that I don't get along with."

Cozie laughed. "It's not like it's such a huge challenge to take care of Miss Peggy, anyway."

Will bent his head to whisper in Rita's ear, "I thought she stopped smoking that stuff a few years back."

"What is it with y'all?" Will shook his head when the tray passed by. Though the scent of Rita's cooking had his stomach growling, the prospect of humbling himself to his mother dampened his appetite but good. "Has my mother taken you to raise?"

"No way." Jillie took her small square of corn bread and shifted it from one of her cupped palms to the other and back again. "If she had taken them in for more than a tea party, they'd be clawing over one another's bodies to get a seat on the Jillie and Rita Memphis roadtrip tour bus posthaste."

"Sounds like you need a break from Mother."

Jillie smiled. "Maybe I need my own kind of redemption."

"What do you think, Will?" Rita put her hand on his arm.

When he looked in her eyes he saw so much trust that it humbled him. She trusted him to do the right thing no matter what the cost. Had he believed he needed a thank-you for his efforts? That look was thanks enough.

"You honestly think folks would say Will West had turned out a fine man?"

Rita looked into his eyes. "Yes, I do."

She could be right. By acting like the man he had forged himself into, choice by choice, he might finally get past his reputation. People in Hellon might see him as something more than a has-been hero and an always-at-the-ready rogue. They might drop the old expectations and finally see him for what he had become. After all these years he might at last enjoy the freedom not to be Wild Billy in Hellon anymore. And all he had to do to realize his fondest wish was let his mother get her way.

His stomach tightened like a fist around a rock, but he did not let his frustration show. He smiled at Rita and his sister, and said, "Okay. Go. I have to stay here to talk to the new workers, make sure they have everything they need. But I can be over at my mother's by late afternoon."

"Thank you." Rita went up on tiptoe to kiss his cheek, her hand gripping his.

He nodded.

"Let's pack," Jillie jerked Rita away. "I don't want to waste any more time. If I had my cell phone, I'd call Paul again right now!"

"I tell you, it's at the church. We'll get it when I take the dishes by."

"Never mind the dishes, I'll take care of them." Every eye turned to Pernel. "Well, don't look so surprised. I did run a restaurant for many, many years. I think I can manage a few dirty dishes."

"We still have to grab a few things for Rita here, then go over and get my—"

A muffled chirping cut Jillie off.

"What the hell is that?" Will asked.

"Somebody has a phone in their purse or pocket, silly. Now like I was saying, Rita, we need to—"

It rang again.

Will squinted. "Does that sound to you like—"

Cozette raised the tray in her hands. "It's coming from the corn bread."

"Rita! You baked my phone into a batch of corn bread?"

"Obviously so. And I would gladly stand here at the heart of the circle of all my nearest and dearest and tell you how stupid I feel for doing that."

"Don't ever call yourself stupid, Rita." Will moved toward her.

She held her hand up and shook her head. "But since Jillie is waiting on a call from her Prince Charming . . . I think we all better dive in and see if we can't answer that phone."

"Mama, why do you do this to me?" He braced both hands against either side of the open door. He had convinced himself that if he got a few things cleared up before he crossed that threshold, it would mean he had not have given in.

"Why do I do what, darling?" She swept her hand out to bid him enter.

He did not budge.

She looked impossibly small today. Pale and plain in a cotton dress set off with simple jewelry and the dangedest little gold shoes. They made the most delicate tappy-tap on the polished marble floor as she took a few tottering steps into the foyer. "You coming along?"

He relaxed his arms and shifted his feet on the welcome mat. "Not until you tell me why you are doing this."

"Whatever you think I'm doing, son, I promise I'm doing it because I want what's best for you."

She motioned him in again, then turned and shuffled, with her hand against the white wall, toward the parlor door. "Let's talk in here. I have the tea already laid out, and the light is better."

What a show. "Mother, where's your cane? Did you have the maid stash it in the parlor so you could hobble around in front me?"

She stepped completely out of sight, then a puff of white hair and one eye peeked out at him from inside the recessed doorway. "You coming in or not?"

"Not until you admit you are a big fake, full of baloney, and that you have most of this town buffaloed and like it that way."

Her small hand gripped the edge of the doorway. It took a minute but her whole face peered out at him, like a small child playing hide-and-seek. "You first."

He groaned and looked skyward. Finally, all he could do was laugh.

"Come have tea with your mama." She disappeared inside the parlor.

He rubbed his face and reminded himself why he had come. He sure hoped Rita appreciated his sacrifice.

Chapter 16

"Isn't it bad enough we're staying in this place? Why do you want to go in here?" Jillie pouted like a five-year-old. She scuffed her pumps practically every step along the teal-and-maroon-patterned carpet. "I know a ton of very nice places . . ."

"This *is* nice."

"It's a hotel lounge."

"A *nice* hotel lounge."

"There is no such thing, Rita."

"Snob," she whispered as she pushed through the swinging door. How lucky could Rita get? She'd walked right into an indisputable excuse to get away from dwelling on Will, from seeing him around, and having to pretend their time together had left her unfazed. She had this trip to Memphis to prove to herself she *could* do something totally unexpected. And she'd found the perfect place to do both.

"Crap! I knew it. This is just . . . just . . . too tacky for words."

"Oh? And waltzing into a room full of people at an early 'happy hour' buffet and hollering 'crap' is just the epitome of graciousness and style." Rita grabbed her friend's arm.

"No, of course not. However, let's consider something." She made quite a show of taking a long, sweeping review of their surroundings.

Rita followed suit and held her serene expression despite the view.

"Let's see. Dark paneling. Antique gilt frames on the sold-by-the-roadside-style artwork. Unflattering yellow lighting from those same damned candleholders Pernel loved in the Palace." Jillie hit Rita with a hard glare. "Hollering 'crap' might well be tacky, also rude and vulgar, but what can I say? I'm a victim of my environment."

"Some days, Jillie, I swear I can't picture any greater satisfaction in life than just to pinch your head off."

"Couldn't you relieve us both and poke my eyes out instead?"

"If you're going to stick around this place, I'd have to lop your ears off too, I'm afraid."

"Oh my word, I'm afraid to ask why."

Rita ignored her companion, turned to the hostess, and smiled like the woman was her new best friend. "When does the karaoke start?"

"Oh, Rita, no. Just climb behind the bar and beat me senseless with that guitar-shaped whiskey decanter now and save us both further grief!"

"Only staff allowed behind the bar." The waitress took the request in stride, making Rita wonder how often someone made that kind of plea around there. "Starts at seven. You can hop up onstage anytime after that."

"Pretty quiet right now. Does it pick up much in the evenings?"

"Hmmm." She squinted one eye at the people shuffling along the early buffet. "Typical weekday crowd—a few out-of-town businessmen and a busload of senior citizens on a Memphis/Nashville/Dollywood summer bus-tour package. Don't expect it to pick up much more than that."

"So, this is a bad time?"

"If you hope to play to a packed house, yes. But we love to have someone get up and start the ball rolling."

Rita put her hand over her heart. The lady expected *her* to start things . . . "Rolling?"

"I personally know a couple of the older gents are just champing at the bit to show off their Elvis moves for the ladies."

"Kill me now. I tell you, Rita, run me through a wood chipper and sell the pieces for bait. I swear I'd enjoy that more than an evening listening to karaoke."

"Even if it's me doing the singing?"

"You? You'd never get up the nerve to stand up in front on all these people and sing."

"Why not?" She scooped on an extra helping of bravado as much for herself as for Jillie and the waitress. "We don't know anyone here. It'd be a hoot and a half."

"Oh, it's *two* hoots and a half if it's a peep." The waitress smacked her hands together. "No sense in being shy. Come back after seven, grab the mike, and knock yourself out!"

"That's the first sensible suggestion I've heard since we walked in."

"Stop your grumbling or you're going to hear some suggestions from me that make your tacky, vulgar, rudeness sound like a new-member tea at the Junior League." Rita snagged the waitress by the arm for one last question. "Um, can you tell me what kind of music you have?"

"Well, Elvis—that goes without saying. And some disco and old rock and roll. You know, the regular stuff that comes with the equipment."

"Uh-huh"

"And Patsy, of course."

"Yes." She shut her eyes and sighed.

"Patsy?" Jillie sounded like a poodle sneezing when she repeated the name.

"Patsy Cline." Rita put her hand over her heart in a mix of reverence and the perverse pleasure of knowing the show would embarrass Jillie. She turned to the waitress. "Do you have 'Crazy'?"

"If they are out of crazy, they can for sure borrow a cup from you."

"Don't mind her." Rita spoke in a tone of invented conspiracy to the woman in the black pants and shabby silver vest. "She's just cranky because she hasn't eaten in two or three... years."

"I'm cranky because you made corn bread out of my cell phone and now I don't know if Paul called me back or not."

"Then we'd better get upstairs and see if we can nibble down to the key pad enough to call him again." Rita took Jillie's arm and spun her toward the door. "C'mon, you have a reprieve from this place until seven."

"See, y'all tonight!"

Rita waved over her shoulder to the waitress. "We'll be here with bells on."

"Mine will be around my neck so when I throw myself into the river, I'll sink faster." Jillie hit the doors and went gliding out into the hallway. "Why are you doing this?"

"Your brother."

"He drove you insane." She slapped the heel of her hand to her forehead as they waited for the elevator. "Yes, it makes perfect sense now."

"He inspired me to try something new."

Jillie folded her arms. "So goes the talk around town."

"Big mouth."

"Big talker."

"It's not big talk if it's true." Rita stole a sidelong look at her friend.

"I'm just going to pretend you're implying my

brother awakened you to greater emotional depth, to a higher consciousness, or, perhaps, just better living through carpentry."

"Got it."

Ding! The elevator doors whooshed open.

"End of discussion." Rita stepped aside to allow the people inside the elevator out.

Greater emotional depth? Higher consciousness? Well, maybe her time with Will had opened her to some new avenues of thinking, but those weren't what made her skin prickle every time she heard his name. Even just a playful conversation about him gave her a light-headedness that she recognized as a danger sign. She had to get that man out of her system. "You know, Jillie, I was just thinking . . ."

"Oh, Rita, don't make me go back in there and arm-wrestle that waitress for that guitar-shaped bottle."

"Hmmm?

"If what you're thinking now is any loonier than this karaoke idea of yours, I need that whiskey and will be fully prepared to conk myself over the head with that ceramic decanter."

They got on the elevator and jabbed the button for their floor.

"Well, wait until after I call Lacey Marie and you call your mother and you leave another message for Paul."

"This must be bad."

"Why say that?"

"You want me to get my affairs in order first."

"Jillie, honey, you haven't been able to get your affairs in order in the last twenty years. What makes you think you could do it in four hours?"

"Are you giving up on me, Rita?"

"You know better than that." She twisted a piece of Jillie's hair around her finger, then unwound it again. "In fact, I trust you so much I'm giving you a shot at something you've wanted to do for a long time."

"You don't mean it."

Rita grinned and nodded. "You know a good hair salon that could work me in and a dress shop that doesn't cater exclusively to scarecrows and cadaver-sized women?"

"Hot damn!" If Jillie had been the old-school Southern religious type, she might have lifted her hands to the Lord and danced in the Spirit, Rita ventured. "Okay, the bottle can stay where it is."

"Good. 'Cause after you're through with me I might need it."

Jillie hugged her.

The door slid open, and they stepped out and headed for their room.

This was it. Today she would hand herself over to her best friend's care. Finally, she'd dare to look like the new—or respectably a little less like her old self—woman she had become. Tonight she would sing her heart out and not give a damn what people thought. If that worked, she would be letting go of all that could never be. And she could rest easy once again knowing she had replaced it with a nice, safe, sane alternative.

*   *   *

"More tea, son?"

"I hate hot tea. Why anyone would take an out-standing beverage, created to be drunk cold and sweet from large ice-filled tumblers and serve it hot from a silver pot into dainty pink-and-white china is beyond me." Will held his cup out for her to refill.

A curl of steam rose from the dark brew as she topped off his drink. "You want another cookie, too?"

"Naw. I mean, no thank you."

"I don't blame you. They're supposed to be good for you." She set the heirloom silver teapot back with the rest of the ornate service. "Miss Cozette brought them by yesterday as a kindness for some advice I'd given her. There's something just not right about that, is there?"

"You can say that again." Will examined a large brown cookie just chock to the brim with dried fruit and what looked and tasted to him like old hay. "Anybody coming to you for advice has to be a bit touched in the head."

"You behave, young man."

He put his elbow on the arm of the cherry-wood-and-velveteen settee and locked into her gaze. "You first."

She laughed.

He held the cup between his hands and gazed down into the dark liquid. "You know I've been here for twenty minutes, Mama, and you still haven't answered my question."

"What question?"

He rubbed his forehead. "Why do you have to make everything so hard all the time?"

"I don't set out to make your life harder, son." Her teacup rattled on its saucer as she set them both on the silver serving tray. "Honestly, I don't."

He shut his eyes. For days he'd nursed an anger with his mother that had burned hot as hellfire. Now came the time to cut loose and let her know about it, and he just couldn't.

He blamed Rita, of course. She'd gotten to him. While he wasn't looking she crept into every molecule of his being and changed it—just enough to leave him a better man.

"Tell me, William. I want to hear what's on your mind."

"You know, Mama, when Norrie was pregnant and she and I were broken up and I was the world's biggest jackass?"

"I have a vague recollection of the time," she deadpanned. "What about it?"

"Only one person was good enough to look me in the face and tell me the truth."

"Oh?"

"Rita didn't pull any punches then. She hasn't let me charm or bellyache my way out of anything since I've been back."

"Good for her."

"She's a good person, Mama. And having spent time with her, I've concluded I want to be a better person, too."

"Will I be needing my checkbook to make a contribution at the end of this testimonial?"

"To hell with your checkbook, Mama. But we *are* going to take a page out of Rita's book today. We are going to cut through the bullshit and talk to each other in plain, unvarnished terms."

"In this house 'bullshit' *is* a plain and unvarnished term, son."

He acknowledged his mother's peeve with his language by holding up his hands in surrender. "You're right, of course. Good manners before bad temper, isn't it?"

"I may make a gentleman out of you yet."

"Don't get your hopes up because here comes the rest of what I have to say about your shams, schemes, and shenanigans."

"I'm listening."

"I hope you are. Because just once I want you to see that what you deem high-minded, above-board ambition often comes across to me like a low-down, underhanded imposition."

"That skirts mighty close to an accusation, William."

"Only skirts close to one?" He put his hands on both knees. "Then maybe I didn't make myself clear enough."

"If you have something to say, don't hold back on my account."

"All right. For one petite, cultured, affluent, old-blood Southern gentlewoman, you play awfully dirty, Mama."

"I'm not *playing*." She folded her hands under her chin and her eyes grew darkly somber. "Not where my children are concerned."

"Don't lie to me, old woman. You're playing— playing hardball. You always have. And Jillie on the receiving end of it more than her fair share if we're going to get it all out in the open."

She blinked as though startled and trying to find her bearings.

He wondered, had he gone too far? Damn but he wished Rita were here to help him do this right. He wished Rita were here, period.

Finally, his mother dabbed her lace-edged napkin to the corner of her mouth, then let her shoulders fall, slightly. "You are right, son."

"I am?" He shook his head and cleared his throat. "I know I'm right, but you're agreeing with me? Admitting it?"

"Yes. Lord knows how I've struggled to bite my tongue about your sister's actions. However, I'm afraid if I did that every time she acted up?"—she stuck her tongue out and pinched the tip of it between her thumb and forefinger—"I'd thald lide dhis."

"Being adorable won't get you out of it this time."

"Fine then." She put her hands quite precisely in her lap. "Then I reckon the truth will have to do."

"About time."

"I did my best with both of you children. But my best never seemed to work for your sister."

"She is hard to please."

"No. No, that's not it. I see how Rita is with her, and I know she is reachable, but maybe not by me. Maybe not in a way that I'm comfortable with."

"Doesn't help you're both stubborn as mules," he muttered.

"Did you *bray* something, my dear?"

He shook his head, grinning.

"Knowing your sister and I had this gap neither of us could seem to bridge, I found new ways to try to get through to Jillian. Why do you think I have such a broad range of people in my social circles and an unrelenting drive to keep up all those connections?"

"Because you like the attention and the status it brings you."

"Well, there is that." Her fingers flitted lovingly over each piece of her cherished silver service. "But I also do it for your sister."

"For Jillie?" He started to reach for his cup again, just to keep his hands occupied. "How does that help her?"

"It helps because I can't seem to be consistently emotionally supportive of her."

His hand froze halfway to the cup handle.

"I said it." She nodded as if lending a steely-eyed reassurance that he had not heard wrong. "I know you and half the town have thought it. Now I've said it, and we all know it's true. I'm not the kind of mother your sister has most needed. That's why I try to keep people in our lives who can set a better example."

"Example?" He dropped his hand to his leg again. "Like Pernel?"

"The man who spit in the eye of local convention and the entire Hellon social structure? You can damn well bet I like his influence on your sister."

"Why are you talking to me like this, Mama?"

"How am I talking?"

"Honestly."

"It's probably my frailties acting up." She fanned herself and coughed none too convincingly.

"You're fine, and we both know it. Just like we both know that I came here for Rita's and Jillie's sakes, not because I'm bowing to your royal command and phony illness."

She dipped her head in acknowledgment. "Maybe I am fine now, but I won't always be, you know. I simply wanted to know that you would come should I sincerely need you."

"What a treacherous ploy to use on your own son, Mama. Treacherous and mean-spirited."

"I never intended . . ." Her eyes became suddenly bright with the threat of tears. "How so?"

"Testing me. Insulting enough on its own, but using a means that would serve as a reminder of how I failed the baby and so close to the anniversary of his death . . ."

"Oh, Will. Darling, no!" Her hand went to her throat, then to cover her mouth, when she finally closed her fingers over her small cameo necklace, they were trembling. "No, I never thought of that. Oh, sweetheart, can you forgive me?"

Forgive her? She'd asked it so many times of him over everything from forgetting to pick him up after ball practice to speaking unkindly of the baby's mother. Not once had it altered her behavior or soothed his aching heart. This time, though, felt different. "You mean that, don't you? You really do see the hurt your antics caused."

"I always see it, William." She lowered her head. Her narrow shoulders rose and fell in a sigh almost as big as she was. "I may not often admit it, but I never lose sight of what a truly flawed individual I am."

It was not the kind of thing that Margaret— "Call me Peggy, just like Margaret Mitchell"— Curtis Morgan West would admit just to gain a dollop of sympathy. She'd have marched into hell with her lips sealed and her head high rather than say a thing like that if she didn't mean it with her whole heart.

He moved from the chair to kneel at her side. He covered her hand with his. "Aw, Mama, you're too hard on yourself."

"I'm too hard on everyone, darling." She laid her forehead against his and worked up a watery smile. "Too hard, too much, and too dang old to change my ways now."

"You're not *that* old. You could change if you wanted to, at least a little bit."

"I might give you the same advice."

"Me? Why would I have to change? I'm perfect, remember? Wild Billy West? Local legend?"

"You aren't any more that than I am what this town has me pegged as—the poor pitiful mother of two wayward, ungrateful children."

He took both her hands in his, chuckling.

"I have not been an ideal parent, Will. Some people aren't. But I did the best I could. Some people aren't cut out to be parents, I suppose, but in my day it was simply expected."

"Since when have you done what's simply expected?"

"I didn't. That's why I became a mother a scant six months after marrying your father." She looked heavenward as if asking forgiveness.

Will looked up, too, but only noticed that the ceiling needed painting. "If you knew you didn't have the temperament for parenting, why have Jillie?"

She pressed her lips together.

He pushed up from where he knelt and walked across the room to the fireplace. "Oh, wait I know this one—because you thought Father deserved to have his *own* child, one with his blood to make up for having to raise some other man's bastard."

"Your father loved you."

"And some days that makes me feel worse, Mama, not better."

"Then that's your choice."

"My *choice*?"

"Will, you are adult enough to understand that feelings are often as much about choices as actions are. When you think of the baby, do you care for him less today because he wasn't your blood? Or do you choose to remember him with the same abiding love any father would have for his son?"

Will spread his open hands across the mantel and clenched his jaw.

"William?"

He knocked the toe of his boot against the heavy black andiron. "When did you turn into the tribal wisewoman, Mama?"

"Since I already had a pair of wiseass children, it just wasn't much of a leap."

"You are a card, I tell you." He chuckled and stood straight. "I don't suppose telling Rita to be more careless with her heart was your handiwork, was it?"

"What did she tell you about that?"

"Passing reference." He shrugged.

"That girl." She clasped her hands in her lap and shook her head.

"Don't start on Rita, Mama. I won't abide it."

"I wasn't about to start on anyone, unless it would be to chide myself again."

"You?"

"I said a lot of things to the girls that I hoped would resonate with them, encourage them to realize what wonderful young women they are." Her chair creaked as she sat back in it and rolled her head to the side to look out the window. "But in light of Miss Rita not sleeping in her guest bed last night, I don't think I made myself very clear."

"I thought we were through playing games." He moved from the mantel to block the light streaming in from the long, narrow window. "I don't need your high drama or the lecture on morals. And I won't warn you again I won't stomach your faulting Rita for anything."

"I'm saying it's me. My fault, not Rita's." She picked up her napkin, set it down, reached for her teacup, but hesitated and placed her hand to her temple instead. "Perhaps *carefree*. *Carefree* with her heart, not careless. That would have been a better way to phrase it. Careless is so . . . I did warn her not to be careless with her body. I should have added not to be too careless with her future as well."

"I'm not having a discussion about mine and Rita's personal business, but if it eases your mind any, we were not . . . careless."

"Oh, grow up, Will." She snapped her fingers. "I am not talking about birth control here, I am talking about Rita taking control of her future."

What a day of surprises. He and his mother both concerned about the same thing for Rita. Of course, they did have one fairly drastic difference of opinion. "Are you saying I'm bad for Rita?"

"Can you tell me you're not?"

He parted the sheers with one hand and stared out into the courtyard without focusing on any one feature.

"I thought you had matured enough to see that not everything is about you, son."

"Not everything, but this is . . ."

"I worry for Rita. I worry that she sold herself short."

"By coming to me last night?"

"By settling for sex when she could have had love."

He dug his fingers into the back of his neck and groaned softly. "Suddenly all this honesty and motherly wisdom is giving me a headache."

"That's not the kind of carelessness I would ever encourage, most especially in a remarkable woman like Rita."

"She is remarkable, isn't she?"

"You just now noticing?"

"No."

"Then why the hell are you here arguing with a woman you are never going to get the best of when you could be in Memphis with her?"

"You just said—"

"I said she shouldn't sell herself short. She shouldn't have settled for an affair when she has enough love to give for a lifetime."

Let's see, he had spent a lot of years misjudging his mother and battling with his baby sister. Now he realized that the one person he had come to help—his big shot at redemption and finally getting to be a real hero—he had, in fact, treated her like a dog. She had a lifetime full of love to offer, and he had convinced her that giving of herself for more than the moment was a waste of time.

"You're right, Mama."

"Of course I'm right, and I might give you the same advice."

"Me? Advice?"

"It pains me to inform you of this, son, but you are not so perfect you could not benefit from a whomp upside the head. Why are you enduring a rootless existence filled with people who barter and trade their friendship for your goodwill but who don't love you?"

"I'd rather those hairy, tool belts pulling their pants down below the equator contractors and suppliers that I work with keep things platonic, Mama, if you don't mind." He gave her his most disarming smile.

Her gaze did not lighten one iota. "I'd rather you had people in your life besides just the ones you work with."

"But love, Mama?" He shook his head. *Love?* No. He would never say it to his mother, but he was too damn selfish for that emotion. Hadn't he proven that already with his child? Hadn't he proven it again with Rita? "Remember when I told you Rita spoke the truth to me about the baby?"

"Yes."

"She called me an 'immature, irresponsible, self-loving donkey-headed bastard.' "

"Isn't that amazing?'

"What?"

"That she could know you so well and still love you so much?"

"Rita does not love me."

"Maybe you don't know she does yet. Hell, maybe even she doesn't know it. But if she didn't love you, why would a woman like Rita have been so careless with her heart around a self-loving donkey head like you?"

"Neither of us mentioned love, Mama."

"So you're a pair of fools. At least you'll have that in common to keep things interesting."

How could one small woman tie him up in knots like this? He pinched the bridge of his nose.

"I know where they are staying. I even know where they will be tonight. Jillie called just before you came over to complain to high heaven about it."

"Don't tell me Rita is finally asserting herself with Jillie?"

"Maybe you should go see for yourself."

"I can't. Somebody needs to stay with poor, sickly Mother."

She shook her napkin out into her lap. "Oh, I'm all right."

"I knew it."

"Don't gloat, son, it's rude." She took one of the chunky cookies, broke it in half, and held it up as if it were the missing piece of evidence in a murder mystery. "Besides, I am never more than a phone call away from mobilizing a network of people that would be the envy of one of those master criminals in those English spy movies."

He did not know about love, but he did know he wanted to see Rita. Half a day apart, and he already missed her. "Okay, I'll go."

"Good." She raised her chin to encourage a

quick all-purpose good-bye, thank you, and "yes mother" kiss.

He went to her chair, put her cookie aside, and helped her to her feet. Then he wrapped her in the most heartfelt hug he had given her since childhood. "Thank you, Mama."

"You're welcome, son." She hugged him back.

He shut his eyes and smiled, then pulled away and helped her to sit again.

She sniffled. He retrieved her napkin, which had fallen to the floor, and handed her one of the cookie halves, taking one for himself. "If your advice works out, I'll thank you with a much higher quality of cookies."

On his way out the door he heard the woman supposedly on death's door with lingering, debilitating ailments bellow like a construction worker on a noisy site. "To hell with the cookies! If my advice works out—give me grandchildren!"

Chapter 17

EVERY DIXIE BELLE WORTH
HER SALT IS INSPIRED TO:
*Be careless with your heart. Not hasty and irresponsible
but if the cause is worthwhile, then fearlessly throw
yourself into the fray even if you know it could tear you
apart.*

She had lost her ever-lovin' mind. That's the only
way she could explain it.

A spattering of strangers gaped at her.

Her head spun. She raised her gaze to counteract the dizzying effect of the flashing light from
under the plastic panels of the stage in the hotel
lounge. Karaoke music blared behind her.

"She gonna sing or what?" A bald man in a tan-
and-black sports coat asked the circle of ladies at
his table.

"Shh. She's working up to it." The woman next
to him slapped his hand. The glitter on her Graceland T-shirt flashed as she moved closer to the
candlelight on her table. "Don't mind him, honey,
he's an old poop. Go on with your song."

The smell of stale cigarette smoke stung Rita's

nose. Every eye in the room homed in on her. Despite her brand-new, fit-like-spun-magic-from-a-fairy-godmother red dress, she felt positively naked.

"Go, girl!" Another of the older ladies from the nearby table shouted. A smattering of applause rose to urge Rita on.

"Two, three, four." Under her breath she counted the beats until the crescendo of the chorus. When the music swelled she could swing into the spirit of things with full force.

"Careful now," the waitress cautioned a patron as she handed over a frozen margarita.

"Five, six, seven eight." The chorus came. And went. She bowed her head forward and a strand of her freshly highlighted hair fell across her eyes.

Out in the darkened lounge she heard Jillie whisper, "Do it, Rita."

The only thing Rita wanted to do was run away. Lacey Marie was right. She couldn't do this. She was a stick in the mud. She'd never change and she was stupid to try.

The rhythm of the music came up through Rita's new shoes, but she could not move.

What had she thought? Because she slept with the sexiest man she'd ever met, because a man who could have anyone had wanted her, that made her something special? If she was so special, where was he now?

Her mouth went dry as a desert. Her focus grew bleary. Only her thoughts raced on, keeping pace with the driving beat of the music and her raging pulse.

Will hadn't wanted her for the long term. And even though she had always known and accepted that she didn't need a man to make her complete, damned if she didn't wish the man she loved was standing there now to give her courage.

Loved? Will? As if her pulse hadn't gone haywire enough already, she had to think of *him*, then go and admit to herself how she really felt! Of course she loved him, but she couldn't have him. She had always known that.

Still, she had convinced herself she could take her taste of heaven once and be forever satisfied. Now, having acknowledged her love for Will, she wondered how she would ever be satisfied with any man, with her old life, again?

"You okay, sugar?" Tressie Lynn, the waitress who moments ago had jumped on the stage and dubbed herself the "Miss Tress of Ceremonies" for the evening asked from the side of the stage.

Rita blinked at her, trying to recall the instructions Tressie had given earlier.

"Start with something upbeat that everybody recognizes," she'd suggested. "Set a fun tone for the evening, and that way you won't have to worry about forgetting the words. People will just get carried along no matter what comes out of your mouth."

The only thing Rita feared would come out of her mouth right then was her dinner.

"Jump in anytime, honey." Tressie fiddled with the knobs on the machine. "The words are on the screen if you need them."

"Thanks, I . . ." She tapped one finger to her throat and shot her most pathetic puppy-in-distress look at the woman.

"Got a tickle?"

She tapped harder and bugged her eyes out, hoping to convey that she had suddenly lost her voice entirely.

"Who is gonna tickle her?" the bald man wanted to know.

"Not you," one of the ladies shot back.

"She's got something stuck in her throat," another explained.

"Shut up, you old poop," the Graceland T-shirt lady commanded.

Spontaneous laryngitis, she wanted to shout out. "I have spontaneous laryngitis!" Instead she improvised a dry, feeble cough. She had not taken into account how the microphone would carry the sound.

"I'll say she got something stuck in her throat. It's like a cat with a hairball," baldy announced before tossing back his drink.

The tour-group ladies hushed and shushed and tsk-tsk-tsked his outburst.

So far in her singing debut she had her very own heckler, had become the object of pity to strangers, and had yet to croon a single note! Stupid, stupid. She wanted to get out of there and back to the safety of her dull, take-no-chances life.

"You poor thing." The waitress cut the music.

Rita let out a sigh of thanks for her answered prayer and took a step toward the edge of the stage.

"Here, take a drink of this." The waitress met her with a glass of ice water. "And when you're ready, I'll start the song over again. Remember, relax and enjoy yourself."

Enjoy? She had not come here to enjoy herself. She had come to *prove* herself.

"What she up to now?" the bald man demanded of his table mates.

"Show a little respect," a maternal voice said.

"Shut up, you old poop." *Graceland* took his drink away.

As the cold water flooded her mouth and throat, Rita reviewed her predicament. She had come through so much, and this was her graduation ceremony. If she walked off this stage without squeaking out at least a couple songs, she would walk off a failure. She would be looking at the aftermath of the twister that her friends had unleashed on her—that masculine sexual force named Wild Billy West—and choosing to live in the rubble.

"Don't you dare have put me through everything up till this, then chicken out." Jillie's whisper penetrated the fog in her mind.

However, if she stood her ground and poured her heart into the music, she could go back to Hellon a survivor. She would be safe on the other side of the storm, stronger and with something new to build upon. She put the glass down on the table where Jillie sat at the side of the stage.

Her friend gave her a thumbs-up.

Rita wet her lips and raised the mike in a white-knuckled grip. The opening chords of the perkiest pop tune on the play list vibrated through the plastic panels of the stage floor. She took a deep breath.

The first word came out softer than a baby's sigh. The next wasn't quite that audible. She cleared her throat and wheezed out the last phrase of the opening stanza.

"Louder. I can't hear a damned thing. What is wrong with her anywa—"

"Shut up, you old poop!" the whole crowd chimed in unison.

Shut up. What good advice, Rita couldn't help thinking. Four beats before the next line. That gave just enough time to make a break for it. She looked both ways, saw the perfect spot to lay the microphone down, fixed her gaze on the doors and . . .

A hand took her elbow. Jillie stepped up beside her and belted—nothing else described it better though Rita had heard better noises out of an electric-sander belt—out the next line.

"What are you doing?" Rita whispered.

"Helping a friend."

Her first impulse was to protest. Rita was the solid, dependable one. Rita was the one who stepped up to help. Rita was the one who could be counted upon to hang on and ride out any foolish endeavor on behalf of friendship.

Jillie launched into the chorus with reckless abandon.

This was what Miss Peggy had meant about being careless with your heart. Not hasty and irresponsible, but if the cause is worthwhile, fearlessly throw yourself into the fray even if you knew it could tear you apart.

That's what Rita had done the first time she confronted Will. And what she had failed to do every time since, when she held back just a little because she did not want him to think of her as stupid. Distance and differences were not what had kept her and Will from pursuing anything more meaningful, caution and self-consciousness were.

That and the fact that he did not love her.

He had been her taste of heaven, not meant to last. And though she felt like hell, she would do what she had come to do and deal with her heartache later.

She took Jillie's hand and bent forward so they could share the microphone.

The muggy Memphis summer air got under Will's collar. He yanked his tie loose before he hit the hotel doors. Why he'd gone the suit-and-tie route for this place was beyond him, anyway. Of course he hadn't done it for any *place*. He'd done it for Rita.

What the hell did he hope to accomplish by showing up, anyway? To announce to Rita that his mama thought they loved each other? If he couldn't say it for certain himself, wasn't it just cruel to show up and . . .

And what? he wondered to himself.

Rita had gone to great lengths on more than one occasion to point out his basic flaws. He was selfish and unsettled, the kind of man more available to strangers than to people who cared about him. He thought of all the people in Memphis willing to do him favors, knowing they could count on him in work and socially, but never asking or demanding anything more. He stayed away from Hellon because no one there saw the real man or spoke the hard truth to him, but if he examined his closely crafted life here in Memphis, was it any better?

He looked at the glass door with the starlit parking lot beyond.

"Hey! What are you doing here, big brother?"

His mama would have had his hide if he'd said out loud what he thought just then. Instead he forced his gritted teeth into a big old grin and turned to greet the women he'd come from Hellon to see. Only she wasn't with his sister. "Where's Rita?"

"Still back there." Jillie jerked her thumb over her shoulder, paused then flung her arm out and pointed again.

He stretched out to peer around the corner and down the short corridor. RIVER REVUE LOUNGE glared back at him in gold-painted letters on glossy black doors.

"If you came for the performance of a lifetime, you missed your chance."

"Is Rita done singing already?"

"Once she got started, I couldn't get her to shut up for nothing. You should see her, Will."

"Should I?" He asked it of himself more than to get an opinion.

"Well, you will. She'll be out here in a minute to catch her breath. Between the lights and the stuffiness, you pretty much have to get out for a few minutes before you sing again."

"Since when did you become an expert on lounge singing?"

"Since tonight." Jillie had a lightness about her he hadn't seen in years. "That great performance you missed was me!"

"You? Sang karaoke?"

"And the earth did not open up and swallow me alive! Can you believe it?"

"It's the age of miracles, truly it is. First Mother gave me what seemed at the time to be sound advice, now this."

"Mother! That's why you showed up here tonight?"

"I'm losing my grip on reality, aren't I?" He caught a glimpse of himself in the mirror behind the check-in desk. Tie hanging loose, hair still wet and looking unkempt from his pushing his fingers through it—he looked the part. "It all started when you talked me into working on the Palace."

"Don't be too hard on yourself." Jillie started straightening his tie. "Mama and her nutty talk about following your heart is why I'm on my way right now to try to reconcile things with Paul."

"He finally call you back?"

She nodded. "He admitted he was stupid. I admitted I was stupid."

"Ahh, a match made in heaven." He took over adjusting his attire.

"I reckon." She laughed. "We decided that we were too pathetic to turn loose on other unsuspecting people and ought to be together. Besides, having already seen the worst about each other, we still want to be together."

"Good for you." He kissed her forehead. "I mean that."

"Thanks. I have to run. You going to stick around a while and hear Rita sing?"

"I *was*."

"Second thoughts?"

"You're her best friend. What do you think I should do?"

"Do you care about her?"

"Yes."

"Do you love her?"

He clenched his jaw.

"I don't know, then, Will." She lifted her shoulders, then eased them down again. "If you want to hear her sing, she's on the list to do another number. She's right after Skippy and Daphne, the fun girls of the senior citizens' Tennessee bus tour, doing their tribute to disco."

"Hard act to follow."

"Rita can do it. She can do anything if she gets the right encouragement and lets herself try."

"I know." He shut his eyes. "She's amazing."

"She's been through a lot."

"That a warning?"

"That's . . . something to keep in mind." She smoothed his jacket sleeve, fit her hand into his, and gave it a squeeze. When she moved away, she glanced over her shoulder. "This is a warning—she just came out of the lounge."

He stiffened, his gut in knots.

"I'm headed that-a-way." She motioned toward the hotel parking lot. "You?"

"Are you kidding? Wild Billy run from a confrontation?"

"*Wild Billy?*" She arched her sketched-in-place eyebrow.

He had said that, hadn't he? Funny, after the talk with his mother, the nickname no longer wounded him, even if it did still sting a little. "Go see Paul."

"I know whatever you decide about Rita will be the right thing."

He gave her a quick hug and sent her on her way wondering if she understood how her faith in him had both humbled him and made him want to beat his head against a brick wall?

With that in his mind and his chest gripped with conflicting emotions, he turned to greet Rita.

Chapter 18

Rita put her ear to the lounge door. A shy businessman from Philadelphia, who until a couple of songs ago hadn't so much as raised his eyes from his club soda and pretzels, was tearing up the room with a spirited rendition of "Heartbreak Hotel."

She smiled. She certainly didn't have the lock on using music as therapy. She took a deep breath and it filled her with a sense of growing bigger, better, stronger. She had done it. Closing her eyes, she savored the moment. No matter what she had to face from here on out, she would do it with a renewed sense of purpose and poise and . . .

"Hello, Rita."

"Good gravy!"

"I beg your pardon?"

She opened her eyes. "It *is* you."

"In the flesh."

"In the flesh," the phrase buzzed softly over her lips. "I can see that but . . . but why are you here?"

"I don't know if I mentioned this, but I live in Memphis."

That's no answer, she wanted to shout at him. Oh, hell, when had she ever had the nerve to shout in public, much less at Will? "Yes, but you're supposed to be in Hellon."

"If I was in Hellon, how could I see you in this sexy red dress?"

Her dress. She'd had so much fun onstage she'd completely forgotten the makeover. This was Will's first glimpse of the new Rita. Well, the old Rita in new-and-improved packaging.

"Rita, I have to tell you . . ." Will took his time looking her over.

If you could feel a man's gaze, she decided then and there standing in the hallway of that less-than-elegant hotel, it would feel hot. And steamy. She liked it.

"This . . . dress is . . ."

"Too much?" She flitted her fingers over the neckline and touched skin instead of fabric. "Or maybe too little?"

"It's just right."

"Maybe if I lost a few pounds?"

"No. It's perfect. *You're* perfect."

"I'd ask if lunacy runs in your family, but . . . I don't want to know."

He grinned. "Perfect *and* smart."

"Not perfect, and I don't know about smart, that doesn't sound like me most of the time, but I certainly am curious."

"Another trait I admire."

"Why are you here, Will?"

"Disappointed to see me?"

She rubbed the tip of her thumb over her lower lip. Disappointed to see Will? Never. Terrified, perhaps. And thrilled.

He shifted his weight, and his jacket fell open.

The force of his presence, the warmth of his body, the width of his shoulders, and the depth of his eyes, in less than an instant she took it all in. Will had followed her to Memphis. What did that mean?

He stuck one hand in his pocket and cocked his head, "Rita?"

"I . . . uh. I thought you had to take care of your mother."

"She's the reason I'm here."

"Oh, dear, I hope nothing bad has happened. Jillie went to—"

"Mother's fine, and I saw Jillie going out."

"That's good."

"*You're* good." He straightened up, his head bowed and his eyes stormy. "You always think of others first. You worry about them. You can't wait to find out how you can get in there and help."

"I thought you were reciting my good traits, Will, not the things you find frustrating."

"Did I say I found those frustrating?"

"Those were the very things you worked to try

to get me to change." She lowered her lashes, hoping to convey a teasing playfulness. She'd never had much practice at flirting or acting coy with a man.

"I was wrong, then. Don't change that about yourself, Rita. It's what makes you perfect, and wise, and make-a-man-crazy-with-wanting sexy."

He made her feel that way, and she wanted more than anything to do something about it. "This isn't exactly the kind of place for talk like that, is it?"

"I don't know. It seems like a damn fine place to remind you of how good you are." He fixed his gaze on the lounge door.

The last strains of "Heartbreak Hotel" resonated through the thin walls.

"Did you . . . did you hear me sing?"

"Yeah." He edged in closer and skimmed his fingers along the side of her neck. "Once."

She shivered.

He smiled.

"Once?" Her whole body tingled with the memory of lying naked in his arms, singing for him alone. The intimacy of that performance had given their lovemaking a taste and texture, a substance she had never known with any man before. And doubted she ever would again. Yet, she could not trust he remembered things the same way. "Once tonight?"

He shook his head.

"Good, huh?" She wasn't asking about her singing.

"Incredible."

"Would you..." She bowed her head. The power rush from singing onstage acted like a kick in the head. It knocked all common sense clean out of her. She would never have dared ask otherwise. But, dammit, the man had come to Memphis. They were in a hotel and... "Would you like for me to ... sing for you again?"

He tipped his head toward the lounge door. "After the disco twins?"

"Is that what you came for, the ... singing?"

"No."

In light of everything between them, everything tonight represented, she should have welcomed his bluntness. She didn't.

He took her hand. "I didn't even know the disco twins would be here tonight."

"Funny." Her fingers fit between his and she pressed their palms and wrists together. "Why did *you* show up here tonight?"

He looked at the lounge door, his brow creased.

The music pounded around them as someone muddled his way through an old Hank Williams cheating song.

"How long before you go on again?"

"It's just for fun." She shook her head. "If I miss my turn, they'll work me in someplace else. If I don't go back in at all, no one would notice."

"I find that impossible to believe."

"I have a room upstairs."

"I have a house across town."

"Mine's closer."

"Tempting." Will studied the way her fingers entwined with his and could all but picture their bodies fitting together just as easily, skin to skin, pulse to pulse, naked and intimate. "Very tempting."

She dipped her head so she could meet his gaze. "But?"

"Yeah, there is a 'but.' "

"I guess I should have known." She pulled her hand away.

"The thing is, Rita, I think we need to talk."

"That can't be good, can it?"

"Hmm?"

"Man's offered no-strings-attached sex, and he prefers to talk."

"I'm beginning to think that's a myth."

"That men don't like to talk?"

"That there is such a thing as no-strings-attached sex."

"I thought we were living proof that it exists, thrives even."

"Rita, look me in the eye and tell me that our making love didn't tangle up your heartstrings just a little."

She looked into her open hand, the one he had been holding only seconds ago, and brushed her fingers over her palm.

"At the very least tug at your conscience some?"

He only knew that she nodded her agreement when the loose curls of her new hairdo bobbed.

"Then don't you think we should talk instead of jumping into bed again?"

She settled her back against the wall, looking all wise and wistful, and sexier than the law should allow. "You're not wild at all, really, are you?"

"You mean outside the bedroom?"

"Yeah." She wet her lips. Her very-un-Rita-like high heels rasped over the patterned carpet. "You're not really wild at all, outside of the bedroom *or* outside the narrow box that people in Hellon have put you in."

"No," he whispered. "I'm not wild. Not when it comes to things that really matter."

He could tell that she wanted to ask him if she was one of those things that really mattered.

"I noticed a couple chairs in the corner of the lobby," he said, before she could ask him a damned thing. "Shall we go over there to talk?"

"Is that why you came all this way tonight?" She walked with him to a pair of blue-green chairs, which sat at angled toward each other. "To talk?"

Why had he come tonight? Now that the initial fire of his mother's influence had died down, he could not say with unerring certainty. He waited for her to take a seat, then settled into the other chair. "I can't rightly say why I came, Rita."

"Well, it's not like you were in the neighborhood."

"No. But being back in the neighborhood— being in Memphis again—it does put things in a different perspective for me."

"Things do tend to lose their rosy glow when you strip away the magical spell of the Pig Rib Palace, don't they?"

He chuckled, but it did not lighten his mood to do so. "You're not making this easy on me, Rita."

"I tried making it easy, Will. In fact I think I went out of my way to make things as easy on you as possible."

He rubbed his forehead. "And that's only made things more difficult."

"You're scaring me, Will."

"Scaring you? How?"

"Because you're building up to something. I can feel it stirring and twitching under the surface."

"Twitching, huh?" He scratched at his scalp. "Maybe I should see if there's an ointment for that."

"You know exactly what I mean." She aimed a no-nonsense Southern woman of substance glare at him. "There's something you've been trying to contain inside you for a long time."

The longest time. He folded his hands and kept his thoughts to himself.

"And right now you're this close to letting it loose on me."

"*That's* what I want to avoid, Rita." The power of this one truth made his voice go low, hoarse with emotion. His secrets were not so deep nor his sins so desperate that he dared not share them with anyone. Quite the contrary, he'd had a charmed life—a damned charmed life. Unloading his petty grievances on anyone, especially Rita, was not an option. "I'm not going to dump a lifetime's worth of pain at your doorstep. You don't have to be scared of that happening."

"You've got it wrong."

"How so?

"I'm scared you *won't* do it."

"What?"

"Because you don't respect me enough or revere my opinion enough to trust me with your pain, Will. To trust me to help you the way you have helped me—to move beyond the past."

"I don't want to do that to you, Rita."

"You can."

"I can. Of course I *can*. And be like everyone else that gravitates into your life and expects you to help them hold their worlds together."

"Will, haven't you been paying attention? There is no everybody else."

"What?"

"Jillie was the last one left. Pernel has moved on with his life, Lacey Marie has grown up, Cozie has up and created a whole alternative universe of activity that doesn't involve me in the least."

"And Jillie finally decided to throw out the poor-pitiful-rich-girl routine and take responsibility for her own actions."

"That just leaves me." She held her hands out.

"What are you looking for? A project?" He smiled as he said it, but the words drove deep. Is that what he feared? Becoming Rita's pet project? It would be so easy to let himself slide into that role. But that wouldn't be moving on really, would it?

"What I'm looking for is a little honesty, Will."

"You want honesty? From me? *About me?* You have that, Rita. You had it six years ago when you had me pegged. I am a selfish bastard. One who never deserved any *other* name ever given him, nor any other honor—from town hero to having that precious baby boy christened as my son."

"Will, is that what's troubling you?"

"You said it once before when you said you knew what I wanted, what everybody wants. Remember?"

"I said you wanted your life to have meaning?"

"Yes."

"And that you wanted someone to miss you and mourn for you."

"And to be really good at something, to hear praise for my work and know it's earned."

"And you don't think you've earned the high opinions that people have of you?"

"I haven't."

"You've earned mine."

He shook his head. "That from a woman who told me to my face that if I were a changed man, my life would be different."

"I was hasty and unfair."

"You were right."

"Maybe then, but not now."

"Nothing has changed since then."

"Do you honestly believe that?"

He sat back in the chair, his hands curved over its overstuffed arms.

She sighed. "For a man who came to talk, you're sure not saying too much."

"Rita? You out there, honey?" From around the corner and down the corridor a woman's voice called out. "Skippy and Daphne are winding it up. Come back in if you're going to sing."

"Go on." He got up from the chair and offered his hand.

"Are you going to stay and listen?"

"I'd love to see you on that stage." One hand on her back, he guided her inside the lounge without making any promises.

They slipped inside the door just as a pair of women wearing sequin-spangled jeans and satin tops waved and headed off the stage.

"Are they just darling or what?" A woman in a waitress uniform delicately clapped her fingers against her wrist while holding the microphone. "You did good, girls."

The women took another bow from their seats.

The applause swelled again.

Rita tried to say something to him, but he motioned like he couldn't hear it. It was a jerky thing to do, but then he'd warned her more than once not to expect better of him.

"I swear, y'all have more energy than a weekend crowd!"

Rita pointed to the front of the room.

He gave her a push in that direction.

"There are plenty of seats," she said.

"I'll stand."

She looked at him. In the darkness of the room she found his eyes and let her gaze sink in.

"Okay, we're geared up tighter than an eight-day clock in here tonight so let's not waste no more time." The waitress looked at a slip of paper in her hand as she worked with the karaoke machine. "Let's welcome our next singer up here—*again*!"

For one moment he thought Rita would say something more to him, then it passed. She sighed, nodded, and made her way toward the stage.

He watched her go, unsure of how he felt. Stirring and twitching just below the surface—Rita's simple interpretation had been so apt.

His mother had spoken of love. But Rita had spoken of trust, of letting him lean on her. He had come to Memphis because he missed Rita. But despite her kind words and sweet flirtations tonight, she had come to make a break from him.

"Rita's picked a hard one this time," the woman working the machine said. "She's going to need all the support y'all can conjure up."

Even if he did love her, which he just could not make himself admit, if she did not return the feeling, what would his coming here accomplish? And if she *did* love him?

He held his hand up to signal a passing waitress so he could order a drink.

"What can I get you?" The redhead held her tray on her hip between them and turned so he could speak into her ear.

"Just a beer."

The small but exuberant crowd let up a cheer.

"You going to sit?" The woman blocking his view of the stage flung her arm out toward the many empty tables.

"Rather stand, thanks. Not sure if I'm staying."

She looked him up and down once, probably trying to decide if he just needed to get his nerve up before hopping on that stage and cutting loose with a song.

He stuffed his hand in his pocket and did his damnedest to look like the anti-Elvis. "My beer?"

"Back in a jiff."

"Welcome Rita back on our stage tonight!"

"This is going to be my last song this evening."

The redhead pivoted and joined the rest of the room in a collective protest.

Will pressed his back to the wall and waited. His pulse hammered out the seconds before the waitress moved on and Rita came into full view.

"You've all been so kind and so patient."

Rita—in red. Patience was not the attribute the sight inspired in him.

"Well, not *all* of you." Rita pointed out into the room.

How could she have seen him all the way back here? How could she have known . . .

A whole table of women jabbed and pointed at the lanky fellow who sat right in Rita's line of vision.

Even from where Will stood he could see the

man blush straight to his hairline—which ended just above the back of his neck.

Everything isn't always about you. Hadn't his mother just reminded him of that?

"This has been such a positive experience for me," Rita said into the microphone, looking like an old pro at handling the spotlight.

It *had* been positive. Will could see that. Her eyes sparkled, her skin glowed. He wasn't crazy about the new hairstyle and sensed Jillie's hand in that. Still, the overall effect of that red dress caressing Rita's breasts, clinging to her hips had its own positive effect—positively uplifting, in fact. He managed a tight grin at that and flexed his hands at his sides.

Rita pulled her shoulders straight. "I came here tonight to see if I could even do this."

"You can do it all right, Rita, honey." The man in a tan-and-black coat waved his arm. "If you'd just stop yakking an' get around to it!"

"Oh, Clive!" Rita laughed.

Was it Will's imagination, or was there a certain sadness beneath her smile? If he had ever done anything to cause her sadness . . .

The ladies at Clive's table crossed their arms and aimed an angry wave of killer looks in the man's direction.

Clive half rose from his seat in a bow toward the stage as he said, "I know. Shut up, you old poop."

Everyone laughed.

Even walking in so late and standing in the

very back, he could feel Rita's influence on the mood of the crowd.

The waitress brought his beer, and he paid for it.

"The point is that y'all may not know it, but I learned so much on this stage tonight. Everything from the real words to 'Mack the Knife' to the truth about myself and the relationships that are important to me."

Will lowered his drink without taking a sip.

"After this I can go back to my hometown and do what I have to do."

"Like what?" Will asked himself quietly.

"Starting with putting a karaoke stage in my restaurant."

While his brain immediately set about calculating how to make that a reality, his heart sank at her intentions. He might act a fool sometimes, but he did have his flashes of insight. Renovating the restaurant to the basic standards was his idea of a smart move. Anything less, and it would trap Rita there, unable to sell or to increase revenue enough to free her from worrying over every nickel and dime. Anything more and she'd have to hang on to it longer to repay incurred debt and start showing a profit. Add in promoting even an amateur floor show—she'd never leave.

Not that she had to leave Hellon to be happy. That much he could admit. It was not the hell on earth he had remembered it being. It had grown and changed, letting much of the old ways that held it back fall by the wayside. Could he say the same of himself? Who was he to judge a whole town, then?

"And not stopping until I put my heart and all I've got into . . . all that I go after." She looked to the back of the room.

If she saw him there, he did not know. He did nothing to draw her attention or reassure her that he was there and he had heard her plans.

"And so if you'll indulge me one last time."

"If only I could." He set his untouched beer on the nearest unoccupied table. He had not come there to talk. Or to find out if Rita loved him or if he loved her. Those were pointless endeavors. He had come to say good-bye.

What else could he do? He could profess his love for her, but to what end? Who would that benefit but himself? He would find in Rita a loyal, loving, unquestioning woman with yet another weight on her shoulders, another person depending on her to be his anchor.

"I want to do now the song I came here tonight all the way from Hellon, Tennessee, to sing."

The familiar opening of Patsy Cline's classic "Crazy" swelled from the machine by the stage.

Rita bowed her head.

Will gritted his teeth, trying not to swear. He blindly made his way to the door. He had to get out. If he heard her sing, he knew he would never leave. And he had to leave for Rita's sake.

He pushed into the lighted hallway outside the lounge just as Rita began the heart-wrenching song about being loved and cast aside. He rubbed his eyes as her voice sank deeper and deeper into his soul.

Tomorrow he would make a few last calls. He'd set her up with the best people in the business to finish the job at the Palace—and put in that stage or anything else she wanted.

What Rita wanted was the thing. Letting Rita move on and rebuild a life without him weighing her down was the first totally unselfish act he'd done in a very long time and his last hope at finding the redemption he'd needed for so long.

He would not stay now and fail her.

Chapter 19

EVERY DIXIE BELLE WHO'S
HAD ENOUGH FINDS OUT:
A girl's best footwear might just be her walking shoes.

She knew he wouldn't stay. Why *would* he stay?

Rita stepped into the elevator, pushed the button, and slipped out of her shoes. The elevator lurched upward, and the sway of her red dress drew her eyes to her distorted reflection in the polished chrome doors. Poor, pitiful, plain Rita. The girl who thought putting a karaoke machine and a few new booths in Pernel's Pig Rib Palace would change everything.

No wonder Will didn't stick around. He probably had to leave to keep from laughing out loud at her.

Safe, sane, and secure outcomes, that's what she wanted for her life. Those, she had thought, promised the key to stability. They were her plan for self-sufficiency, her protection against loneliness, and her path to happiness.

Ding. The elevator stopped two floors below hers.

She had clung to her standpoints with a single-mindedness that had pushed aside all other options. And look at what it had gotten her. Did she feel powerful? Had she staved off loneliness? Was she happy?

"No, no, and no," she whispered, as the door slid open.

The woman waiting to get on waved her not to hold the doors as she retreated from the elevator's threshold.

Manners dictated that Rita explain she wasn't shooing the woman off with her stream of negatives. *Good manners before bad temper.* Well, to hell with that. She jabbed the CLOSE DOOR button, and the elevator pitched upward again.

Moving on. How many people had tried to tell her *that* was the key? She eyed her blurred image again. "Work with Wild Billy. Go to college. Sell the Palace. Do something with your hair."

She leaned in closer. That last one she could have done without.

Ding. The doors whooshed apart again.

Ignoring the startled faces of the people waiting, who found her bending forward with her nose just inches from the opening, Rita stood up. Taking a shoe in each hand, she held one up like a royal wave and strode off toward her room.

Will hadn't stuck around. Well, he was intended to be the tornado, the thing to get her life going again. No one can live in the eye of the storm. Rita knew that too well because she had done it too long.

She had let her friends' lives circulate around her, taking far too much comfort from their chaos. She needed her own chaos, and Wild Billy West had brought that to her. It was right he should go. The work of putting her life back together, of finally following in her mama's wobbling footsteps, was Rita's alone to make.

Yes, her mama's footsteps. Following her mother's example by standing on her own two feet, not by walking away from the people she loved. She would always be there for her friends and family, but she would no longer put her own life on hold for them.

She unlocked her door, went inside, and threw her high heels on the bed. There, all on her own in a big, strange town where no one needed her to hold the world together, she vowed that the next set of footwear she'd put on would be her walking shoes.

"You're no fun anymore." Dina, an ex-Miss Arkansas, a constant fixture on the beauty-pageant circuit and a sometime dinner date of Will's pushed her food away practically untouched.

"What do you expect out of a selfish, donkey-headed bastard?" He considered pushing the plate right back under her upturned nose. How he ever put up with her ordering the most expensive thing on a menu so she could take one bite and groan over how much she'd have to diet to make up for it, he'd never understand.

"Don't talk that way about yourself." She reached across the candlelit table and put her hand on his.

Okay, so he had to pay a fortune for her not to eat, at least he could count on the woman to feed his ego.

"When you call yourself things like that, it doesn't reflect well on me." Her hesitation before she laughed made him realize she was only partly joking.

"Thanks for the support." He pulled away from her touch, picked up his fork, then set it down again and rubbed his forehead.

"You used to be a lot more fun." She put her hands in her lap.

This was her "I'm pouting at you and you better *say* or *do* or *buy* something to rectify that immediately if you want to get lucky tonight" look.

"Yeah, well." He tossed his napkin onto the table. "I used to be a lot of things." Like satisfied with meaningless sex with women so skinny they don't make a dent in my mattress and so self-involved they don't leave an impression on my heart. "You ready to go?"

"So soon?" She ran her finger along the rim of the wineglass. "What do you have in mind?"

"Making an early night of it." He signaled for the check.

"Oh?" She leaned over the table, her breasts falling forward in her scrap of a dress. "Maybe you are still fun after all."

"Maybe you were right the first time." He handed a credit card to the waiter without looking at the check. "Listen, Dina, this . . ."

A tiny tremor from his pager interrupted his train of thought.

"What is it?"

"Hang on." He held his hand up as he pressed the light to better read the message. "It's my sister. She wants me to call her. Do you mind?"

"Go ahead, call her back." She turned in her chair and pulled a small silver object from her beaded handbag. "Here, use my phone even. Make the call right from the table. Don't mind me. It's not like you're actually all here participating with me on this date anyway."

The guilt trap. It set his teeth on edge. Was there any woman in his life who did not employ it to get her way with him?

Rita. The answer sprang into his mind so fast he had no time to counteract the effect of her memory on his emotions. That happened all too often, but he had decided he could learn to live with it. What other choice did he have?

"If you don't mind, then." He took her phone, oozing charm like he had no clue she had only offered it to try to manipulate him. "I really need to call her back. It might be about my mother."

"You and your family." Dina rolled her eyes. "You are so tied to them. It's really not becoming in a man your age."

"You calling me a mama's boy?" He flipped the phone open, laughing at the very notion.

"Worse. I'm saying you're a family man."

"Me?" He laughed again, only this time the humor wasn't so heartfelt. "I guess it may seem like that since I spent so much time home this summer."

"Home? Since when did you start calling Hooterville home?"

Good question. When had Hellon become home again to him? He wasn't sure. Still, sitting here in this overpriced, soulless restaurant with a woman who cared only about the level of fun he could provide her, it sounded so right. "The town's name is Hellon. It's where I was raised and where my family still lives. Why shouldn't I think of it as my home?"

"I don't care if it's Mayberry and Andy, Aunt Bea, Opie, and the gang are all your next of kin. You've never thought of anyplace but Memphis as home as long as I've known you."

Memphis? Home? He punched in Jillie's private number. "Look, maybe I just reconnected with my roots a little more lately. What's so bad about that?"

"Lately?" She rolled her glass in her hand so that the wine glowed in the candlelight. "When we first met you led me to believe any ties you had with your family were . . . tenuous at best."

The phone rang in his ear. "So?"

"So? It's hard enough for a girl to compete for a man's attention with all the other beautiful women around."

"It's not a competition." If it was, it would be one competition where a woman like Dina couldn't even place as runner-up. Not against his family and certainly not compared to . . .

"Hello?" Jillie picked up on the third ring.

He knew she would. Will smiled. Mama had a rule that no lady ever answered the phone sooner than the third or later than the fifth ring. Something about perception and manners. "Hey, girl. What's up?"

"You *have* to check on your mother tonight," Dina grumbled.

"Will? Wow, that was fast."

"I thought something might be wrong with Mama."

"Just now coming to *that* conclusion?" Jillie sighed. "No, Mama's right as rain."

"Would that be acid rain?" They shared a laugh.

"A week ago you had to cancel a date because your sister rolled into town *uninvited*," Dina droned on, making sure she hit the highlights loud enough for even Jillie to hear. "Insisting you meet some man named Paul."

"Who are you with? Where are you? Are you doing something important?"

"I often ask myself those same questions."

What he'd intended as a quip rang quietly poignant in his own ears. He cleared his throat. "That's nothing. Go on, why did you call?"

"Nothing? Are you referring to me as *nothing*?" Dina slapped her napkin down.

"Would you hang on just a sec, Jillie?" He covered the mouthpiece. "Can we have this conversation later—like when I'm not already having *another* conversation?"

His date bristled the way that only a gorgeous, pampered Southern belle can. It was an art form in itself and often left lesser men trembling and bewildered. Will skewered one of her broiled shrimp with his fork and took a bite, saying as he ate, "I won't be long."

Her eyes narrowed to slits. "You are not the same man I remember having such a good time with last spring."

He started to argue that point, then stopped and looked at the phone. He looked at the food that last spring he thought was the finest in the city but which he now found bland and pretentious. Then he looked at the woman across from him who looked like she'd just fallen out of the pages of a magazine and would just as easily fall into bed with him, expecting nothing more than a good time from it. All he could really see, all he had been able to focus on these last six weeks since he'd returned to Memphis, was Rita.

"You know, you're right, Dina. I am not the same man."

The waiter placed the receipt in front of Will.

Dina gave the young man a sly once-over before he got away. "What do they say? The first step in getting help is admitting you need it?" She beamed him an aren't-I-clever smile.

Still holding the phone, he grunted and pulled a pen from the pocket inside his jacket. "The man you remember from last summer would have hung up on his sister and spent the rest of the evening trying to get back in your good graces—not to mention your bed."

"That's still not an impossibility, provided you're willing to spoil me with a lot of—"

"Bullshit."

"I heard that," Jillie said, even though she was still waiting for him to talk to her again. "What's going on there, Will?"

"Sorry, Jillie, hang on just a second longer. I was having a . . . moment of clarity."

"That's not boy-code for something I don't want to know about, is it?"

"No. Just bear with me a little bit longer." He lowered the mouthpiece.

Dina flipped her hair back so fast he marveled it didn't give her whiplash. "What did you just say to me?"

"You heard me. This game between us. It's nothing more than a big steaming pile of—"

"Wasn't everything to your liking, sir?" The waiter, who had come back for the signed receipt looked very concerned that Will might use the word again.

Will smiled. "Everything was fine. Or will be when you call the lady a taxi."

"A taxi? You can't just send me home in a taxi."

"If you prefer the bus . . ."

She stood and held her hand out. "That's my phone."

"I'll wrap this up before you leave."

"A gentleman would drive me home."

Will stood, too. "Good. If you find a gentleman hanging around, that'll save me the cab fare."

She yanked her arm away when he tried to take it to escort her out of the dining room.

"Don't act all high-and-mighty with me now. You've taken your fair share of late-night cab rides both to and from my house; you're just mad because this one was my idea."

She gave him an icy glare over her shoulder. "You really aren't the same man."

"No, I'm not. And I do apologize for not taking you home, but you see I'm heading in the other direction."

"Your house is not in the opposite direction of mine."

"No, but my home is."

"Your . . . ?"

"Jillie?"

"Uh-huh?"

"I'm guessing at this point you didn't page me for anything urgent."

Dina whisked past him to the ladies' room.

"No, I . . . I . . . well, I shouldn't have even

bothered you really. Knowing how you left things here and all."

"Is this about Rita?"

"Given that you told me not to bring up 'that name' I was going to say it's about the Palace."

"Is something wrong?"

"No, it's just . . . well, what with the grand opening tomorrow and Rita . . ."

The taxi pulled up front. "Okay, hon, I have to go. Whatever you have to tell me, I hope it can wait."

"How long?"

"Say, ninety minutes, give or take?"

"You're coming to Hellon?"

"Should I come out to the house first or—"

"Go straight to Rita's, you might still catch her there."

"Catch her? What are you—"

"Bye-bye, Billygoat. I can't stand here blabbing. I need to go make sure Rita doesn't run for cover."

"Run for cover?"

"Yeah, sounds like her very own tornado is blowing back into town."

"Have I done the right thing?" Rita asked.

"I *have* done the right thing." Cozie's voice seemed to boom in the bare-walled kitchenette. "Remember, you are what you say you are."

"Then I am . . ." Rita stared at the few boxes of things she planned to take with her from her old apartment. "Out of here."

"Good for you." Cozie came up from behind and wrapped both long arms around her in a welcome hug. She laid her cheek against the side of Rita's head. "Did you make one last sweep of the place to make sure you're not leaving anything you want to keep?"

What could she have left here? The idea of walking through this room, dredging up the memories of the summer gone by, did not sit well. It was never a home to her. She had left most of her things in storage when Pernel's hasty sale of their old house had forced her into this cramped place.

"You do it, please? I'm afraid if I head anywhere but for that door, it will take a backhoe to get me out of here."

"You got it. But you know, even if you did leave some belongings behind, I think the new landlords wouldn't mind you coming back now and then."

"Careful what you wish for," Rita warned, as her friend headed off toward the bedroom.

"Rita? Cozie? Y'all still up there?"

"Jillie?" Rita went to the stairway door. "What are you doing here? Are you lost?"

"Lost?" Jillie's beautiful curls bounced as she climbed the steps.

"The grand reopening isn't until tomorrow morning."

"I know that."

"Did you also know that people are working here?" Rita put her shoulder to the doorframe. "If you come up, you may have to lift a carton or tote a suitcase back down."

"I'll risk it." Jillie pressed by, taking long enough to eyeball Rita's softer haircut and new color—which was actually her old color. "Where's Cozette?"

"Right here." She emerged from the other room with Rita's old Dixie Belle Duchess crown in her hand. "Rita, don't forget this. You left it hanging on the vanity mirror."

"Thanks." She took it and set it on top of her purse. "Well, one more load in the car and . . ."

"You're not driving to Memphis tonight, are you?"

"Well, I was. Just to take a load of things to the new place. I'll be back first thing tomorrow in plenty of time for the ribbon-cutting ceremony."

"Oh, but you don't want to go tonight."

"Jillie, Rita's on the brink of a whole new adventure. College in Memphis, a new apartment . . . why should she hang around Hellon another minute longer than she has to?"

"Be . . . cause . . . because . . ." Jillie's dark eyes darted back and forth. "Um, because . . ."

Cozie put one hand on her hip and braced the other against the counter. "Yeah, we got that part."

Rita crossed her arms. "Jillie, what are you up to?"

"Not a thing. Not one damn thing, Miss Suspicious. Can't a person feel . . . can't she . . . can't I . . ."

"Oh. I get it." Cozie pushed off from the counter

and put her hand on Jillie's shoulder. "Without sarcasm you're virtually speechless, aren't you?"

Jillie glared at the older woman.

"Don't you get it, Rita? Your oldest friend in the world just isn't quite ready for you to leave."

"Is that it, Jillie?"

She nodded her agreement. "That'll do."

"What this calls for is some kind of grand gesture. Something we can take away with us—to mark the occasion and celebrate the conclusions of what proved to be a life-altering summer." Cozie spread her hands wide.

"We're having a party tomorrow," Rita reminded her.

"Not a party, a *ceremony*."

Jillie slashed her hand through the air. "I refuse to dance naked in the moonlight."

Naked in the moonlight. The memories flooded back of joking with Cozie, Jillie, and Miss Peggy, then of the tender time with Will. Rita swallowed. Her eyelids fluttered to hold back the promise of tears. She could cry her eyes out all the way to Memphis and every night after she got there if that's what it took. Tonight, Cozie was right. They needed ceremony, they needed to celebrate. "Jillie, why don't you go see if your mama will join us?"

"My mother? Dancing in the moonlight? She'll never do that, even in her best pegnoir, much less buck nekkid."

"I wouldn't be too sure." Cozie laughed.

"Maybe she won't dance, but she will drink champagne." Rita wiggled her eyebrows. "Go get her. Cozie, you go downstairs and steal a bottle of you know what from the kitchen."

As they scrambled to their missions, Jillie asked, "What are you going to do?"

Rita plunked the glittering tiara on her head and smiled. "I am going to finish loading my car. That way when we all meet in the back parking lot—so nobody can see us and spread the word we're up to no good—I will be ready to march headlong into my new life."

"Well, we've toasted everything but marshmallows, what now, girls?" Miss Peggy, who was indeed wearing her best pegnoir as Jillie had roused her from an early bedtime, waited for a refill from Cozette.

"Think you've drunk enough to dance, Mama?"

"Who needs to drink for that?" Miss Peggy spread her arms and swayed gracefully from side to side.

They all laughed.

It felt good to laugh. It had been a while for Rita, ever since . . . "I want to thank you all for coming out here with me tonight. I needed this."

"I needed this, too," Miss Peggy announced. "No one ever comes to my door and invites me to come out under the stars anymore. Thank you girls for including a foolish old lady in your moment." Hardly half a heartbeat went by before she added, "And if my daughter tries to tack 'Mama you're not that old' onto my charming old and foolish lady remark, I will chase her through the street of Hellon with my cane flailing."

"I was going to say you're not that *foolish*, but now . . ." Jillie drew her mother into a sideways hug. "Oh, hell, you're really not near as foolish as you pretend to be and nowhere near as foolish as I used to think you were."

"Don't you dare make me cry, young lady." Miss Peggy sniffled.

"You're all going to make me cry." Since Rita expected to drive later that night, then turn around and come back at the crack of dawn, she had had only a few sips to drink. Still, her head was light and she felt warm in ways that had nothing to do with alcohol. She adjusted the tiara on her head and tipped her chin up. "Thank you again for this fitting end to an . . . interesting summer."

"To all the summers yet to come, may they be as . . . memorable." Miss Peggy lifted her champagne flute.

Rita's pulse quickened. She didn't think she could survive a summer more memorable than this. Of course, she was game to try. That much had changed about her.

"To summers." Cozie's glass joined Miss Peggy's in the circle. "And to new endeavors—for all of us."

"To new endeavors," they echoed.

And Rita's stomach knotted tighter.

"To caring friends," Jillie stepped up.

A car's headlights swerved across the front of

the Palace, and tires crunched on the gravel drive.

"Who'd be driving up at this time of night?" Cozie started to move out of their circle, but Jillie caught her arm and pulled her back.

"To caring friends," she started again.

Rita drew in her breath and held it.

"And careless hearts."

The car door slammed.

Rita curled her fingers around the narrow flute and put it to her chest. "No! You didn't . . ."

"And the wild winds that rearrange the best-laid plans." Jillie clinked the rim of her glass to Rita's. "I think you've got company, girl, and nowhere left to run for cover."

Chapter 20

EVERY DIXIE BELLE WHO LOVES
HER MAN LEARNS AT LAST:
He apologized, explained himself, and said he loved you.
Only a damned fool would ask for anything more.

"I can't believe you drove over here at this time of night expecting . . . well, heaven only knows what you were expecting." Rita's voice carried down the stairwell as he walked behind her.

He considered telling her to save it until they got all the way upstairs and could shut the door but he doubted she would take the advice kindly. He also held no illusion that the threesome who had met him in the dark parking lot, then rushed him upstairs after a retreating Rita, would let a little thing like doors keep them from listening in for whatever morsel they could hear.

"I can't believe you're here now, tonight. The timing is just so . . ." She made one of those female sounds of utter aggravation, a mix of a groan, a moan, and a sigh pressed through clenched teeth. "I just can't believe it."

"And I can't believe . . ."

At the top of the stairs she turned and flipped on the light in the kitchen.

He stopped a scant three treads down from her and just took in the sight. He had not seen her in six weeks, had not spoken to her. And here she was.

She took his breath way.

"And I can't believe," he said as he moved up another step and reached out, "that you are wearing this thing again."

"Oh, I forgot about that." Her hand went to the sparkling crown to remove it.

He stopped her. "Don't. It becomes you."

"An old beauty-pageant crown? I don't think so."

"I was thinking more of a princess or—"

"A goddess?" She narrowed one eye, daring him to cross the line with her.

He took the next step up so there were only inches between them.

"Thought we determined that goddesses did their outdoor frolicking buck nekkid."

The line of her mouth was grim, but there was a wavering deep in her lovely eyes. "When you look at me like that I *feel* naked."

He wanted to touch her hair, her cheek, to take her hand. He grabbed the banister instead. "Rita, I . . ."

"Did you want to come in to talk or what?"

He wanted to "or what." He wanted to "or what" with her until the whole town buzzed with gossip about their staying locked in Rita's apartment for days on end. He wanted to "or what" with her until neither of them could move another muscle and both of them understood that they truly belonged together.

"Well?" She tipped her head.

"I'd like for us to talk."

She moved aside and motioned him to come in.

The place looked wrong.

She flipped on the lone light over the kitchen table.

It illuminated the familiar shabby rug, walls, and furnishings. Everything as he remembered it. But somehow it all seemed so impersonal now. Empty.

He glanced at the old refrigerator and realized the photos and colorful magnets were gone. "Where are your things? What's going on?"

"Me." She pulled a wooden chair out and sat down. "I'm going on."

"Moving?"

She nodded.

"You can afford to do that after paying for the renovations? Wouldn't it be wise to wait until the Palace started bringing in a real steady income to make that kind of move?"

She sat up straight. "You disapprove of my finally getting up the courage to change a few things?"

"Not disapproving." He took the seat to the left of hers at the table. "I'm worried about you."

"Is that why you came back to Hellon tonight? Worry over me?"

"Actually I told myself I was coming because I missed my family. And because I had just realized that while I am still every bit the donkey head you once spotted me for, I am no longer a self-involved bastard."

Her face paled. "I don't understand."

"I don't know if I do either, except to say that when I told Jillie I wanted to come to Hellon tonight it was because I genuinely wanted to see my family, to come home."

"Home? You think of Hellon as home?"

"I thought that was all it was, until she mentioned your name. Until I walked up those stairs and saw you standing there with the light behind you and that damned tiara on your head."

Her hand shot up, but before her fingers brushed the headpiece, she sank them into her hair and blinked. "And?"

"And then I understood it wasn't the place I wanted to come home to, it was *you*, Rita." He held his hand out to her.

Her? He'd come back for her? How many times these last few weeks had she dreamed, even prayed for this very thing to happen?

Now it had. He'd done it. The ball was in her court. She shifted her head, and the Dixie Belle Duchess crown wobbled. *Stupid, stupid!* Once again he'd caught her looking a fool. Taking so long to come up with any kind of response to his amazing statement only made it worse. *Stupid, Rita. Stupid, stupid . . . wait. No!*

She refused to beat herself up like that. She was not stupid! She was strong and resourceful. And she was not going to let someone who broke her heart, then had the gall to show up again talking about home, make her retreat into her worst fears.

"Well, if you've come to Hellon to make a home with me, Wild Billy, leaves-a-girl-all-alone-on-a-hotel-lounge-stage, West . . ." She stood, not caring that it made her crown slip to the back of her head. "You are too damn late."

"I know."

"You know?"

"I'm not so self-centered that I'd think that I could walk back into your life armed with nothing but an apology and—as you said—a 'too damn late' profession of love and hope to make up for what I did."

His what? She waved her hand in a slow, jerking motion. "Back that train up. Your profession of what?"

"Love. I love you, Rita."

"Damn it, Will." She whipped around so he would not see the tears in her eyes or read the emotions on her face. She had no idea what emotions he might see there, of course, and that made it all the more frightening. Would he pick up on her frustration? Her anger? Her joy? Her confusion? Or worst of all, would he see that despite the way he had behaved, she loved him right back? "Why are you doing this?"

"Maybe because I finally realized a taste of heaven wasn't enough for me, Rita. That's why I left you that night in Memphis. And that's why I've come back."

"It can't be both!" She whirled around, her arms out. "It can't be the reason you left *and* the reason you came back."

"It sounds impossible, but that's the truth of it." He pulled at the knot in his tie, and his jacket rustled against his cotton shirt. "I left because by staying I knew I'd become another excuse for you to keep things the way they were. I left for your sake."

"What made you think you could make that decision on my behalf?"

"It was one of the hardest things I ever had to do, Rita, I swear it. Made more difficult by the fact that I knew the one thing you despised in this world was someone who didn't stick around for the people he loved."

"But you walked out anyway."

"I had to. And I hope you'll let me tell you why."

"I'm listening." She stood behind a chair, gripping its back so hard it felt like the wood grain was being burned into her palms.

He hung his head for a moment but as he talked, he raised it again and looked toward the curtainless kitchen window. "All my life people have wanted things of me—put their expectations on me."

"The first son in the West family. I can believe that."

"The first son. Not a West, though. Not by blood."

"What are you saying?"

"Now, do not hold this against my mother, she's done her penance in spades, and it's a matter between her and my . . . my daddy." He looked at his hands, then out the window again. "But Jillie and I have different fathers."

"Things like that *do* happen." She felt herself smiling, and for only an instant wondering if Will's biological father had been one of those gentlemen callers who bade Miss Peggy to come out in the moonlight. "If Pernel hadn't decided to marry me in high school, Lacey Marie might have called another man her father in time."

He nodded without meeting her gaze. "Then there's the whole Wild Billy, football-hero stage of my life. Suddenly I'm just a kid but I'm carrying the responsibility and reputation for even more names that were not rightly mine. You know there were times in the past I sort of wished we had lost that state championship."

"Lost? You could never have held your head up in town again."

"Naw, they'd have gotten over a loss quicker than they did that win, and you know it. Thing was I didn't deserve to become a local legend. I was part of a team but when people talk about the championship, Wild Billy West is the one who gets the credit."

"You felt guilty about that?"

"Not at first." He gave her a sheepish grin.

Then he sighed. "But later, yes, guilty and more than a little stifled. Spending your life under a mantle you don't really believe you earned takes its toll, Rita."

"I can see how it would."

"As problems go, that one is petty, and I admit it. But it affected me in ways that worked themselves into the rest of my life. After I left Hellon, the reason I couldn't come back is because I couldn't let myself live under other people's expectations anymore. Especially if those expectations were that anything I did was fine, even if it was foolish."

"Like the story of Midas, having everything you touch turn golden is not as great as it sounds to others."

He laughed, but his face reflected no joy. "I've spent a lot of time making sure no one put their expectations on me again. What I've realized is that meant I never had to strive to do things that I knew were beyond my reach."

"Welcome to the club." She put her hand on his chest.

"I never had to grow up as Wild Billy in Hellon, and in trying to escape that I created the same situation, only it was my own fears and stubbornness that kept me from growing. The one exception was when you told me off, Rita."

She shut her eyes and groaned.

He touched her cheek. "There I was feeling sorry for myself for having another title thrust on me that I didn't merit, feeling sorry for myself, hiding behind my past and you . . ."

"I never did anything like that before. I never have since, really. But I had always wanted more children, and there you were having a baby, not even caring about your own flesh-and-blood child."

"He had my name. And he was *like* me."

"Of course he was. He was your son." She rested her hand on his shoulder.

He looked at her with those same, aching, haunted eyes he had the first day he'd come to the Palace. "He was like me because he had the name of a man who was not his blood father."

"Will." She started to sit again, then felt too restless for it. She walked the few steps to the counter, turned, and studied his weary expression. *One of the reasons Norrie never became Mrs. West was that she had a rather relaxed approach to fidelity.* Cozette's tidbit of gossip rushed back into Rita's mind. "And I said those awful things to you. I am so sor—"

"No." He stood. "Don't apologize for that. Never apologize for being the one person in my life who had just enough faith that I could do the right thing that she would dare to speak the truth to my face."

"But I didn't know the whole story. There I went on and on berating you for not being supportive of Norrie and putting your selfish pleasure above the needs of your unborn baby . . ."

"A baby who *needed* a decent father. You were right to do that, Rita. That tiny boy deserved a decent father more than anything on earth."

She hung her head and sniffled.

"You gave me another kind of glimpse of heaven then, Rita." He came to where she stood and lifted her chin with his finger. "By allowing me to know for even a preciously short time what it meant to be an innocent child's daddy."

Tears washed onto her cheeks, but she did nothing to wipe them away.

"After the baby passed, I understood more deeply than ever what it was I had lost. I had lost my one tiny sliver of heaven on earth."

"That's kind of what children are, aren't they?"

"That's what love is, true love, *unselfish* love." He took her hand. "I didn't know it when I came here, but that's where I would find my peace of mind again. In loving you, physically, spiritually, and unselfishly."

"This is all so much to take in, Will." She drew her fingers out of his grasp so slowly that she felt every nerve tingle at the parting touch. "You say you love me, but that night in Memphis you walked out."

"Because I realized that night that I wanted you too badly, that I cared about you too much to let you use me as another crutch to keep from going after your real dreams."

"You did." She sank into her chair again.

"Yes. I did."

"No. I said 'you did.' Not a question. A statement of fact. When you walked out of that lounge and there was no one left around for me to play martyr to, I had to take a good long look at myself and my life at last."

"And?"

"And I came back to Hellon the next day, got the paperwork to enroll in college in Memphis, and sold the Palace."

"Sold it? That fast?"

"I had a motivated buyer."

"Who?"

"Cozette and her husband. All this time they've been getting financial advice from your mother about how to invest money they made from selling off lots of the farmland."

"My proper mother, who gave herself the name Peggy to honor Margaret Mitchell, still holds formal tea parties and rules this town's social set with an iron cane, gave financial advice to aging bohemians? Telling them to buy a half-gutted pig rib restaurant?"

"No."

"No?"

"Your mother was against them buying the Palace. But once Mouse heard about the stage he was sold. Being vegetarians, they did dump the whole rib thing. They're calling the place the Java Palace and—" She sank into her chair and started to laugh.

"What?"

"Well, we started out talking about love and then you told me that incredible story about your son and finding peace again then I told you about Cozie and Mouse and now we're onto the Palace."

"The conversation has had more twists than—"

She held her hand up. "Don't say it."

He knelt in front of her. "Then what should I say, Rita?"

What more could he say? He had apologized, explained himself, and said he loved her. Only a damned fool would ask for anything more.

"Say absolutely nothing." She leaned forward and kissed him passionately, lovingly, carelessly.

They would still have so many things to work out, but she was a smart woman, and he was a decent man. Together, they could handle anything that life threw at them, and they would still be standing—together.

Pernel Stark Presents an Epilogue
(after a fashion)

So, Rita got her own story.

Should you stop into the Java Palace or the Cozie Mouse, the boutique the new owners just opened upstairs and brought me in to run—it ain't turned a profit yet, but it sure has got a few boxers in a bunch (and that's better than money around here any day, if you ask me) . . . Anyway, if you find yourself passing through Hellon, Tennessee, one day and decide to stop at the Palace and ask about Rita Butcher Stark people will . . . Now, first thing, they'll correct you. It's Rita Butcher Stark West, and she kindly asks you lop out the old last names. I ain't offended at that especially now that there's a new Mrs. Stark, who doesn't mind sharing my closet space and the occasional fashion tip. It's just good sense.

And before we get too far along I will tell you

that folks will still want to tell you about that tornado. Good stories do not die easy in a place where not much happens.

That is one reason they will go on about The Wedding. Now, not just any wedding, this is The Wedding. The Wedding to which all weddings heretofore in Hellon will forever be held up against and find themselves lacking. Nobody would expect anything less than big doings for the only daughter of the West family. Jillie not only had the most beautiful dress and the handsomest husband going, they had the happiest matron of honor and best man ever.

Will—someday if you want to see him grin real big, sneak up on him and call him Wild Billy—Will and Rita had a small ceremony at a church in Memphis. They never did go much for fluff and folderol. Besides, Rita said, she was far too busy with her fall classes at college to plan a big affair. And she did not want to compete with Jillie for the honor of most-talked-about wedding. And she would have, too, what with the likes of Lacey Marie, Cozette, and Jillie as bridesmaids and Miss Peggy and me fighting (false) tooth and (press-on) nail over which one of us would be flower girl. That would have been an event most folks in town would have paid to see.

So, if you do drop in some morning and ask after Rita, that's what you'll hear. That and the tornado story—*again*. But first you'll want to order yourself up a piece of pie, or cobbler or, if it's not too early in the day, a hefty slice of red velvet cake—they still use Rita's recipes though no one ever quite made them as good as her. Don't be shy about ordering plenty, either. Because no one will get around to telling you anything about Rita West until they've made sure you know down to the last detail all about that summer when Rita tore the Pig Rib Palace apart, then tore away everything holding her back and took off. Just like her mama. Just like we all knew she would once she got the right wind under her wings.

Call me Sugar, Sugar, Sugar Cookies

Don't tell Cozie they aren't health food—sometimes it's healthy just to eat food that makes you feel good.

---

4 c. flour
½ c. sour cream
1 c. soft butter
½ t. salt
½ t. baking soda

½ t. nutmeg
1 t. baking powder
1 t. vanilla
1½ c. sugar
1 egg

Sift flour, powder, soda, salt, nutmeg. Cream butter, sugar and add egg then sour cream and vanilla. Add the flour mixture and blend well. Chill overnight. Divide dough into four parts. Roll out one section at a time. Return other parts to the fridge. Cut with cookie cutters and bake at 350°F on greased cookie sheet for 8–10 minutes.

Peanut Butter Cheese Torte

Some Southerners have more sophisticated tastes than
fried peanut butter and banana sandwiches, y'all.

Crust:
1 c. graham cracker
   crumbs
1/4 c. melted butter
1/4 c. packed brown
   sugar
1/2 c. chopped peanuts

Filling:
2 c. creamy peanut
   butter
2 c. sugar
2 t. vanilla

2 pkg. soft cream
   cheese—16 oz.
2 T. soft butter
1 1/2 c. stiffly
   beaten whipping
   cream

Topping:
4 oz. semisweet chocolate
   chips
chopped peanuts—
   optional
3 T. plus 2 t. hot coffee

Combine all crust ingredients. Press into the bottom and halfway up the sides of a 10-inch spring form pan. Chill. For filling, beat peanut butter, cream cheese, sugar, butter, and vanilla in a large mixing bowl on high until smooth, about 2 minutes. Fold in whipped cream. Gently spoon into crust; refrigerate 6 hours or overnight. For topping, melt chocolate with coffee until smooth. Spread over chilled torte. Refrigerate until firm, about 30 minutes. Garnish with chopped peanuts if desired.

Pucker Power Pie

Pucker up and say "Yum!"

---

7 T. cornstarch
1½ c. sugar
2 **c.** water
¼ c. butter

dash of salt
4 egg yolks
½ c. lemon juice

Mix cornstarch, salt and sugar. Boil 1 cup water. Add cornstarch mixture to 1 cup cool water and stir. Stir in boiling water and cook 4 minutes. Mixture should be thick and clear. Add about ¼ cup hot mixture to egg yolks and combine well. Add egg mixture gradually to hot mixture. Cook 45 seconds. Add lemon juice and butter, mix well. Cool. Serve in graham cracker crust. Top with whipped cream if desired.

Taste of Heaven Divinity

Be an angel and make a batch.

---

2 c. sugar
1 t. vanilla flavoring
1/8 t. salt

1/2 c. water
2 egg whites
1/8 t. cream of tartar

Combine sugar, water, salt, and cream of tartar. Cover and boil for 5 minutes. Uncover. Wipe sides of saucepan with a damp cloth. Boil without stirring to firm ball stage (245°–248°F). Pour slowly, beating constantly, over stiffly beaten egg whites. Add flavoring. Continue beating until candy holds its shape when dropped from a spoon. Drop by teaspoonfuls onto waxed paper. Sprinkle with chopped nuts if desired.

Slap-Together Cake

Slap a bib on and dig in!

---

1 c. fruit cocktail,
  drained
1 c. sugar
1 egg
1 t. baking soda
¼ c. brown sugar

¼ c. liquid from
  fruit cocktail
1 t. vanilla
1¼ c. flour
½ t. salt
¼ c. nuts

Put fruit cocktail, liquid, sugar, vanilla, and egg into bowl. Sift into same bowl the flour, soda, and salt. Mix everything together until only moist. Do not mix too much. Sprinkle brown sugar and nuts on top. Bake at 350°F for 35–40 minutes in greased and floured 8-inch pans.

Mint Ice

Well, it ain't a Julep, but it'll cool you down just fine on a hot day.

---

1 c. sugar
2 egg whites
a few grains of salt
$\frac{1}{4}$ c. lemon juice

$1\frac{1}{2}$ c. water
green food coloring
mint flavoring

Combine sugar and water. Boil 10 minutes. Cool. Add lemon juice and salt. Flavor with mint. Add food coloring until desired tint is obtained. Mix thoroughly. Pour into tray of mechanical refrigerator. Freeze to mushy consistency. Remove from tray. Place in chilled bowl. Whip until light. Carefully fold into stiffly beaten egg whites. Return to tray. Freeze until firm. 6 servings.

CAUTION: If you are worried about using uncooked eggs, do not use this recipe!

Red Velvet Cake

*An old favorite that Rita made her specialty,
the Perfect Princess cake, by adding strawberries dipped in
white chocolate—it'll make you feel like royalty!*

½ c. butter or margarine,
   softened
2 large eggs
1 t. baking soda
2 T. cocoa
1 T. white vinegar
2 t. vanilla extract

1½ c. sugar
2½ c. cake flour
½ t. salt
1 c. buttermilk
2 (1-ounce) bottles red
   liquid food coloring

Beat butter and sugar at medium speed with an electric mixer until creamy; add eggs, 1 at a time, beating until blended after each addition. Stir together flour and next three ingredients. Stir together buttermilk and next three ingredients. Add flour mixture to butter mixture mixing alternatively with buttermilk mixture, beginning and ending with the flour mixture. Beat at low speed just until blended after each addition.

Pour batter into three greased and floured round cake pans. Bake at 350°F for 17–19 minutes, or until a wooden pick inserted into the center comes out clean. Cool in pans on wire racks for 10 minutes; remove from pans and cool completely on wire racks. Spread frosting between layers and on top and on sides of cake. Cover and store in refrigerator.

Boiled Icing:
1½ c. sugar
1 t. vanilla flavoring
2 egg whites,
* stiffly beaten*
⅛ t. cream
* of tartar*
¾ c. boiling water
a few grains
* of salt*

Combine sugar, water, cream of tartar, and salt. Stir until dissolved. Boil to soft ball stage (236°F). Pour slowly, beating constantly, over egg whites. Add flavoring. Beat until thick and creamy.

Aunt Bette's Church Lady Chocolate Brownie Cake

*A favorite Southern funeral food that won't be turned away
at a Fourth of July picnic or as a groom's cake at a
church basement wedding reception.*

---

2 c. sugar
1 c. water
1 stick margarine
1 t. baking soda
6 T. cocoa

2 c. flour
½ c. shortening
2 eggs (beaten)
1 t. vanilla
½ c. buttermilk

Sift flour and sugar together. Bring to boil the
water, shortening, margarine and cocoa. Pour this
hot mixture over flour, sugar mix. While hot, add
buttermilk, eggs, soda and vanilla. Pour into
large cookie sheet (mix will be thin) and bake at
400°F for 20 minutes.

Icing:
1 stick butter
6 T. milk
1 box powdered sugar

4 T. cocoa
1 t. vanilla
1 c. nuts (optional)

Bring to boil the butter, cocoa and milk. Add powdered sugar (sifted), vanilla and nuts. Spread over cake while icing is still hot so it will melt into cake.

Brandy Slush

When plain old sweet tea or lemonade just ain't enough!

Boil two cups water and steep four tea bags in it. Dissolve two cups sugar in the tea. Add twelve ounces frozen orange juice, twelve ounces frozen lemonade, seven cups water, and two cups brandy. Mix well and freeze. Makes one gallon. Keep in freezer. Put some slush in a glass and fill up with 7-Up (about half slush and half 7-Up). Carries a real kick!

Bunco Night Brand-Name Bliss

All the girls at work will ask for the recipe.

---

1 pkg. Double Oreo
   cookies

1 stick butter (or
   margarine) melted

Pour butter or margarine over crushed cookies. Stir until cookies are coated with butter.

2 (8 oz.) Cool Whips
1 (8 oz.) cream cheese
   (room temperature)

1 c. confectioner's
   sugar

Mix well in large bowl: 12 oz. instant chocolate pudding (mix as directed). Alternate layers beginning with cookies/ filling/ pudding, ending with cookies.

Cousin Nancy's Famous Cheese Pocket Pie

*Just right for when guests drop in unexpectedly
like they do around here.*

---

2 premade pie crusts
1 T. lemon juice

1 (8 oz.) cream cheese
½ c. sugar

Place bottom crust on aluminum foil on cooking pan. Mix cream cheese, lemon juice and sugar well. Spread on bottom crust. Place second crust on top and crimp edges. Push foil up to crimped edges. Cut four slits in top crust. Bake at 425°F for 25 minutes. Top pie with powdered sugar, water and vanilla glaze. No clean up is needed as you just throw away the aluminum foil and put the cooking pan away.